Mrs Bates of Highbury

A prequel

Inspired by Jane Austen's Emma

Allie Cresswell

Introduction

My story is set some thirty years before the beginning of Miss Austen's novel *Emma*. In my book Mrs Bates—very elderly and almost entirely silent in Jane Austen's novel—takes centre-stage. We meet her in her late forties, just recently widowed. Her daughter—the garrulous spinster Miss Bates—is as talkative aged twenty nine as she is in her later iteration. Fans of Emma will know that Mrs Bates had a second daughter. She is mentioned by name just once—her name was Jane. Her only importance in Emma is as the deceased mother of the elegant and accomplished Jane Fairfax but in my story she plays a much more central role.

Mrs Bates of Highbury is the first of a trilogy which will trace the pre-history of Emma and then run in parallel to it. Fans of Jane Austen need have no fear; I have no intention of deviating from her plot and in the end she and I will be on exactly the same page. For those readers unfamiliar with Emma, I hope Mrs Bates of Highbury will be enjoyable as a stand-alone novel.

Chapter 1

Frederick Bates was the fourth and youngest son of Squire and Mrs Bates of Hazelwoods Manor in the county of ___shire.

The oldest boy, Albert, attained his majority, departed for an extensive tour of Europe and settled in Florence where he married a beautiful but penniless Contessa. There he waited until such time as his father's decline—or his death—should require a return to Hazelwoods and an assumption of the mantle of inheritance.

Jeremy, the second boy, chose the Navy, was bought a commission and went in due course, with admirable determination and an epaulette fairly soaked in the tears of his mama, to do his duty abroad. Here he was heroically wounded in one of the first engagements with the enemy and subsequently retired on a full Captain's pension to a small property on the south coast.

The third son matriculated at Cambridge and determined to go into the law, where a man with no pecuniary expectations can be enabled to amass his own fortune from the misery or tangled machinations of others. Being of a manipulative and an avaricious bent, and rather careless of the feelings of those not closely connected to himself, this excellently suited Edgar Bates, and he was soon ensconced in the chambers of Whitsniff, Beakie and Bates as a junior partner.

This left Frederick with the church, an occupation which suited his gentle, contemplative nature as well as his vocation. He relied on becoming the incumbent of the prosperous living situate in his father's parish as soon as it should become vacant. He looked forward to doing much good amongst the poor cottars of his father's estate as well as the wealthier neighbours, equally —or perhaps more—in need of salvation.

In that expectation Frederick took a wife quite soon after ordination, making Miss Marie Winkle into Mrs Bates when she was not much more than seventeen years of age. Miss Winkle was as rich in natural goodness, grace and simple beauty as she was poor in fiscal means, but she was an ideal helpmeet for a parish priest and the two settled into the two rooms of their city curacy, served their parishioners with kindness and humility and awaited the news that the occupant of the vicarage of Hazelwoods had been called to minister elsewhere.

A daughter was born to them, Henrietta, a slight, rather sickly child given to nervous convulsions and hysterical spasms. Mrs Bates cared for her daughter with all the tenderness of her sacred namesake and prayed that the time might come when their service in the rough streets of the city parish might draw to a close, transporting the child to the wholesome fresh air and healthful surroundings of Hazelwoods.

Providence, however, dealt them a bitter blow. Squire Bates suffered a fall while riding to hounds. His grievous wounds were compounded by an inflammation of the brain and he expired before a week was out. He survived long enough for the junior partner of Whitsniff, Beakie and Bates to get to his side and rearrange financial matters to his own satisfaction. The oldest boy—now a portly and pompous individual—arrived from Florence as the funeral cortege departed the steps of Hazelwoods Manor. His sun-tanned complexion looked more blue than brown as he shivered in the bitter November air, perished with cold in spite of the numerous shawls and rugs closely tucked around him in his closed conveyance. Frederick awaited his dear departed father's arrival in the old stone church which was to have been his living, numbed by grief and shock to the penetrating chill of that draughty building. By kind permission of the presiding priest, he committed his beloved father's body to the earth and his soul to the Lord with a voice which trembled with emotion.

Captain Bates declined to attend, having promised his cronies at the Club to make a fourth for bridge.

Not many weeks had passed after the old squire's interment before it became clear to Reverend Bates that if he continued to wait for the living of Hazelwoods to become available, he would wait in vain. A letter from his mama informed him of wholesale changes at Hazelwoods. The new squire had many alterations and improvements in hand at the manor in order to make it suitable to house the Contessa. Family heirlooms were being removed for the accommodation of Mediterranean artefacts more likely to comfort that superlatively European lady. Sleeping chambers were being refurbished into lofty boudoires and a marble mosaic installed in a new atrium. The letter-writer had contemplated removal to the lodge, either as a temporary or a permanent arrangement, whichever the Contessa should prefer, but Edgar had succeeded in meddling so thoroughly in the estate's affairs that the lodge, traditional refuge of the squire's widow, had been let, and their London house also. 'I am by no means able to discover,' the widow went on, 'where the rental monies are being deposited. But you can be sure that whatever hand Edgar has had in the affair, he will not be the poorer by it. As a result I have had no alternative but to remove to Brighton, where dear Jeremy has made over two rooms on the first floor of his house for my use and enjoyment for as long as I might require. I need not tell you how comforted I am in his kindness and how glad I am to be able to offset his additional expenses from a moiety of my marriage portion. As much as a daughter would have been a comfort to me, I am glad to have none in so far as the need to provide for her is concerned. I fear that between them Bertie and Edgar have the whole estate firmly in hand,' the letter concluded, 'and you will be the loser. I will do what I can for you. The income from what remains of my portion shall pass to you when I die, for your lifetime. But I must advise you that when the living at Hazelwoods becomes vacant they are unlikely to think of you. I advise you therefore to look to your own resources.'

Accordingly Reverend Bates began to look about him, and to revive old University and clerical acquaintance in the hope of finding a suitable living. His own exceptionally good character, quiet good manners and gentlemanlike bearing, the sense and simple charm of his lady wife plus a word in the ear of a certain Mr Knightley, squire of Donwell Abbey, hard by the village of Highbury, soon resulted in the little family quitting the cramped rooms of the city for the pleasant vicarage in that charming settlement.

The reverend soon established himself as a popular priest. On Sundays the pews of the picturesque stone church were well-filled with worshippers who found his sound good sense and practical sermons eminently palatable. His gentle officiation of the sacraments calmed squalling babies, soothed the nerves of wedding candidates and smoothed the passage of the elderly to the peace of the hereafter.

Some three or four years after their settling at Highbury, news arrived at the vicarage of the demise of Frederick's mother. Frederick travelled to Brighton to officiate at the interment and returned with a sorry account of his brothers; Albert, the new squire, had become corpulent and had treated Frederick with distant disdain. Jeremy, the Captain, had been friendlier although a confirmed invalid, full of complaint. Edgar was very much the man of business, miserly on his own account but a generous spender of other men's money. He had agreed, however— reluctantly, and only on production of the old letter which had been carefully preserved against such an objection—to divert the income from their mother's capital to Frederick's account.

Six years more saw an addition to the happy little family at Highbury vicarage. A second daughter, Jane. In contrast to her sister—now aged thirteen—she was quick and lively, with the pleasing countenance of her mother and the intelligence of her father. She showed none of the nervous unreliability of her older sibling and soon became a favourite amongst Reverend Bates' congregants, both high and low. Frederick and Marie had considered the possibility of sending Hetty to school, but rejected it as soon as it was mooted. Henrietta had insufficient stability of character to support such a remove from home and hearth. In spite of her parents' most diligent efforts she had grown into a girl with sudden, irrational anxieties and wild imaginings. Extremely garrulous, her mouth was an immediate and unfettered conduit for every peculiar fancy which entered her mind. And that mind was unretentive, equally unable to remember the date of the Battle of Hastings as the simplest instruction to the cook. Though kind of intention, and desirous of doing good, she was a girl who needed constant guidance and reassurance, seeing evil—actual or potential—in the slightest trifle. No, to be sure, Henrietta was not suited for school. It soon became apparent that for Jane, school was too good. If Hetty was flighty, Jane was steady. Where Hetty was scatter-brained, Jane was brilliant. She soaked up her father's lessons like a sponge, eager, hungry for more. If school would have been wasted on Hetty, then Jane would be wasted on school. No, Frederick decided, and Marie whole-heartedly agreed, better that both girls should stay at home, the one to be protected, the other to be nurtured.

Highbury, during the twenty-seven years of Reverend Bates' incumbency, saw an enlargement of its population, in particular an influx of comparatively well-educated and well-to-do middle-class families who gave dinners and drank tea and occasionally danced at delightful balls held in the rooms above the Crown Inn. The village, in short, grew and thrived, and, at its centre, indeed, at its very hub, the reverend and his family lived and ministered. They were, if not in wealth, certainly in popularity and esteem, considered to be the first family of that bustling, respectable little town. They entertained with elegant, understated generosity, and their own easy manners ensured that they moved seamlessly from the august drawing room of Donwell Abbey to the cluttered confines of farmhouse kitchens and were welcomed everywhere.

The girls likewise developed large acquaintance with the better-off families in the town and amongst the simple farmers and cottars of Highbury and Donwell. Hetty made herself useful carrying messages hither and thither around the parish for her papa and baskets of charitable provisions for her mama. Her intention was to be useful, that is, and she set off with every desire to do good, but nobody—least of all her parents—held very sanguine hope in the efficient or timely performance of her errands. She would stop to speak to whomsoever she might meet, giving out disjointed accounts of her parents' health, the cook's rheumatism, the blight on the asparagus crop and a pair of mislaid stockings at the same time as assimilating half-understood tittle-tattle and imperfectly remembered intelligence and allowing it all to get confused with the messages and charitable gifts. The whole would mingle in her mind, grow like leavening bread, assume awful connections and catastrophic outcomes so that she often arrived fevered with anxiety or pale with doleful predictions. The message to the bailiff would get delivered to the blacksmith. A pie for an invalid would be left with the squire. Quite separate tidings of the miller's new baby, a blocked dyke or a loose bullock became conflated in the mile between Abbey-Mill Farm and Ford's until it was quite certain that the miller's baby had been trampled by the bullock, strangled by the lost stockings and then drowned in the dyke.

'I do fear that Hetty is not safe to be out alone,' Marie confided to her husband one evening, when the girls were in bed. 'Her imagination makes upset into tragedy. Mrs Ford tells me she worked herself up into a terrible state because a blue button rolled off the counter and fell between the floorboards, yesterday. It was mother-of-pearl, quite pretty, and one of only four left in the box. "What use are three buttons to anyone," she wailed, apparently, before sinking onto a chair in a swoon. Mrs Ford had to fetch smelling salts. To think we live so comfortably, here, with nothing to vex or threaten us. Highbury is the safest, most settled, quiet little town. And yet even here she finds alarm and disquiet round every corner. How she will manage if real tragedy strikes, I cannot think.'

'She will have you dear,' said Reverend Bates, 'and that will be sufficient, and if it were not, she will have Jane, who has enough sense for both their heads.'

Chapter 2

Tragedy *did* strike, as it is wont to do, and Marie Bates found herself a widow. As sudden and crippling as her bereavement was, she was allowed scant time to mourn or accustom herself to her loss. A new incumbent was almost immediately found to minister to the inhabitants of Highbury and of course the vicarage must be vacated so that he could establish himself there. With two daughters as well as herself to be accommodated, and scarcely any visible means of income—the reverend's stipend naturally having devolved onto the new man—Marie wrote to Frederick's relatives in the hope of assistance. But a reply from Edgar Bates (now senior partner in the firm) lamented their inability to offer any and, heaping coals upon the widow's head, declared his intention of withdrawing the small amount of income which had derived from their mother's portion. The pecuniary consequence of this was severe indeed. But she read his letter with a face which barely betrayed any of the bitter disappointment of feeling which must inevitably have been the result of such a grievous blow, and got on with the task of packing up the family's belongings. Jane, then aged sixteen and, like her mother, practical and firm of character, set off with scarcely a tear to Donwell Abbey where she was engaged to assist the squire's elder boy George—aged 8—in his lessons, preparatory to him being sent to school the following term. Hetty read the letter with many a shriek and apostrophic outcry, making up, with her excess of emotion and ungoverned force of feeling, for the fortitude and restraint of the others. She clutched her apron, her hair and her mother, fell against the mantel and threw herself in a paroxysm of nerves onto a nearby window seat.

'Oh Mother! What will become of us? How will we manage?' she cried, and without waiting for the calm reassurance of her mother's response, went on, 'Oh! We're quite destitute. We shall have to go to the poor house! If only I had had a proper education, I could go out to teach. But, you know, papa always said he couldn't get a fact to stay in my head more than ten minutes. Not like Jane, who, he said, would have matriculated if she had been a boy. Or if I could sew, I could make dresses for wealthy ladies. Or poor ones—

I should not be too proud to make the simplest shift or pinafore. But you know my buttons fall off as soon as ever I have sewn them on, so what good should I be? Perhaps I could work in Mrs Martin's dairy. She told me only last week that she can't get a dairymaid to stay more than a fortnight at Abbey-Mill Farm. But I am so afraid of cows, I am not sure that would do. Oh Mother, indeed, what shall we do? We shall have to walk the roadways. We shall be reduced to sleeping in the undergrowth!'

That evening, George and his father sat a while by the vast parlour fire. Two or three dogs, exhausted by a day of following their master from field to farm, flushing out pheasant and throwing themselves into the mill pond, lay on the rug at their feet. Mr Knightley had a book on his lap, but he was not reading it. George, likewise, held a book but paid no attention to its pages.

'Papa,' he said at last, 'I wonder if we could not do something to assist Mrs Bates.'

Mr Knightley stirred himself, uncrossed his legs and reached down absent-mindedly to stroke a dog's muzzle. 'I esteem Mrs Bates very highly,' he said. 'I have rarely met such a genteel, lady-like lady who, at the same time, has such simple, delightful, unaffected manners and practical good sense. She makes herself agreeable wherever she goes. The loss of her husband, at her comparatively early age, is a grievous blow, but I should think it very probable that she will marry again.' The squire, at this time a sprightly sixty-two years of age, had been a widower for only the last of them, and was by no means confirmed in that state for perpetuity. It would have been unseemly, so early in Mrs Bates' bereavement, to have thought of her in any matrimonial context whatsoever, nevertheless he spoke from the heart, with a warmth George had not often heard in his father's voice unless in connection with a particularly fine bull or a prodigiously good crop of barley.

'To be sure, sir,' George replied. 'But in the meantime, I gather, there is a little difficulty. Without the vicar's stipend, they have no income, and, of course, they must quit the vicarage.'

The squire roused himself a little more, and gave his son a keen look. 'No income? What? None whatsoever?'

George shook his head. 'Reverend Bates has family, I believe, well-provisioned, but they have declined assistance.'

'Absolutely declined?'

'Yes, sir. Jane came today to help me with my lesson, you know …'

'A bright girl. Pretty too. She'll marry well, I have no doubt.'

'No doubt, sir,' said George, warmly, wishing himself ten years older, 'but she is very young, and even if she does marry advantageously, there is still Mrs Bates, and Miss Bates …'

'Ah yes, Miss Bates. Well she's a different case altogether.'

'Exactly my point, sir.'

'Well, George, I am very pleased with you for taking this proper, paternal interest in these worthy people. It is just what the future squire ought to do. And what do you suggest?'

George squirmed a little in his seat. He had not expected to be called upon provide a solution to Jane's problem, only hoped that, by raising it, his father might do so. But he took a deep breath and answered his father stoutly. 'Sir, if *I* were squire, I would make discreet enquiries amongst the better-off gentlemen of the town, and I could see what could be done between us to provide Mrs Bates and her daughters with a modest home and a small income.'

Mr Knightley nodded. Encouraged, George went on, 'It is the duty of those who have much to provide for those who have little. The Bible tells us so, as well as good sense and common decency. I understand she has served us—the parish, I mean sir—for twenty odd years, and now it is time for us to repay in kind. For myself, if I had a vacant cottage somewhere on the estate, I would happily give it over to her use. Although it might be more rustic than she has been used to, and she might not like the remoteness from the village, it would be something. I would be happy to contribute to a fund which would provide them with an income. Many of us here about have orchards, flocks, crops and good things in abundance, sometimes in over-abundance. Our own supplies of rhubarb and spinach this year seemed never-ending; I was heartily sick of both in the end. There is no reason why the surplus could not be offered to them if they will do us the kindness to take it off our hands.'

'And what if Mrs Bates declined to be the recipient of the charity of her neighbours? Some people might find it demeaning.'

'I do not think Mrs Bates has that kind of pride,

Father, but I suppose the money could be offered in such a way as to keep its source a secret?'

'My goodness, George, my boy,' Mr Knightley burst out, 'what a Solomon you are! If only men twice—nay, three or four times—your age had your sense and innately charitable heart, the world would be a better place indeed. It is a pity that I need you to take over the estate when I am gone. To be sure, I think I had better begin training John to do it for I see that you will be wasted here. Your place is in politics!'

George blushed. He had rarely heard such praise from his father. 'Thank you, sir,' he stammered.

Mr Knightley reached for his pipe. 'Now, off to bed with you sir, before you shame me into giving succour to every poor widow-woman in the county!'

George stood up. 'Good night then, sir. But, as for Mrs Bates ..?'

'Yes, yes, I will look into it. Good night now, son.'

And so it happened that not many days had passed before Mrs Bates received a call from John Abdy. John had been the reverend's clerk for the whole period of his incumbency, a worthy and respectable man treated

with warmth and affection by the vicarage family
whether visiting on business or for pleasure. But on
this occasion he seemed flustered and discomposed,
kneaded his hat in his hands and looked at the carpet,
the fireplace, the casement—anywhere, indeed, than at
Mrs Bates herself. The summary of his news, when he
had managed to stumble it out, was that 'a small but
significant paragraph had been found in the church's
founding articles, that was to say, in the town's
charter, or at least, mentioned in the one and detailed
more fully in the other, which stated that in such a
case as hers it was incumbent upon the parish, on the
one hand, and on the guilds and local institutes upon
the other, or any properly constituted body so located,
overseen by an obscure department of the bishop's
office, who devolved responsibility for it back onto
the clerk, to provide, in short …' the clerk took a
breath, and fumbled with a sheaf of papers bound in
red ribbon. 'In short, Mrs Bates,' he concluded, in a
rush, 'I have the happiness to tell you that, should you
require them, a suite of rooms above Pellins' the
grocers is available for you, free of rent. Two
bedrooms, a parlour, small indeed but with two
windows overlooking High Street, a scullery below, at

the rear, and, in the attic, room for a maid. And an annual allowance of coals and a sum of £50, payable for your lifetime, madam, or until your … but it seems indelicate to mention …'

'Until I remarry?' Mrs Bates provided.

'Yes, indeed, Madam. May I tell the gentleman, that is, gentlemen of the … the committees variously concerned, that you are happy to accept?'

'Oh yes,' Marie said, a catch in her voice. She advanced towards the clerk and took his hand warmly, 'and please to inform those gentlemen, whoever they are, that they have the gratitude of my heart for their great goodness.'

It was the work of only a few moments for the ladies to attire themselves and walk the quarter mile to the High Street. In a shadowy angle of a half gable, rather obscured by creeper, a small door next to the grocer's revealed itself to them.

'Well, I declare,' Henrietta said, gazing at it with wonderment, 'that I never noticed this door before, and I have been to Pellins' more times than I can count. But it is so narrow, and in the shadow cast by the gable, almost disappears in the gloom. The ivy, there, is very thick—quite overhanging the lintel. And then, the pavement is much fractured just here, and I daresay there's a puddle every time it rains. I have probably avoided it, for fear of tripping …'

'Or of drowning?' Jane put in quickly. 'Good morning, Mrs Pellins! A fine day indeed! I thank you, quite well. No. Very dry. Look at our shoes! Not a mark upon them!' She turned to her mother. 'Come on, Mama, let us go in.'

The door was not locke —it yielded at their push. A narrow passageway led past the stairs to the scullery and kitchen. The stairs themselves were also narrow, and gloomy, unlit by any window. A sharp turn towards the top and a final, unexpected step brought them to the parlour and the sleeping accommodations beyond. A thorough inspection of the rooms found them just as the clerk had described. The ladies walked around them, one in wonderment, one in thankfulness, one in doubt.

'I declare,' Hetty said, 'I did not know these rooms existed. I suppose Mrs Pellins has used them for storage, or for the accommodation of an elderly relative—although I never heard of one. Perhaps someone grew old here, and was unable to manage the stairs. They lived here for years, I surmise, unvisited, as, perhaps, we shall do. It may be haunted! Didn't you feel, on the stair, an odd draught? How the floorboards creak! And what is that strange moaning sound?'

'Oh Hetty,' Jane said, testily. 'Why must you be so gloomy? I felt nothing. It is a little chill but it is October and I expect the rooms have not been aired lately. The wind in the chimney makes the noise you hear. There is nothing a good fire and our own familiar belongings will not lay to rest in a moment.'

'A sound roof over our heads. A warm fire in the grate. To be able to live here, in the heart of Highbury, where everything is so familiar to us, and where we are known,' Marie sighed. 'It is indeed a blessing. People are so good.'

With hearts mainly filled with thankfulness, and having no alternative in view, of course the Bateses agreed to take the rooms, and Marie and Jane surveyed the room's proportions to decide upon which furniture could be accommodated from the vicarage, and which would have to be dispensed with.

'Our fireside chairs will arrange themselves perfectly here, with plenty of room for the sideboard there behind,' Jane observed, 'which will mean that nice china dinner service papa bought you from his first month's income can come with us, after all, Mama.'

'Plenty of shelves already provided, for your papa's books,' Marie pointed to the alcoves beside the chimney. 'And this window will be the perfect situation for our dining table—not the large one, I mean the smaller one which has been in the morning room and which we have used for breakfast these twenty years past.'

'Oh yes,' cried Jane. 'And the window seat, there, behind the table—which I can already see in my mind's eye, the perfect size and proportion—will double as a dining chair for one or even two persons, if we do have people to dine (which, I know, is not likely), but if we did …'

'Indeed, Jane,' said Marie. 'That's a very practical suggestion. We will work here, too. The light from the window, you see, will help us see to sew, or read, or write letters, and we will be able to look down into the street and see our friends and neighbours as they go about the village. Will that not be pleasant, Hetty?'

'To be sure, it will,' Hetty agreed, 'but I doubt that we will be able to persuade many to come up to visit. The stairs, you know, are so very narrow, and that step, at the top, by the turn, is very awkward.'

'Our friends will brave a narrow stair and an awkward step, to wish us well, I am sure, Hetty. Do you not hear yourself finding fault again? I am sure Mama has spoken to you about it a thousand times.'

Hetty looked shame-faced, and turned away. There was so much she had not commented on: the gloominess of the two bedrooms, for example—their small windows let in scarcely any light, and the view from them! All grocers' yards and lean-tos, and a mean little alley and a—she shuddered to consider it—a shared privy. And all the while that they had been inspecting the place she had heard Mrs Pellins haranguing her husband in the shop below. But she must be brave, as her mother and sister were being brave, so she turned back into the room and said, as brightly as she could, 'It occurs to me that the good carpet from the parlour might fit in this room very well. I wish I had brought a measure but I forgot.

Perhaps we could pace the distance, Jane?'

Marie gave Hetty a warm smile of approbation. 'Very good, Hetty, very good.'

Later, towards the end of the day, Marie slipped into the church by a side door which connected to the vicarage gardens, and took a seat on the front pew. Looking up at the pulpit, she could almost see her dear Frederick there, where he had so often stood and ministered to his flock, smiling and nodding, and the tears which poured from her eyes blurred her vision of him, and of the sunlight which streamed through the beautiful stained glass window of the west transept.

And so Mrs Bates and her daughters quit the vicarage and moved into the rooms above Pellins', and took with them Martha, maid-of-all-work, to prepare their meals and deal with their linen. They found that the south-facing aspect of the parlour made it light-filled and pleasant during the day, and, as predicted, afforded a constantly changing scene of village life below. Jane and Hetty shared the larger of the two bedrooms, Jane accommodating her sister's frequent change of preference of one side of the bed over another—one being too near the window, and too draughty, the other too near the wall, which—apparently—emanated odd creaking noises and strange scufflings in the dead of the night. Mrs Bates took the smaller room, and wore the already rather bald carpet out with her knees as she gave thanks to God each night. They continued to go out and about in the village, to visit the sick in humble cottages and to drink tea in well-appointed parlours. Indeed they found that, if anything, their daily invitations increased, so if their domestic portion of mutton was reduced, their necessity of sitting down to it was likewise diminished as dinner, tea and supper engagements took them away from their own table. And not very many days went by without the maid finding a basket of surplus fruit, a brace of pheasant, some fresh-dug vegetables or a jar of homemade preserve on the scullery steps, anonymous gifts from friends and well-wishers for the Bateses. Some of these even found their way, occasionally, to the ladies' table, although many were mislaid in the direction of the maid's mother's cottage.

Chapter 4

That evening, George and his father sat a while by the vast parlour fire. Two or three dogs, exhausted by a day of following their master from field to farm, flushing out pheasant and throwing themselves into the mill pond, lay on the rug at their feet. Mr Knightley had a book on his lap, but he was not reading it. George, likewise, held a book but paid no attention to its pages.

'Papa,' he said at last, 'I wonder if we could not do something to assist Mrs Bates.'

Mr Knightley stirred himself, uncrossed his legs and reached down absent-mindedly to stroke a dog's muzzle. 'I esteem Mrs Bates very highly,' he said. 'I have rarely met such a genteel, lady-like lady who, at the same time, has such simple, delightful, unaffected manners and practical good sense. She makes herself agreeable wherever she goes. The loss of her husband, at her comparatively early age, is a grievous blow, but I should think it very probable that she will marry again.' The squire, at this time a sprightly sixty-two years of age, had been a widower for only the last of them, and was by no means confirmed in that state for perpetuity. It would have been unseemly, so early in Mrs Bates' bereavement, to have thought of her in any matrimonial context whatsoever, nevertheless he spoke from the heart, with a warmth George had not often heard in his father's voice unless in connection with a particularly fine bull or a prodigiously good crop of barley.

'To be sure, sir,' George replied. 'But in the meantime, I gather, there is a little difficulty. Without the vicar's stipend, they have no income, and, of course, they must quit the vicarage.'

The squire roused himself a little more, and gave his son a keen look. 'No income? What? None whatsoever?'

George shook his head. 'Reverend Bates has family, I believe, well-provisioned, but they have declined assistance.'

'Absolutely declined?'

'Yes, sir. Jane came today to help me with my lesson, you know …'

'A bright girl. Pretty too. She'll marry well, I have no doubt.'

'No doubt, sir,' said George, warmly, wishing himself ten years older, 'but she is very young, and even if she does marry advantageously, there is still Mrs Bates, and Miss Bates …'

'Ah yes, Miss Bates. Well she's a different case altogether.'

'Exactly my point, sir.'

'Well, George, I am very pleased with you for taking this proper, paternal interest in these worthy people. It is just what the future squire ought to do. And what do you suggest?'

George squirmed a little in his seat. He had not expected to be called upon provide a solution to Jane's problem, only hoped that, by raising it, his father might do so. But he took a deep breath and answered his father stoutly. 'Sir, if I were squire, I would make discreet enquiries amongst the better-off gentlemen of the town, and I could see what could be done between us to provide Mrs Bates and her daughters with a modest home and a small income.'

Mr Knightley nodded. Encouraged, George went on, 'It is the duty of those who have much to provide for those who have little. The Bible tells us so, as well as good sense and common decency. I understand she has served us—the parish, I mean sir—for twenty odd years, and now it is time for us to repay in kind. For myself, if I had a vacant cottage somewhere on the estate, I would happily give it over to her use. Although it might be more rustic than she has been used to, and she might not like the remoteness from the village, it would be something. I would be happy to contribute to a fund which would provide them with an income. Many of us here about have orchards, flocks, crops and good things in abundance, sometimes in over-abundance. Our own supplies of rhubarb and spinach this year seemed never-ending; I was heartily sick of both in the end. There is no reason why the surplus could not be offered to them if they will do us the kindness to take it off our hands.'

'And what if Mrs Bates declined to be the recipient of the charity of her neighbours? Some people might find it demeaning.'

'I do not think Mrs Bates has that kind of pride,

Father, but I suppose the money could be offered in such a way as to keep its source a secret?'

'My goodness, George, my boy,' Mr Knightley burst out, 'what a Solomon you are! If only men twice—nay, three or four times—your age had your sense and innately charitable heart, the world would be a better place indeed. It is a pity that I need you to take over the estate when I am gone. To be sure, I think I had better begin training John to do it for I see that you will be wasted here. Your place is in politics!'

George blushed. He had rarely heard such praise from his father. 'Thank you, sir,' he stammered.

Mr Knightley reached for his pipe. 'Now, off to bed with you sir, before you shame me into giving succour to every poor widow-woman in the county!'

George stood up. 'Good night then, sir. But, as for Mrs Bates ..?'

'Yes, yes, I will look into it. Good night now, son.'

And so it happened that not many days had passed before Mrs Bates received a call from John Abdy. John had been the reverend's clerk for the whole period of his incumbency, a worthy and respectable man treated with warmth and affection by the vicarage family whether visiting on business or for pleasure. But on this occasion he seemed flustered and discomposed, kneaded his hat in his hands and looked at the carpet, the fireplace, the casement—anywhere, indeed, than at Mrs Bates herself. The summary of his news, when he had managed to stumble it out, was that 'a small but significant paragraph had been found in the church's founding articles, that was to say, in the town's charter, or at least, mentioned in the one and detailed more fully in the other, which stated that in such a case as hers it was incumbent upon the parish, on the one hand, and on the guilds and local institutes upon the other, or any properly constituted body so located, overseen by an obscure department of the bishop's office, who devolved responsibility for it back onto the clerk, to provide, in short …' the clerk took a breath, and fumbled with a sheaf of papers bound in red ribbon. 'In short, Mrs Bates,' he concluded, in a rush, 'I have the happiness to tell you that, should you require them, a suite of rooms above Pellins' the grocers is available for you, free of rent. Two bedrooms, a parlour, small indeed but with two windows overlooking High Street, a scullery below, at the rear, and, in the attic, room for a maid. And an annual allowance of coals and a sum of £50, payable for your lifetime, madam, or until your … but it seems indelicate to mention …'

'Until I remarry?' Mrs Bates provided.

'Yes, indeed, Madam. May I tell the gentleman, that is, gentlemen of the … the committees variously concerned, that you are happy to accept?'

'Oh yes,' Marie said, a catch in her voice. She advanced towards the clerk and took his hand warmly, 'and please to inform those gentlemen, whoever they are, that they have the gratitude of my heart for their great goodness.'

It was the work of only a few moments for the ladies to attire themselves and walk the quarter mile to the High Street. In a shadowy angle of a half gable, rather obscured by creeper, a small door next to the grocer's revealed itself to them.

'Well, I declare,' Henrietta said, gazing at it with wonderment, 'that I never noticed this door before, and I have been to Pellins' more times than I can count. But it is so narrow, and in the shadow cast by the gable, almost disappears in the gloom. The ivy, there, is very thick—quite overhanging the lintel. And then, the pavement is much fractured just here, and I daresay there's a puddle every time it rains. I have probably avoided it, for fear of tripping …'

'Or of drowning?' Jane put in quickly. 'Good morning, Mrs Pellins! A fine day indeed! I thank you, quite well. No. Very dry. Look at our shoes! Not a mark upon them!' She turned to her mother. 'Come on, Mama, let us go in.'

The door was not locke —it yielded at their push. A narrow passageway led past the stairs to the scullery and kitchen. The stairs themselves were also narrow, and gloomy, unlit by any window. A sharp turn towards the top and a final, unexpected step brought them to the parlour and the sleeping accommodations beyond. A thorough inspection of the rooms found them just as the clerk had described. The ladies walked around them, one in wonderment, one in thankfulness, one in doubt.

'I declare,' Hetty said, 'I did not know these rooms existed. I suppose Mrs Pellins has used them for storage, or for the accommodation of an elderly relative—although I never heard of one. Perhaps someone grew old here, and was unable to manage the stairs. They lived here for years, I surmise, unvisited, as, perhaps, we shall do. It may be haunted! Didn't you feel, on the stair, an odd draught? How the floorboards creak! And what is that strange moaning sound?'

'Oh Hetty,' Jane said, testily. 'Why must you be so gloomy? I felt nothing. It is a little chill but it is October and I expect the rooms have not been aired lately. The wind in the chimney makes the noise you hear. There is nothing a good fire and our own familiar belongings will not lay to rest in a moment.'

'A sound roof over our heads. A warm fire in the grate. To be able to live here, in the heart of Highbury, where everything is so familiar to us, and where we are known,' Marie sighed. 'It is indeed a blessing. People are so good.'

With hearts mainly filled with thankfulness, and having no alternative in view, of course the Bateses agreed to take the rooms, and Marie and Jane surveyed the room's proportions to decide upon which furniture could be accommodated from the vicarage, and which would have to be dispensed with.

'Our fireside chairs will arrange themselves perfectly here, with plenty of room for the sideboard there behind,' Jane observed, 'which will mean that nice china dinner service papa bought you from his first month's income can come with us, after all, Mama.'

'Plenty of shelves already provided, for your papa's books,' Marie pointed to the alcoves beside the chimney. 'And this window will be the perfect situation for our dining table—not the large one, I mean the smaller one which has been in the morning room and which we have used for breakfast these twenty years past.'

'Oh yes,' cried Jane. 'And the window seat, there, behind the table—which I can already see in my mind's eye, the perfect size and proportion—will double as a dining chair for one or even two persons, if we do have people to dine (which, I know, is not likely), but if we did …'

'Indeed, Jane,' said Marie. 'That's a very practical suggestion. We will work here, too. The light from the window, you see, will help us see to sew, or read, or write letters, and we will be able to look down into the street and see our friends and neighbours as they go about the village. Will that not be pleasant, Hetty?'

'To be sure, it will,' Hetty agreed, 'but I doubt that we will be able to persuade many to come up to visit. The stairs, you know, are so very narrow, and that step, at the top, by the turn, is very awkward.'

'Our friends will brave a narrow stair and an awkward step, to wish us well, I am sure, Hetty. Do you not hear yourself finding fault again? I am sure Mama has spoken to you about it a thousand times.'

Hetty looked shame-faced, and turned away. There was so much she had not commented on: the gloominess of the two bedrooms, for example—their small windows let in scarcely any light, and the view from them! All grocers' yards and lean-tos, and a mean little alley and a—she shuddered to consider it—a shared privy. And all the while that they had been inspecting the place she had heard Mrs Pellins haranguing her husband in the shop below. But she must be brave, as her mother and sister were being brave, so she turned back into the room and said, as brightly as she could, 'It occurs to me that the good carpet from the parlour might fit in this room very well. I wish I had brought a measure but I forgot.

Perhaps we could pace the distance, Jane?'

Marie gave Hetty a warm smile of approbation. 'Very good, Hetty, very good.'

Later, towards the end of the day, Marie slipped into the church by a side door which connected to the vicarage gardens, and took a seat on the front pew. Looking up at the pulpit, she could almost see her dear Frederick there, where he had so often stood and ministered to his flock, smiling and nodding, and the tears which poured from her eyes blurred her vision of him, and of the sunlight which streamed through the beautiful stained glass window of the west transept.

And so Mrs Bates and her daughters quit the vicarage and moved into the rooms above Pellins', and took with them Martha, maid-of-all-work, to prepare their meals and deal with their linen. They found that the south-facing aspect of the parlour made it light-filled and pleasant during the day, and, as predicted, afforded a constantly changing scene of village life below. Jane and Hetty shared the larger of the two bedrooms, Jane accommodating her sister's frequent change of preference of one side of the bed over another—one being too near the window, and too draughty, the other too near the wall, which—apparently—emanated odd creaking noises and strange scufflings in the dead of the night. Mrs Bates took the smaller room, and wore the already rather bald carpet out with her knees as she gave thanks to God each night. They continued to go out and about in the village, to visit the sick in humble cottages and to drink tea in well-appointed parlours. Indeed they found that, if anything, their daily invitations increased, so if their domestic portion of mutton was reduced, their necessity of sitting down to it was likewise diminished as dinner, tea and supper engagements took them away from their own table. And not very many days went by without the maid finding a basket of surplus fruit, a brace of pheasant, some fresh-dug vegetables or a jar of homemade preserve on the scullery steps, anonymous gifts from friends and well-wishers for the Bateses. Some of these even found their way, occasionally, to the ladies' table, although many were mislaid in the direction of the maid's mother's cottage.

Chapter 5

Christmas came, and Mrs Bates and her daughters celebrated it in the lofty hall of Donwell Abbey with the squire's carriage to convey them there and back again.

'After dinner there is to be other company, and dancing, I dare say,' Mrs Bates informed her daughters as the carriage took them through the pleasingly undulating park of the Abbey. 'Although we are in mourning I will not deny you girls the pleasure of standing up with such good friends and neighbours as will be present. But I rely on you to remember your manners.'

'I shall not remember my manners to Mrs Winwood,' Jane declared, stoutly, 'since she has been so remiss in remembering hers.'

'You will not be called upon to converse with Mrs Winwood,' Mrs Bates soothed. 'It will be sufficient that you are civil to her girls.'

'I do not like Ursula Winwood,' Jane grumbled. 'She loses no opportunity to remind me that the bedroom which used to mine is now hers. She intends to strip off the rosebud wallpaper, she says.'

'Of course they will wish to make alterations,' Mrs Bates said.

'She will be very sorry if she attempts any such thing,' Hetty said. 'You will not remember it, Jane, but the workmen who put that paper up had no end of trouble with it. The plaster underneath is unstable and the gable wall is very damp. If they could get it to stick at all it would not stick smooth. Do you not recall, Mama?'

'I do,' Mrs Bates nodded. 'That is why we put all those pictures up on your wall—to hide the damp and uneven patches. But we will keep our recollections to ourselves. Miss Sophia is an energetic, friendly girl, I think. Perhaps you will strike up a friendship with her.'

'Sophia is a determined flirt. She speaks of nothing but beaux. And I will strike up no friendship with any member of a family which snubs mine.'

'As a favour to me, Jane, you will be polite to all the squire's guests, whoever they may be. Refuse no gentleman who asks you to dance but if you are *not* asked, observe and share the pleasure of others who are. Do not sulk. Drink sparingly of the punch and,' with a particular glance at Hetty, 'let your companion's conversation dictate your own. Respond briefly to their observations, return their enquiries and encourage them to talk. If they are taciturn, or little inclined to conversation, remember silence, and a smile, can be as articulate as—and a good deal more polite than—a tirade of ill-considered verbiage.'

'If all else fails, talk about the weather,' Jane declared. 'That's what *I* do.'

'Very wise, Jane.'

'The weather will prove an interesting topic, I conjecture,' said Hetty, looking out of the carriage window. 'Snow clouds are gathering on the horizon, or, if they pass over, there will be a heavy frost. The squire's coachman will be unhappy about turning out to take us home whichever comes to pass. The carriage may well overturn. At the very least the horses will slip and skid. I wonder many of the squire's guests will risk setting out, such are the hazards.'

'I hope they are more sanguine than you, at any rate,' Jane laughed. 'I wish to dance, since Mama says we may, and although George Knightley says he will stand up with me, I hope for more equal partners also.'

'George is as far above you, in one sense, as he is below you in another,' Hetty remarked. 'He will be squire, one day, owner of Donwell, with all the influence his father has now, and more. Ten years more and he will be marriageable. Could you wait that long?'

'Good heavens, Hetty, how your imagination runs away with you!' Mrs Bates cried. 'From a simple dance to matrimony! What a leap!'

'George is a sweet boy, but he is a child. I cannot imagine him grown. And I do not expect to spend the next ten years in Highbury,' said Jane.

'Do you not?' Marie asked, turning to her daughter.

'No, Mama. I wish to see more of life than Highbury can offer. Is that wrong of me? Does it upset you?'

'I think you had much better stay at home,' Hetty said, with a shudder. 'The evils of the world are innumerable. Think of the dangers! What bad characters you may encounter—charlatans and scoundrels. Pestilence and disease.'

'What friends I might make! What sights I might see!'

Jane replied, wistfully.

'And here we are at Donwell,' Marie said, to put an end to the discourse. 'How beautiful the Abbey looks—the candles in the windows, the wreath on the door, and there is our good friend the squire, coming out to meet us. How kind he is! Come, girls. Let us not keep him waiting.'

Squire George Knightley of Donwell was a well-looking man in spite of his years. A life spent out and about on his estate had kept him lean and hale. He had such height as gives a man stature and authority without making him looming or ridiculous. His face—to be sure, a little weathered, a little lined, a little grizzled about the eyebrow—was benign, his eyes clear and kind and his voice low. His mind was businesslike but his heart was compassionate and his words generally reflected both. He worked diligently for the good of his community, running his estate, treating his tenants well, sitting on the bench in Kingston and overseeing parish matters. He had married rather late in life, when all expectation of it had been given up by his acquaintance. A distant cousin had been destined to inherit in due course when a young lady of a good

Kingston family had caught the squire's attention and won his heart. Considerably his junior in years she had been his equal in respectability and gentility and had adapted herself quickly and perfectly to the role of the wife of the squire. For ten years they had been happy. Two boys had been born to them, the second coming into the world as his mother slipped out of it. The squire lamented her passing of course—lamented it bitterly. But he had his estate to run and his boys to bring up. He had lived most of his life as a single man and he had readapted himself to that condition with comparative ease.

Squire Knightley rarely accepted invitations even from the higher ranking families of Highbury. He declared that in the course of his business he encountered quite enough of them to know how they did; he did not need to eat his mutton at their table to know more. He liked offering hospitality in ways which removed, rather than enforced social boundaries; his annual harvest supper was held in one of his vast barns. The great and the good of Highbury could expect to mix with the humble and hard-working and any lady who supposed herself too high to sit next to the miller's wife or to dance with a ploughman had better stay away. Accordingly, for Christmas, the squire had invited a broad cross section of Highbury and Donwell society to celebrate with him. The lofty hall rang with laughter as twenty people sat down to dinner, the Yule log burned brightly in the vast fireplace and the table groaned with the squire's generosity.

After dinner the table was cleared and the furniture pushed back as more guests arrived to join the festivities; Reverend Winwood, his wife and children, representatives from Highbury's better families, Mr and Mrs Ford the haberdashers and other tradespeople as well as some of Mr Knightley's more prosperous tenant farmers, the miller and the steward. Hot cider punch was served and the sideboard laden with pies and sides of ham, salads and cheese. Soon the hall of Donwell Abbey was thronged with merry-makers and the fiddlers began to play.

George quickly claimed Jane as his partner. Mr Knightley sought to engage Mrs Bates for a quadrille and the *Sir Roger de Coverley* but she declined both. 'I do not mean to dance,' she said, smoothing her black mourning gown, 'much as I enjoy it. It would seem … disrespectful.'

Mr Knightley bowed and withdrew, but he was very disappointed. Presently he led Mrs Stokes to the head of the set. He danced with surprisingly light and rhythmic step. Mrs Stokes, a widow of some years standing who ran the Crown, was a comely woman, Marie Bates' equal in years and almost as beautiful. She danced with energy as well as grace—the two made a very attractive couple. The squire's period of mourning was over and he was free to seek another wife.

'Do you see?' Mrs Bates' friend Mrs Weston remarked as she observed the two. 'She has not birth, but she has a good business head on her shoulders I think. We always suspected it was she, and not her husband, who managed the Crown so successfully, and she has proved us right. Since he died, it has become more successful than ever.'

'Indeed it has,' Marie agreed, 'but I do not think the squire would choose such a one as her to be a mother to his boys.' She could not precisely say why, but Mrs Bates felt a vague discomfort about Mrs Stokes. She knew nothing in particular to that lady's discredit and yet it was so. What kind of lady could work in an inn and not be in some way tainted by the roughness of the place, the drinking men, the foul-mouthed coach drivers?

Mrs Weston gave a knowing look. 'It is not always *maternal* qualities a man looks for in a wife, you know. But there is Abel Larkins taking your Hetty in *Le Boulangere!* Well, that will test him!'

And indeed it did look as though Abel rather regretted his dance partner, all arms and legs as Hetty was, spinning off here and putting in extra twirls there, and fizzing all the while and likely to explode while Abel— a heftily built man—puffed and wheezed and struggled to keep up.

Since she had decided not to dance, Mrs Bates made herself useful by overseeing the arrangements of the supper table and making sure the older guests had chairs and were adequately served with all the good things Mr Knightley had provided. She directed some of the younger people away from the cider and towards the elderflower cordials, and encouraged the shyer youths to engage the girls in dances. From time to time she sent the maids back to the kitchens, that they might enjoy the servants' celebrations there.

'We will manage quite well here for half an hour,' she told them. 'You go and have something to eat in the servants' hall. I will send if we need anything in the meantime.'

The girls gave her a grateful smile, put down their pitchers and scurried away. She would not go so far as to appear as the hostess—that would be a presumption too far—but in many small ways she ensured the smooth running of the affair.

Finding Mrs Winwood alone near the supper table with no one to talk to, she undertook to engage that lady in conversation. They exchanged cool pleasantries—the splendour of the spread, the number of couples, the likelihood of snow.

'Reverend Winwood is decidedly against it,' Mrs Winwood declared. 'He says the wind is in the wrong quarter.'

'*Does* he, indeed?' Mrs Bates replied, wondering what Reverend Winwood might know of it, such a recent resident in the area. 'And how are you all settled, in your new accommodations?' The slight emphasis of her question invited Mrs Winwood to return it. The vicarage, after all, was not the only residence in Highbury to have a new family in it.

But Mrs Winwood refused the bait. 'Such a great deal to arrange and improve,' she said, archly. 'I doubt we will be fully settled until Easter. I certainly could not think of entertaining until then.'

Her remark called for no rejoinder, and Mrs Bates made none. She busied herself by rearranging the dishes on the supper table, and, when she saw that something was amiss with the ham joint, sending one of the squire's menservants to remedy it.

'Upon my word, Mrs Bates, I do declare,' Mrs Winwood burst out. 'You make yourself uncommonly at home here at Donwell Abbey. Anyone would take you for the lady of the place! I fear you rather over step your mark, ma'am.'

'I do hope not,' Marie replied. 'I have known the squire for many years. He and my late husband were intimate friends. When Mrs Knightley was alive, she was mine. I am quite confident of my place in Mr Knightley's esteem to be sure that I do not trespass.'

Mrs Winwood glanced toward the centre of the room,

where Mr Knightley danced with Mrs Stokes once more. 'What a handsome couple. The discrepancy in their ages nothing at all—no impediment. And she is such a handsome woman, is she not? And widowed these past five years I understand. Well, *that* is a very proper period of mourning, I think.'

'I would not presume to have any opinion on the topic,' Mrs Bates said. Very soon the ladies found themselves separated by the press of others at the table and Marie was able to make her escape. In the guise of surveying the whole room, she watched the squire and Mrs Stokes. Though it pained her to admit it, they *did* make a fine couple. For all her confidence when challenged by Mrs Winwood, she did wonder if she had perhaps gone too far in presuming to manage matters for the squire. Accordingly she found a seat in an alcove, where the draught from a slightly open window cooled her heated face, and where she could rest unobserved for a while.

It was not long, however, before Mr Knightley found her out. 'There you are!' he exclaimed, 'half hidden behind my great grandfather's armoire. I wanted to thank you. I am only just at liberty for a moment from the dance and the discourse of the men around the cider jugs but I wanted to say I have seen you making up for my lack. My hospitality lacks a woman's touch. I am grateful for you making it good.'

'Not at all, you are all generosity and provision. I have simply been helping some of the matrons and older gentlemen.'

'And curbing the high spirits of the young people, and overseeing the servants. I have seen it all but I have not until this moment been able to get close enough to you to say how much I appreciate it. Are you sure you will not stand up with me?'

'If I were to stand up with anyone, it would be you,' Marie said, 'such an old friend as you are. The very first to bid us welcome when we came to Highbury, the very first also to come when Frederick died and offer condolences. And all you have done since—do not think am I ignorant it Sir. If I could repay you with a dance, I would do it. But I have decided not to dance and I must not allow my gratitude or the delights of the day to sway me from my resolution. It is but three months since I became a widow. I do not think it would be seemly and I would not expose either of us to malicious comment.'

Her voice held genuine regret and indeed as she looked up at him—so handsome in his most elegant coat, a white froth of lace at his neck, his thick, curly hair—she was glad he did not powder it or cover it with a wig—she found she was very full of regret. She would have liked to have danced with him. She had missed a man's embrace. The feeling of wanting to be held swamped her momentarily. Mr Knightley saw her blush, saw the glisten of a tear on her lashes, but misconstrued the cause.

'I have distressed you, ma'am,' he said, withdrawing. 'Forgive me.'

Among the Highbury contingent for dancing and tea was one Lieutenant Weston. Now the Westons were a respectable and long-established Highbury family who, although starting in trade, had risen beyond their original rank to not inconsiderable wealth and importance. Mrs Bates was intimate with Mrs Weston; they moved within the same circles, drank tea at one another's houses and worked together on a number of philanthropic projects amongst the poor and needy of the parish. Two sons had gone into the family business but the Lieutenant, James, had chosen a career in the militia and been absent from the locality for some years. He had distinguished himself, risen to the rank of Lieutenant and bore his uniform with exceptional dignity and grace. He was single, and had good prospects, either from his own wit and bravery in his chosen sphere, or from his family. In appearance he was an exceptionally good-looking man, with an open countenance and frank, grey eyes. By reputation he was open-tempered and uncomplicated, genial and well-liked wherever he went. He moved around the room now greeting old acquaintance with every evidence of delight and affability, shaking hands with all and sundry, smiling and nodding, drawing every eye.

He drew the particular eye of Miss Sophia Winwood. Miss Sophia had not taken sparingly of the hot cider punch and was already making an exhibition of herself by speaking much too loudly and dancing with outrageous abandon. She had gathered around her an entourage of other silly girls—two Miss Coxes and a Miss Snell, as well as her sister Ursula. They all crowded round Lieutenant Weston, blushing and giggling until he had engaged each of them for two dances. Jane, Mrs Bates was pleased to see, kept herself at a distance from their shenanigans, bouncing little John Knightley on her lap when she was not dancing with his brother or playing with the younger sons and daughters of the yeomanry. She danced with the miller's son and a young apprentice of the farrier. Hetty had not danced since standing up with the steward. She stood in conversation with some of the Highbury matrons.

Mrs Bates gave a sigh. If only Lieutenant Weston would notice Hetty. Although *she* would never have couched it in such vulgar terms, he would be a catch for any woman who managed to take his eye. Highbury and its environs did not boast so many sons of good family and excellent prospects that its marriageable daughters could afford to let one pass without exerting themselves. George Knightley, as Jane had pointed out, was too young. There were sons at Clayton Park but they were destined to marry women of rank and fortune; if Hetty had ever had a chance with one of them, it had passed. Mr Snell, the lawyer, had two sons but both were away at University and one, at least, was reputed to be running rather wild. Neither would do for Hetty, who would be considered by both as old enough to be labelled an old maid. The steadier of the two might take Jane if the lack of dowry could be overlooked. But it was a distant prospect and not an especially desirable one—Jane deserved better. Mr and Mrs Ford had a son who would take over the business after them. He was a year or so older than Hetty, and the Fords were respectable people. Mrs Bates was the last person in the world to scruple at their being in trade, and if Hetty had liked him she would not have raised an objection. But the man was known to be mean-tempered and moody. He had not even deigned to come to Mr Knightley's party, preferring his own company on Christmas night to that of his neighbours. No, she did not think Obadiah Ford could make Hetty happy.

Enumerating these prospects of husbands for her girls was not pleasant for Marie, but it was necessary. The news that Jane wished to quit Highbury for a wider sphere had not come as a surprise—her intelligence and strength of character had always suggested it as a probability—and in many ways it was glad tidings. If

Highbury could not supply a man good enough for Jane, the wider world, surely, would do so, if only Mrs Bates could somehow get her launched. But Hetty was a different matter. She was already rather past the ideal age for marriage. Her excitable character meant that she needed a husband who would handle her firmly, but with understanding. A calm, even-tempered man. Where, in Highbury, was she to find such a one? But now, here was James Weston. That *he* was unexceptionable marriage material Marie had little doubt. But whether he would see Hetty in the same light was a different matter.

As she had tallied the eligible men in Highbury, Marie now reckoned the unattached young women with whom Hetty would have to vie for the attentions of Lieutenant Weston. She soon came to the conclusion that apart from Hetty, Highbury could supply few young ladies likely to meet Lieutenant Weston's requirements. The oldest Miss Winwood, Hermia, was of the age (or, perhaps, even a year or so beyond it) when marriage might be looked to, but she was bookish and introspective and had a pronounced over bite. There was a Miss Clayton at Clayton Park, but it seemed unlikely James Weston would look so high. Mrs Coxe had daughters aplenty but they were all silly, insipid girls and the Coxes came from a lower order even than the Westons. Hetty was equal—perhaps even a degree or two superior—to Lieutenant Weston in rank and an ideal three years his junior. Her lack of fortune might not weigh too heavily with him, a man who would be wealthy by his own diligence or as a result of his family's fortune. The more Marie thought of it, the more desirable the match seemed, and there was little time to waste. There was no knowing how long the lieutenant would be in Highbury or when his next visit might be.

Mrs Bates looked about the room to find her daughter, with the idea of giving her some little directions and advice about how she should comport herself when Lieutenant Weston asked her to dance— which he inevitably would, it being his duty as an unattached man to partner as many single ladies in the room as the number of dances allowed. At present he was working his way through Sophia Winwood's posse. Jane was partnered by the miller's boy again—a strapping, handsome lad. How small she looked, against the boy's brawny outline. How pretty and fine her features, and how intelligent, against the rustic blandness of his.

The dance ended and the revellers returned to positions around the room. Many made for the cider tray. Lieutenant Weston returned the Coxe girl he had partnered to her mama, and then approached Jane. His bow was very low, his smile very warm. Jane, Mrs Bates saw, returned his greeting very properly and glanced over at her, to see if she might allow the young man to engage her for a dance. Mrs Bates gave a slight nod, and Mrs Weston bustled up at that moment to make the introductions. The musicians struck up once more, and Lieutenant Weston led Jane to the top of the set.

Small hope now of Hetty catching the Lieutenant's eye. No one, in a room with both girls, would prefer Hetty over Jane. But where *was* Hetty?

Chapter 6

Hetty was sitting within the inglenook with a gentleman who had been introduced as Mr Henry Woodhouse. The name of Woodhouse—the younger branch of an ancient family—had been long associated with Highbury without, in living memory, ever being represented there. The vicissitudes of court life, the expediencies of war and the vagaries of fortune had removed them from a county where, however, they were still counted as very much at home. Now, this Mr Woodhouse had come back to the area to settle and was seeking to buy land whereon to build himself a house. He had met Lieutenant Weston on the coach and the two had fallen into conversation. A mutual liking had sprung up although the two were rather unlike in character; Weston all openness and geniality, overcoming every obstacle with a bound, Woodhouse rather morose and tending to caution, seeing impediments in the slightest thing. Mr Woodhouse had been bound on personal business some miles west, as far as Oxfordshire, intending to return to Highbury to find his plot when his business was concluded, but Lieutenant Weston's enthusiasm had been compelling; the healthful air and pleasant countryside around the place, the worthy families there resident, the availability of good land, timber and stone. Compounded with a little reluctance felt on the part of Mr Woodhouse to address the business in Oxfordshire, they had persuaded him to linger. The intelligence that Lieutenant Weston intended, at some time in the future, to buy property there, had convinced Mr Woodhouse that he could do no better than break his journey and look about the place before travelling on.

Mr Woodhouse was a man in his early thirties, but, in appearance, demeanour and habit, some twenty years beyond that. He was tall, but walked stooped, with a stick. In figure he was somewhat lean, but so swathed in shawls and wraps and spare waistcoats that he seemed almost portly. He tended not to exert himself to be sociable—shrinking from the crowd around the supper table and walking the full perimeter of the room to avoid rubbing shoulders with the jostle of dancers at its centre—but when society came to him and met him on his own terms, he was sociable enough. In manner he was very gentlemanlike. His bearing was elegant if his clothes were not. His name alone commanded the respect and awe which his person left somewhat wanting and, all in all, he had excited a deal of interest and curiosity amongst the squire's guests. Many had wanted to talk about him but few had wanted to talk to him, and it had been left to Hetty—at that moment unengaged in the dance— to entertain the newcomer.

Having quickly induced her to think the dance floor a great deal too crowded and boisterous, Mr Woodhouse consented to be attended by Hetty and they agreed to take a seat by the fire. 'I do not venture out in the evenings, in general,' he announced. 'I find the evening air to be chill and ill-conducive to a man with a weakness in the chest. Indeed, even if it does no actual harm I can hardly think it does good to any, even those most blessed with health. And yet,' with a sigh, 'I know gentlemen who think nothing of walking a mile or more to spend an evening at cards with their friends. They don't think it worthwhile putting their horses to for such a short distance.'

Mindful of her mother's advice, Miss Bates re-joined,

'Oh yes, and so it is here in Highbury. I can count on only one hand the number of families who even keep a closed carriage and I vouch none of them would think of using it for such trifling distances as one thing is from another, here. The vicarage—where, you may know, until recently, my family resided—is the farthest house out of the village, a quarter of a mile, perhaps, down Vicarage Lane—apart from Randalls, which is a sadly broken down place, all shut up, so does not signify. We all walk everywhere, here! But you are quite right; it might not always be advisable. Think, after the chill air, to come into a room so hot and humid as this, where persons are exerting themselves in the dance! Anyone with a vulnerable constitution would be ill-advised indeed. I am surprised to see the youngest Miss Winwood amongst us, for I know she was crippled with croup only last week and that, you know, can have very serious complications. Young Joshua Hopley almost died of it two winters ago. He was an infant, however. I am almost sure it was croup, but it could have been the whooping cough. But the apothecary attended every day—that I do recall, for Papa paid the bill out of his own pocket. No, no. I assure you, I am quite of your opinion, Sir. No one with a pulmonary complaint should risk an evening party if it can be avoided. Oh, Sir. Are you unwell? The fire is rather fierce. I wonder they did not take your wrap from you at the door. Shall I assist you? No? Oh, well, if you really think… So, what were we discussing? Oh yes, evening parties. Well, I suppose the attraction of such a party as *this*, and the festive season, not to mention the great honour of an invitation to Donwell Abbey (for, I assure you, the squire does not entertain very often, and certainly not in this style) will overcome many a scruple on the grounds of health. So,' she concluded, 'you do not generally go out in the evenings? We are exceptionally fortunate, then, that you have made an allowance on this occasion. I wonder what convinced you to break your usual habit.'

But Mr Woodhouse did not elucidate beyond a querulous, 'I wonder too, now.' He eyed the Miss Winwood in question narrowly. 'Croup, you say? That is a very serious complaint. Is it contagious? I wonder her parents have brought her. Children are delightful, of course, but not always at an evening party, I think. Childhood ailments spread so quickly. I wonder

Knightley is not more careful of his boys.'

'I do not think George or John has known a day's illness! George broke his arm last year, falling from a tree, and he once fell through the ice of the mill pond, but suffered no harm, and a dog of theirs was bitten by an adder, and died horribly. But apart from that, the Knightleys are as hale and hearty as you would wish.'

'Mrs Knightley, I believe, died in childbirth?'

'Oh yes, of course. But I do not count such a complication as that as illness, do you? Tragic though it was.'

'I would not count a broken arm as illness in itself, but if infection sets in, there is no knowing what it can lead to.'

'To be sure,' Miss Bates agreed, warming to her theme—this was just the sort of conversation she enjoyed—'and I recall an incident some years back in which a ploughman suffered so bad a break that the arm never did recover. Slipped on some ice—you know how it collects in the ruts and pot-holes. Over he went and that was that. The limb was twisted and useless ever afterwards. Or was that a leg? I do not quite recall, but it was certainly so, and he never ploughed another field.'

Mr Woodhouse, rather than being gratified by having had his point proven, looked aghast. 'It makes one fear to venture out at all,' he muttered.

'Indeed,' Hetty agreed, cheerfully. She was having a splendid time, and could not have found a companion more suited in opinion and interests. 'So you are staying at the Crown? How are you finding the accommodations there, Sir? Mrs Stokes is very particular as to bed linen, I believe, and fresh sawdust is strewn every day—I know that as a fact. But some inns one hears report of…'

'In general I avoid inns,' Mr Woodhouse said, 'But the Crown came recommended by my friend Weston and I have not found it wanting. Some direction was required as to the fare—I abhor grease above anything, and a superfluity of butter is almost as bad— but once Mrs Stokes understood my requirements she has been most helpful and accommodating. Are you acquainted with my friend Weston?'

'I know Mr and Mrs Weston very well, but I have not seen Lieutenant Weston since he went away to the militia and that would be—let me think now—well, many years. Mrs Weston is prodigiously proud of her son and indeed he is very handsome and quite the gentleman. He is dancing with Sophia Winwood— what an elegant couple they make. He dances very well, do you not think? Very light on his feet indeed, and look how he swings her round quite as though she were no weight at all. This is a merry tune indeed. My feet are twitching.'

'I do not dance, madam, I am sorry to say, or I would be honoured to engage you. But the floor is so crowded and the people are so heated. Nothing would induce me to risk it. I would not recommend you join the revels. You are better sitting quietly here with me. By and by we will see if a bowl of gruel is to be had.'

'I thank you for your consideration, Sir. It had not occurred to me—that is, the heat and press of dancers—and someone is sure to turn an ankle or fall into the fire. I will be guided by you, and be content to watch, and if I can catch the maid's attention I will enquire after refreshment for you, Sir. It is Bessy—I know her very well. She is cousin to our own Martha. Bessy! Bessy! Oh! She does not see me.'

'Pray do not trouble yourself on my account, madam. It grows almost too late for supper. I always think supper, eaten too late, lies heavily on the constitution. It lies heavily on mine. I have been advised to avoid anything after eight in the evening.'

'My papa used to suffer with indigestion but he was an inveterate eater of cheese just before bedtime. He died, you know, in September.'

'From indigestion? I do not wonder at it. Cheese is the very worst culprit of all and when taken late at night it can cause the intestines to spasm most painfully.'

'You mistake me, Sir. My papa died of a stroke. It was very sudden. We had no inkling of illness at all. I know for certain that he had eaten no cheese because cook remarked that what we had in the pantry had gone rancid and been thrown out. She was most vexed about it. But,' recalling her mother's advice, 'do you return to the Crown on foot, this evening, or by carriage? Mr Knightley has been so good as to put his at our disposal, but I am sure we could convey you in it, if you wish. I am sure Mr Knightley would be only too pleased. We live on the High Street, you know, almost opposite the Crown, so it wouldn't be the least inconvenience. And then, Mr Woodhouse, you could be sure of getting home safely. Donwell's driveway, you know, is quite well maintained, and yet, in the dark, for someone who does not quite know the path, there is always the danger of a fall… and one could lie incapacitated all night long. All in all, I think you had much better come in the coach, with us.'

'You are very kind, Miss Bates, but I have hired a coach and four,' said Mr Woodhouse.

'A coach and four?' exclaimed Miss Bates. 'Were you under the misapprehension that Donwell Abbey was a great distance from Highbury, then? Or that the road was very treacherous? I would not have given you that impression, for all the world!'

'Neither, Madam. But I perceived a frost in the air. Even snow, I thought, was not unlikely, and took proper precautions.'

'I too, predicted snow. The clouds over the hills looked grey and heavy as we drove here. I hope Martha has banked up the fire, at home.'

'A properly banked fire is a difficult thing to achieve. If a coal should slip… But I shall not stay but half an hour more, to be sure of getting back before the temperature drops further,' Mr Woodhouse said, ignoring Hetty's blanched expression. 'Boxwell, the coachman, is very steady, I am assured, very steady indeed, but one cannot legislate for a thick frost, pot-holes filled with ice or a horse made skittish by snow and I shall not court risk of any kind. Others may be careless of their personal safety but that is not an accusation which could be laid at my door. I pride myself I have more sense.'

'Well,' said Hetty, 'snow does not often stick here in Highbury. We are so sheltered, you see, by the hills to the west. Having said that there was one winter when it lay very thick, and did not clear for some weeks. I know Mr Boxwell, of course, and he is steady, as you say, and I am sure will partake but sparingly of the punch which is sure to be on offer in the servants' hall. Mr Knightley is so very liberal, and it is Christmas, after all…'

But Mr Woodhouse seemed far from reassured. 'There should be no evening parties,' he declared, squirming in his seat. 'The dangers are legion. I wonder how the weather fares. You, girl,' (hailing a servant), 'go and see if it snows, will you? And tell Boxwell, from the

Crown, that he is on no account to take any punch.'

The girl curtseyed, and, rather exacerbating Mr Woodhouse's fears, offered the tray of hot punch she carried. But he waived it away, requesting a cup of warm water instead, if thin gruel was not to be had, and if either could be brought *quickly,* before eight o'clock. Miss Bates was sorry for the downturn in Mr Woodhouse's humour—she had been enjoying their conversation enormously. They had seemed so like-minded on every subject, but something appeared to have distressed him. In spite of her mama's warning she took a cup of cider and drank half of it at a draught. Thankfully she could see her mama making her way round the room towards her. 'Here's Mama,' she said.

Mr Woodhouse made a performance of rising from his seat, clutching his stick and exhibiting a pronounced stiffness of limb. He made his bow to Mrs Bates.

'Sir,' that lady began, 'I do not think I have had the honour of an introduction, but in a friendly, informal situation such as this, where all are near neighbours and good friends, perhaps it does not signify if we contravene the normal courtesies.'

'This is Mr Woodhouse, an acquaintance of Lieutenant Weston, lately come to Highbury in the hope of finding a place to build a house,' Hetty said, 'at least, so I understood from that gentleman when he was so good as to introduce us. Mr Woodhouse, Sir, may I present my mama?'

'Charmed, Madam,' said Mr Woodhouse, and, indeed, his eye, dull and rather rheumy up to this point, brightened considerably when it lit on Mrs Bates' beautiful face and pretty figure. 'I am happy to have the connection between you and your daughter pointed out to me,' he went on, looking from one to the other, 'for, upon my word, I would not have taken you for mother and daughter, so unlike are you in any case, and, if you'll forgive me, Madam, it seems impossible to me that you could be the mother of any grown up daughter, such as this one.'

'You are very kind,' Mrs Bates said before, in pursuance of her own rule, taking up a subject on which he could not fail to be interested. 'So you are come to Highbury in search of property. And have you found anything to your liking? Randalls, I believe, was a very commodious and imposing property at one time, and has some extensive grounds. Have you viewed it? Perhaps you could renovate?'

'Weston advised me against it. East-facing, he said, subject to a cruel wind when it is in that quarter, and the first house to have snow in winter, due to its situation on a knoll of ground.'

'Its elevation affords some superior views, I believe,' Mrs Bates demurred, 'but perhaps views are not your priority.'

'Extensive grounds, shrubberies and so forth will provide all the vista I require, so long as the air is healthful. In fact I believe I have found just the place—a piece of ground to the west of the village, half a mile or so, just the ideal distance. Close enough for access to the village amenities, even on foot— should it be desired; close enough to engage with Highbury society, but far enough away to afford a certain privacy and exclusivity, for the place to be its own separate entity, as Donwell is, as Clayton Park is, where I had the pleasure to go with my friend Weston to dine, earlier in the week.'

'In mentioning Donwell and Clayton, you give us

exactly the clue we need to understand the extent and air of the house you intend,' Mrs Bates said, altering, in an upwards trajectory, her understanding of the kind of man Mr Woodhouse was, his standing in life, his means.

'Indeed?' her daughter chimed in. 'I wonder where you can mean? I can think of no site that is for sale at present which meets your description. Can you, Mama? Where can Mr Woodhouse have in mind? There is nowhere that I can think of which could accommodate so extensive a property as Donwell or Clayton. Shall you have coverts, then, and a lime walk, and a ha-ha, and plantations?'

'I speak of the house and grounds pertaining to those properties, madam, not their estates. I do not require parkland, simply gardens—a decently proportioned shrubbery suffices for my exercise—and a residence such as will suit a gentleman. The place is called Hartfield. Deer, I suppose, were seen there, in years past. It is now a pleasant piece of pasture with a stand of oak and ash trees behind, bordered by a small stream. The stream gave me cause for concern at first—damp, madam, is anathema to me, and one worries about noxious vapours—but upon viewing the property I find it is but a very small watercourse, inconsiderable, almost no more than a culvert, really, and so my fears were assuaged. The whole extends to some twelves acres or so and I am assured that it can be bought for the right sum of money. But that is business which will not interest a lady.'

'Oh, Hartfield!' burst out Hetty. 'Is that not farmer Cropley's property? It borders the Donwell estate on its eastern side. I wonder at him being ready to sell it! I never heard of the possibility, did you, Mama? But, to be sure, that is a very pretty spot indeed, and, along the stream there, my sister and I have gathered many a basket of blackberries in years gone by. Oh! I hope you will not tear out the blackberries, Sir. People are so wont, these days,' with a rueful glance at Mrs Winwood, 'to tear out perfectly good plants.'

'I cannot promise to leave them,' Mr Woodhouse admitted, 'but I assure you, madam, that I will make good your loss from my hot-houses, when they are built. You shall have all the soft fruits your heart desires. Soft fruit is wholesome, I believe, in moderation, lightly stewed and served without custard or cream. I do not believe anyone can object to it.'

Lieutenant Weston then came to claim Miss Bates for a dance and Mr Woodhouse took the opportunity to excuse himself to say his farewells.

'An extraordinary gentleman,' was the general Highbury opinion, when he had left, in his coach and four, not an hour after arriving and before the moon had risen. 'What age might he be?' and 'Is he married?' and 'How has he got his fortune?' were all the topic of conversation as the young people danced. Thirty years of age, came back the answer, although acting much older, it was agreed, very conscious of his health and prone to think much lacking in it. Mrs Jackson, a farmer's wife whose son was pot-man at the Crown, reported no end of trouble in accommodating his frugal taste; meat without fat, porridge without cream, eggs boiled just so. His family was of high repute—*the* Woodhouses, unexceptionable people, an ancient and very well-established family in the very first tier of society—and Mr Snell, a lawyer who had been instructed to handle the sale of Hartfield on behalf of farmer Cropley, spoke of 'family money, old money but recently inherited, a very comfortable sum.' No wife was known of, certainly he had never mentioned any, and, it was agreed, for a man who had taken no trouble to make himself agreeable, not danced and left so early, he was unlikely to attract one on his own merits. But, as he was to become one of them—as he was by old association with the area, one of them—his oddness must be overlooked. To Mrs Bates, the arrival of Mr Woodhouse gave added significance to the evening. Two gentlemen, unattached, very eligible, in her girls' reach, was something she had not looked for.

Hetty thoroughly enjoyed her dances with Lieutenant Weston, quite forgetting, in her exhilaration, the discomfort of the heat, the unpleasantness of agitated bodies or the likelihood of being thrown headlong into the fire. But as the carriage bore them homeward, it was Mr Woodhouse who remained in her mind. Such a sensible man, she considered, his thoughts so in tune with her own, the only person she had ever met who had not declared her anxieties groundless but, on the contrary, shared and encouraged them!

'I hope Martha banked up the fire properly,' she murmured. 'I fear that one of the coals might have slipped.'

'If Highbury were ablaze we would be able to see the flames from here,' Jane said. 'If you have these fears, I do not know why you should share them. You would scare Mama to death if she were at all persuadable to your starts and alarms.'

But Marie remained silent, looking out into the star-lit night and admiring the glistening contours of Donwell's fields and hedges. The warmth of the squire's earnest farewell hand-shake lingered on her palm. It produced such a confusion of feelings in her, an ache of loneliness and an unsuspected spark of what she, as a married woman, recognised as passion, as well as a strong sense of the inappropriateness of both of these things. She did not know whether to press the hand to her breast, or to wash it in scalding water, and she was glad of the darkness inside the carriage, that her girls might not see the conflict reflected in her face.

Chapter 7

The following morning Lieutenant Weston called at the Crown to wait upon his friend Mr Woodhouse for the purpose of a walk to Hartfield. It took Mr Woodhouse some time to array himself in a sufficient number of coats and mufflers against the sharp, chill air, and to swap his thick boots for some thicker ones, but at last he was ready and the pair set out.

'You missed an evening of great pleasure, Woodhouse,' declared Lieutenant Weston, as they strolled from the village to the turning in the lane which denoted the boundary of the Hartfield property. 'The squire is a generous man, and a few of us were enjoying his excellent brandy until the small hours.'

'I hope there were no ladies in the company, Weston. Late hours are especially injurious to a woman's health.'

'On no! The ladies had left us. There was just myself and Knightley, Mr Snell, Larkins the steward and Hopley the miller. I rather fear that Hopley will find his health less than buoyant, this morning. I predict little milling.'

'Mr Hopley affirms me in my belief that late hours in particular and evening parties in general are to be avoided,' said Mr Woodhouse. 'It was a pleasant enough gathering, I suppose, for those who know each other well, and I hope, in time, to count those people amongst my friends and neighbours. But the lateness of the hour was sufficient for me, and the glass, as I predicted, was plummeting, a sure harbinger of snow.'

'And yet no snow fell,' laughed Lieutenant Weston, 'and I had a delightful walk home, in the moonlight, my feet crunching the thick hoar-frost which had formed. I saw a dog fox, clear as day, just beyond that copse of Knightley's. I must tell him. I suppose you don't hunt?'

Mr Woodhouse gave a shudder and a decided shake of the head, but pursued his earlier train of conversation. 'A very pleasant gathering, I say. I had delightful conversation with a Miss Bates. We were compatible on a number of topics. And then I made acquaintance with her mother, who seemed to me to be particularly agreeable, rather pretty, and quiet-spoken. Except that they bore no resemblance to one another at all, I'd have taken them for sisters.'

'Ah yes, Mrs Bates is recently widowed. Her husband was well-liked and she, too, is a popular member of Highbury society.'

'She is young enough to consider marrying again, I conjecture?'

'In due course, perhaps. But I should think that she is more concerned with finding a match for her daughter, than for herself. Miss Bates wants only a few months of being thirty years old.'

'A very conversable young woman if rather angular in her looks. A want of flesh, especially around the face, can make for a somewhat haggard appearance.'

'We must not be too severe, sir. She takes after her father in looks—he was spare of frame with a narrow face. But I know her to be a kind-hearted young woman, if given to a certain loquaciousness. Indeed, I danced with her last night and I swear her tongue worked harder than her feet! But the loss of a dear papa will not usually improve a girl's appearance or figure.'

'I did not mean to be unkind. I had very pleasant conversation with the lady. She seemed very sensible, as wholly cognisant as I could wish on matters of health and personal wellbeing. And yet, as fully as she entered into my own opinions, I found myself strangely unsettled at the end of our discussion. I am sorry she has taken the death of her father so hard. It speaks much of her sensibility. I shall recommend a raw egg beaten into sherry, to be taken every morning, and abjure sitting in a draught, although I am sure she is far too sensible to expose herself to such danger.'

'The younger Miss Bates has a very pleasing figure and a comely face.'

'I did not see her, but, from what you describe, she must take after the mother. Now, Weston, just here, where the lane bends, is where I envisage the park gates, with a drive leading diagonally across the plot to that slight elevation, where I propose to build the house. The sweep will be short—not much more than twenty yards or so—and one would wish for something longer. But the elevation of the house is more important. It must catch the healthful air. What is your opinion of the scheme?'

The next hour was taken up as the two men paced out the ground and agreed upon the general layout of gardens and terraces, stables and ancillary buildings. A rose garden, covered arbour and shrubbery were positively agreed upon, a pond with a fountain mooted and much screening by trees, both from the prying eyes of passers-by and the prevailing weather, established as an absolute necessity. The size and scope of the house—number of drawing rooms, French doors opening onto a terrace, quantity of bedrooms, servants' quarters—was enlarged upon in some detail, Mr Woodhouse having visited houses he now wished to emulate or even surpass in style and grandeur. Lieutenant Weston suggested the names of architects in whom Mr Woodhouse could put his trust, as well as mentioning—in the interests of absolute transparency—that his own family's concern encompassed the provision of high quality building stone, superior timber and excellent glazing.

'Not that I, personally, have any connection with the business, you understand—that is carried on by my brothers now, my father having retired. I could have gone into it, with them, but I am an independent-

spirited man, and was keen to make my own way, to
have my own adventures, which, I flatter myself, I
have done. I have travelled more extensively than
either of my siblings and experienced more already
than they will ever do, in all likelihood, in their entire
lifetimes. But, sir, it would seem disingenuous to have
met and struck up an acquaintance with you, a man
manifestly intent upon building a substantial and
noteworthy property, and to have helped you, without
making it clear to you also that I have, by family
connection, a concern in the business.'

'I appreciate your candour, Weston,' Mr Woodhouse
said, wiping his shoes very carefully on the verge, 'and
it inclines me to trust and rely on you the *more,* rather
than to draw back in suspicion of you having
something personal to gain. If your family's business is
local to the area—which I suppose it is—what more
natural than that I should instruct my architect to
utilise their services?'

'You are very kind, sir. Do you lunch? Shall we repair
to the Crown and see what is on offer?'

'I never eat luncheon, Weston. A bowl of consommé
is the most that will pass my lips, if you will be so

good as to join me?'

'Thank you, sir. I will be happy to eat a mutton chop while you drink your soup. But see, here are Mrs Bates and her daughters! What a coincidence, after we were speaking of them!'

Indeed, Mrs Bates, Jane and Hetty could be seen taking their morning walk along the lane towards Hartfield, all well-muffled in shawls and shod in thick boots against the brisk December air. They walked thus every day, weather allowing, but, it must be admitted, had chosen this direction today in the light of the news that the Hartfield pastures were to be the site of a new mansion.

Their 'good mornings' were exchanged, hands warmly shaken, the weather remarked upon and the delights of the previous evening's entertainments agreed.

'Oh, Mr Woodhouse,' Hetty cried, when these preliminaries had been concluded, 'how was your journey home? I was quite anxious for you! Mr Boxwell drove you without incident, I surmise, and you suffered no ill effects from the cold? No complaint in the chest? I hope Mrs Stokes had left instructions for a fire in your room and had sheets well-aired? For nobody knows more than I do the perils of a cold chamber and a damp bed.'

'Yes, indeed,' Mr Woodhouse said, struck by the alignment of her concerns with his. A well-warmed room and properly aired sheets had been principal amongst his instructions to Mrs Stokes. 'Madam, I am honoured by your interest in my well-being.'

'I was struck by your sensible caution, sir, and worried all the way home in case Martha hadn't banked the fire properly. I made sure to mention to the squire, also, the great honour you had done him in accepting his invitation, last night. I do not think he had quite comprehended how far from your natural habit you had condescended to move, on his behalf. He seemed, indeed, quite amazed, when I explained it.'

'He was so good as to send me a message this morning, enquiring after my health,' Mr Woodhouse said. 'I am honoured by his concern, I must say.'

In the fresh morning air Miss Bates looked better than she had the previous evening. She was thin, to be sure, but her eyes were bright and her smile almost pretty. Her concern for him was very flattering. He noticed that she wore an extra spencer against the December chill, a warm knitted bonnet and thick, woollen gloves, of which he thoroughly approved.

'The squire is a most considerate man,' Mrs Bates agreed. 'When it comes to his compassion for others, there is no one to surpass him, I believe. We, too, received a message with his compliments today, and a parcel of victuals. Such generosity! Almost an entire ham hock, and a whole pie, and several cheeses.'

Mr Woodhouse turned his attention to Mrs Bates. *There* was a fine complexion; it bloomed with a healthful glow. And her dress was all that it should be—warm and sensible—though in widowish black. Her quiet, mellifluous voice was restful and soothing especially when set against the gush of her daughter's.

'Madam,' Mr Woodhouse said, wishing he had a hamper of comestibles about him to present to the lady, 'but I hope you will not eat the cheese at night.'

'Do you walk far?' Lieutenant Weston enquired.

'To the Hartfield corner,' Miss Bates blurted out, 'to see for ourselves how the ground will accommodate Mr Woodhouse's new property, for it never occurred to us, did it Mama, that such a thing could be, and we are wild to see it, to imagine it and envision it, with our own eyes. For, to be sure, it is very pretty spot, and popular, in summer, when farmer Cropley has set it aside for hay-making, for picnics and the like. *We* have used it so, in any case, and I know others have too, for farmer Cropley is so very agreeable a man, and does not mind, and hardly ever puts his cows in those fields on purpose that the people can use it. For, naturally, once the cows have been in, the ground is, that is to say … And, as I think I mentioned yesterday evening, the blackberries along the stream are exceptionally good, quite the juiciest, although Mr Woodhouse was so good as to promise that he will make good the deficit from his hot-houses, when he has them. But, to think that in a twelve-month, or less, the Hartfield pastures will be enclosed and private, and to go there no more for picnics and the like, we felt that we ought, now, go there very often, to look on it, even though, before this, in short, there were other fields which … Those at Donwell are very pleasant in their way, and there is a particular paddock by the mill pond which might perhaps … but I do not know. It can be boggy after rain, and I never like a damp seat if I can help it …'

Mr Woodhouse's face wore the expression of being somewhat overwhelmed by this tirade of information, opinion and conjecture. The lady certainly could talk and it was not easy to extract, from her tangled morass of monologue, the right thread to pursue.

'Oh, *Hetty!*' Jane said, under her breath, 'stop wittering.'

Lieutenant Weston smothered a smile but Jane saw it, and returned it. The youngest Miss Bates was a delightful girl, he thought, bright of eye, with a graceful, natural air and a very quick understanding.

'We walk along the lane, for twenty minutes or so, and then we return,' Mrs Bates said, firmly. 'This morning, it happens that we walk *past* the Hartfield pastures. Do you return from there?'

'Yes, we have been scoping out the lie of the land,' Lieutenant Weston said. 'My friend Mr Woodhouse is soon to instruct the architects. We had thought to return to the Crown, but there is no reason why we could not accompany you, if you would do us the honour. Miss Jane, I hope you will take my arm. Woodhouse? What say you?'

Jane took his arm with a smile and the two strolled on

without waiting for Mr Woodhouse's answer. Mrs
Bates and Hetty hung back.

Mr Woodhouse found himself suddenly filled with a
sort of panic. Clearly he was expected to offer his arm
to one or other of them, or both, but he had his stick
to deal with, and he hesitated. His marital destiny was
all-but set. His fate awaited him in Oxfordshire. But,
from his current perspective, Oxfordshire seemed like
a trap waiting to spring, a deep, dark pit from which
there would be no escape. Why would he put himself
in its power when here, now, in the light of this
pleasant and benign day, not one but two alternatives
presented themselves? Miss Bates' manner was a little
abrupt, to be sure, and her speech somewhat
disjointed, but the import of her conversation was full
of interest. Mr Woodhouse was not a man of broad
intellect but the ideas he held, he held very firmly,
sometimes against general opinion. It was refreshing
to meet with a young lady so similarly awake to the
hazards attendant on everyday living. It was true that
Miss Bates was no beauty but she was not repugnant
and beauty was not especially important to him. A
judicious, wholesome diet would improve her looks;

he might make some indulgence in the matter of cream and custard to assist in her in the gaining of flesh. A stay in Bath or some sea air might be beneficial. He understood the lady lived in reduced circumstances but that did not matter to him; his fortune was large. If he wanted anything in a wife, it was sympathy, a similarity of taste, a compatibility of ideas. Weston had described her as kind-hearted and *he* was as good a judge of character as any man Mr Woodhouse had ever met. He set great store on Weston's opinion. She seemed an amiable, unaffected woman. She would not expect much in the way of society—the quiet life of a parson's daughter would be admirable preparation for the kind of sedentary life he proposed to live. She had several years of childbearing left to her.

But then there was the mother. She was a beauty—no doubt of that. And there was a motherliness about her, a calm and maternal comfort which made him feel that he would like to rest his head on her shoulder. She would minister to his needs, order up simple, nourishing foods, direct the servants with quiet efficiency and provide everything for his comfort. She would know which salves to administer, which tinctures he should take. She would know the benefit of a good poultice on the chest. She, surely, would know how to boil an egg just as he liked it. That she was beyond childbearing was a consideration but as he was a man of elderly habits, the difference in their ages would not be an insuperable obstacle.

On the other hand, it occurred to him with a sudden jolt, she was seventeen years older than him. She might die before him, leaving him bereft. *That* was not in her favour. No. The younger lady was the more attractive prospect, he believed. Or he thought he believed …

Weston, he could see, was already almost beyond the turn in the lane which would take them into open countryside. Mrs and Miss Bates remained in expectation of his word. He had already walked a vast distance that day. To walk further would be reckless, surely? His legs were tired and, in spite of the bright sunshine, the air was very cold. He felt he really ought to return to the Crown, to sit by his fire and think things over. There again the day was bright and dry, the two ladies would be most agreeable company, it would be of interest to get to know the area better. Much of him wished to oblige, but there was so much of sense to say on the other side of the question and his dilemma would not resolve itself. He abhorred a dilemma of all things—a choice of options was anathema to him as he never could make up his mind. He emerged from these deliberations now with his mind by no means made up.

Weston and the younger lady were already out of sight, screened by thick hedging. He found there really was no alternative but to follow and the decision thus having been effectively made for him he said, 'After you, ladies,' indicating that they should precede him, and the party at last moved off down the lane.

'You enjoyed the dancing, last evening?' Lieutenant Weston asked Jane.

'Oh! *Very* much. I love to dance,' Jane said. 'There has not been a ball at the Crown in months, and we missed the squire's harvest-home because, you know, it was just after poor Papa died.'

'I have not had the opportunity to offer my very sincere condolences on your sad loss,' Lieutenant Weston said, inclining his head towards her and looking at her with his kind, grey eyes. 'The whole parish feels the loss of Reverend Bates most acutely. My parents, I know, miss him dreadfully. My mother has written to me most particularly about it. Not that the Winwoods do not seem to be elegant, genteel people, but twenty seven years is a long time and I know my father counted Reverend Bates a very particular friend.'

'So did everyone,' Jane said, sadly. 'He was an excellent teacher. George Knightley was coming on very well under his tutelage and I miss my lessons with Papa very much. There is so much he did not get round to teaching me! And now, I fear, my education will be lacking for … for whatever sphere in life I might find myself in, in the future.'

'And what sphere do you imagine that might be, Miss Jane, if I you do not object to my enquiring.'

Jane sighed. 'I do not know. I had thought perhaps to teach—there are schools, you know, for girls, which make a real attempt to educate the students' minds— far beyond the usual accomplishments: Latin, Greek, philosophy, mathematics …'

'I should be terrified to encounter such a young

woman,' Lieutenant Weston laughed. 'She would find me out as an utter dunce immediately.'

'No, she would not,' Jane shook her head. 'Like all boys, you were amply grounded in all the disciplines at school. I suppose you know trigonometry, literature, science …'

'If I did, I have forgotten more than half of it.'

'But you have had a better education than any that can be got in the classroom,' Jane said, seriously, 'for you have seen the world. You have seen life. What experiences you must have had!'

'Ah yes. I have something of the wanderlust and I have been lucky enough to indulge it. You sound envious.'

'I *am* envious. I would like to travel, to see the sea, to go abroad. Rome, Florence, perhaps even Athens. I would like to hear foreign tongues spoken. I would like to taste strange foods. I would like to see the works of the masters hanging in their native halls. But,' (with a heavy sigh) 'I know I never shall.'

'Miss Jane, you astonish and humble me,' Lieutenant Weston said, looking down upon her pretty, earnest face. 'I went away from Highbury with the same intention, the same desires in my heart. I could have stayed here and joined my brothers in the family business, you know, but I wanted so much more. And I *have* travelled, heard the jabber of foreign voices, and eaten dishes consisting of I know not what—spicy and pungent. I confess I have not seen much in the way of art, but architecture I have seen—the cathedral in Nantes struck me very particularly, and all the chateaux in that region are magnificent—romantic, turreted and castellated.'

'Perhaps you will tell me of your travels, Lieutenant Weston,' Jane said. 'Highbury is dear to me, and, of course, wherever Mama is will be home, but it is so very parochial. Perhaps I can travel away from it, in *your* shoes.'

Lieutenant Weston pressed Jane's arm, and the two walked on along the lane without seeing anything of the landscape on either side.

Mrs and Miss Bates and Mr Woodhouse followed more slowly behind them. Mr Woodhouse walked very languidly, and stopped frequently to catch his breath. Mrs Bates smoothed over these delays by remarking on the countryside, and pointing out to Mr Woodhouse the landmarks visible to right and left. 'That copse on the hill there is called Widowbower—a very ancient stand of trees—my late husband suspected some pagan associations in times gone by. The farmhouse you see down the track, there, is farmer Cropley's property. A very tidy farm indeed. Mrs Cropley is a worthy woman with a flock that lays superior eggs—I would not recommend you get your supply from anyone else, once you are settled, Mr Woodhouse. This tree is popular amongst the village boys in autumn—horse chestnuts, you know.'

Miss Bates supplemented her mother's narrative with pepperings of information she calculated to be of more interest to the gentleman. 'Oh yes, he thought it not unlikely that nefarious rituals and witchcraft were carried on at Widowbower copse. He discovered an ancient manuscript which suggested it. Personally, I have never ventured up there since, although the hill does afford a magnificent view … Oh no! On no account let Jethro Nidd convince you to take *his* eggs, for his fowl are allowed to nest where they like and the eggs can sometimes be days old when he finds them.

Mrs Coxe told me she once opened one and it was bright green! Oh! The boys and their horse chestnuts! William Larkins suffered a concussion last year when a stick he had thrown up into the tree landed back on his head. I wonder the squire does not have the tree felled, for it is on his land. All this, you know, is Donwell land. Highbury is just a little notch taken out of it. His estate is quite vast although the majority of it is given over to tenants. He farms only a small proportion of it himself.'

'Does *your* family own large estates?' Mrs Bates enquired, both to interrupt Hetty's diatribe and to augment her understanding of Mr Woodhouse's circumstances.

'Vast tracts in Scotland. I haven't been there since I was a boy. The sporting life is not one I espouse and the journey alone is very arduous. There are several properties in the Home Counties, of course, as well as the house in town. But since I am a son of a lesser branch of the main family, I haven't concerned myself with them. One is invited, of course, from time to time, and, as a duty, one must attend. But large gatherings are what I most abhor. A quiet life is what I crave, Mrs Bates. My own home and hearth, solid locks and draught-free windows. A game of backgammon and a dish of thin gruel is all I require.'

'Just what I think, too,' Hetty said. 'Apart from the gruel—I do not know that I would go as far as that! Jane wishes to travel, to see foreign shores, but *I* eschew any such ambition. We are happy at home, are we not, Mama, amongst our own friends, living quietly. Highbury is all the world to us, is it not?'

'We are blessed to be so comfortable,' Mrs Bates nodded.

'Well! 'Comfort!' I would not go so far as that!' Hetty cried, 'when we have known the pleasure of the vicarage, with its commodious accommodations and pleasant garden. Our present circumstances are not *so* comfortable, I think.'

'You still regret the necessity for our removal,' Mrs Bates said, 'but Hetty, dear, what is past is past and,' (in a low but emphatic voice,) 'there is no good to be done in rehearsing it now.'

'I have not seen the vicarage,' Mr Woodhouse remarked.

'It is quite in the other direction,' Hetty said. 'Perhaps, another day, you will take your exercise that way. There *was* a delightful old apple tree in the garden, but it is no more.'

'I think we should consider turning back,' Mrs Bates suggested. Mr Woodhouse looked quite done in and, at his slow pace, there wasn't the smallest possibility that they would be able to catch up with Jane and Lieutenant Weston, who were already a quarter of a mile ahead of them, almost at the crossroads. 'Hetty, why don't you accompany Mr Woodhouse back to the Crown, while I run ahead and tell the others we have turned back.'

Without waiting for their agreement, Mrs Bates walked quickly away in pursuit of her younger daughter. Mr Woodhouse held out a tentative arm to Miss Bates and the two began to saunter back toward the village.

'I am so happy to have renewed our acquaintance this morning,' Hetty said. 'I found our conversation last evening most enjoyable. But you have not told me about your plans for the property. How large a house do you propose, Mr Woodhouse? And I hope, when you come to engage staff, you will consult us, for there is not a soul in the parish that we do not know. Martha's sister Tilly will make an excellent scullery maid for she is very strong and can haul ever so much coal without the least effort. She is of excellent character, I can vouch for that. John Brewer has experience as a footman although he walks with a pronounced limp. He was invalided out of the militia on account of an injury. You will need a housekeeper, as there is no Mrs Woodhouse to manage the household for you. I shall consult with Mrs Lemming, the squire's housekeeper, or Mrs Stokes might be able to recommend someone.'

'Dear lady, you rush ahead somewhat. The ground is yet to be broken. Indeed, the land is yet to be purchased! Dear me, I fear I must stop again and rest for a moment. Here is a stile which I perched on before. A moment or two and I will catch my breath. My chest—I think I mentioned—it is not strong. And your conversation, ma'am, is somewhat … You overpower me, Miss Bates!'

'You must forgive me, sir. In my enthusiasm to have an addition to Highbury society—and such a great one—I am too precipitate. And I talk too much.

Mama is always telling me of it. I am sorry.'

'Your great warmth does you credit and your kindness also. But I feel I must—forgive me,' reaching into his pocket, 'I have some *sal volatile* here. I feel quite faint.'

'My dear sir I would not have you on any account over-exert yourself. Let me hasten to the village and get the gig from the Crown. It could be here in a quarter of an hour.'

'No, indeed, I would not put you to that trouble. And now here is Weston and your mother and sister. Weston will give me his arm, and I shall get along much better.'

And so it was. Lieutenant Weston relinquished Jane Bates' arm—with some reluctance on both their parts—and allowed Henry Woodhouse to lean upon him, and very soon they were in Highbury once more, on the High Street between the Crown and the Bates' lodgings.

'The luncheon hour has long passed and I must go and change, for I am invited to Donwell to dine,' Lieutenant Weston said. 'Ladies, I bid you *adieu*, for the time being.'

'I hope you will come and drink tea with us, this evening,' Mrs Bates said, cordially. Lieutenant Weston gave a bow of assent. He allowed his eyes to flicker towards Jane. Her smile was radiant.

'I know you eschew an evening party in general, Mr Woodhouse' Mrs Bates went on, 'but our rooms are just here,' she indicated their door, 'half a dozen steps will accomplish the distance, and our hours, I can assure you, are very early. The tea tray comes in at six, when we are at home, and is always cleared by seven.'

'I am glad you pointed out the door, Mama,' Hetty said, 'for it is so shadowed, in that corner, anyone might have missed it. Our rooms are very small and the stairs are unconscionably narrow. There's a turn at the top with another step which takes people quite by surprise …'

'I am sure neither Lieutenant Weston nor Mr Woodhouse is the kind of gentleman to be proud or stand-offish on the account of a narrow stair, Hetty,' Mrs Bates said, through a smile somewhat fixed. 'Our home is humble, to suit our status, but it is perfectly respectable and it will be our delight to offer hospitality.'

'I can hardly imagine that Lieutenant Weston or Mr Woodhouse will be disengaged,' Hetty fluttered, 'but if they are, and will condescend to visit us, of course, we'd be honoured.'

'I rather wish to go to Donwell myself this afternoon,' said Jane, 'for George and young William Larkins declare that they will take a dip in the mill pond and I should very much like to see them do it.' She looked at the lieutenant from beneath her lashes. If she hoped he would offer to accompany her, she was disappointed, however.

'You will go nowhere near such hobbledehoy behaviour,' Mrs Bates replied. 'And, in any case, here is Mr Knightley himself. I am sure he will tell you that George's scheme is all bravado and boasting.'

The gentleman had at that moment just emerged from the Crown and could be seen conversing with Mrs Stokes. On seeing the little assembly in the street he walked across to join them. It soon transpired that Weston and Woodhouse were being engaged to drink tea and Mrs Bates could not escape including the squire in her invitation also even though it could only revive and increase her confusion of the previous evening. Even as she issued the invitation, she rather hoped, for her own peace of mind, he might decline it. Indeed she quite expected him to do so. Mr Knightley was not renowned for his tea-drinking. In all likelihood he would have an evening of accounts or letter-writing planned.

But Mr Knightley said, 'I'd be honoured to join you, ma'am,' with a bow and a smile of genuine anticipation.

'I am surprised at young George for contemplating so wantonly dangerous a thing as a swim in the mill pond,' Marie Bates said, perhaps a little more sternly than she had intended.

'Reckless!' Mr Woodhouse said, quite frightened by the idea.

Hetty opened her mouth to begin a homily on the dangers of bathing in winter, the notoriety of mill ponds, examples of tragedies arising from such exploits in the past—hadn't a dog drowned in that very pond some summers past? Or perhaps it was a sheep—but her mother took a firm grip on her arm and gave her a speaking look and she snapped her lips closed before a word of it could escape.

'But enormous fun,' Lieutenant Weston laughed. 'I might even join them. It will shake this languor I have about me, today.'

'By all means, swim if you will,' Mr Knightley said, 'but you will do so without George. I have already scuppered the plan and I doubt young Larkins will be so foolhardy when it comes to the point. There was ice on the pond this morning. Mrs Bates, it will be the easiest as well as the pleasantest thing to walk up to you after dinner to drink our tea. Woodhouse, we will call for you on our way past.'

Mr Woodhouse felt as though, after his exertions of the day, a hot bath, a chest poultice and the liberal application of some soothing unguent to his feet and legs would be all the ministrations he might require before an early night in a well-aired bed, but Mr Knightley had such an imperative tone—he was not the kind of man one could refuse—and Mr Woodhouse found he could voice no demur.

He ordered his bath, and, when he had taken it, requested that two soft boiled eggs and a plate of dry crackers to be brought to his room. He closed the curtains although the day was yet bright with sunshine, and banked up the fire, and sat with his feet in a basin of hot, salted water. The more he encountered Miss Bates, the more he liked her. Her stories of mishap and accident confirmed everything he believed—that the world was a dangerous place, fraught with every kind of calamity for those reckless enough to be unwary. She stirred something in him—she made him feel buoyed up and justified—but mixed in his feelings was an element of the unsettled; a sense of headiness quite foreign to him. Could it be love? The alternative, in Oxfordshire, was unknown. Three unmarried daughters of his late father's old and excellent friend O'Brien. He was, to put it baldly, to have his pick. It was an arrangement which had been the cherished desire of his father and Mr O'Brien both—an alliance between the two families—and he had long been made to understand that this was his marital destiny. All the girls, he had been told, were delightful and sensible; genteel, quiet and compliant. He had seen their likenesses in miniatures—but one could put little store by *their* accuracy. A slight acquaintance claimed to have met one of the Misses O'Brien—but could not remember which—and declared her to be a pleasant enough girl. That was all the recommendation he had.

What was quite certain was that he would not be able to go into Oxfordshire and come back without having secured one of them to be his bride. The pressure of such an undertaking was heavy indeed, the effort required would be immense, especially to a man who little liked to exert himself for any reason. Whereas here, to hand, was a perfectly agreeable young woman, a gentleman's daughter, a resident of Highbury who knew everything there was to know about his new domicile. It was manifestly certain that she shared all his most cherished concerns—would never leave a window ajar, wouldn't dream of leaving home without a proper number of shawls, looked as though she could not stomach the least grease. And with her, an appendage most delightful, which would add to his comforts and supplement any little deficiencies or inexperience of the daughter—a mother, a beautiful woman of gentle voice and genteel manners. It would be nothing to Mr Woodhouse to offer both women a home. Mrs Bates, if she wished, could have her own apartments within the new mansion. The energetic trepidation of the one and the reassuring, assuaging temperance of the other would be a perfect arrangement, certain to complete his happiness. What need had he of Oxfordshire?

Presently, Mr Woodhouse rang his bell and called for paper and ink. 'And send my man to me at five,' he added. 'I will need to dress. I am going out.'

Chapter 8

The ladies spent the afternoon in preparation for their guests. There was a little debate between them as to whether or not some others should also be invited. A married couple, it was posited, would give the event complete respectability. 'After all,' Hetty said, 'we will be three single ladies and, since you included the squire in your invitation, three single gentlemen. People will talk.'

'Nobody will speak of it if you do not,' Jane replied, 'for I declare, Hetty, you are the greatest gossip in Highbury. And, in any case, nobody is more respectable than Mama. Where she is present no sniff of impropriety can possibly exist.'

'I wonder you even thought of such a dubious interpretation on a perfectly decorous occasion,' Mrs Bates said. 'Your mind runs on very peculiar lines.'

'Oh!' Hetty cried, 'so I am a gossip and I am peculiar! What a poor opinion you have of me! But, Mama, haven't you always taught us that our most precious possession is our reputation? It's only that I am thinking of.'

'And very properly,' Mrs Bates soothed, 'but I think we need have no fear. In any case, we have insufficient chairs for more guests.'

'And as for being a gossip,' Jane said, in a conciliatory tone, 'you know that your mouth does run away with you, Hetty, and sometimes things that had better have been kept in are out of it before you know it. I do not mean that you are malicious, or deliberately spread tittle-tattle. But I have known times when you have unwittingly shared information that would have been better kept private.'

'Perhaps,' suggested Mrs Bates, 'you are uneasy about this evening because you feel particularly anxious that one of our guests should find nothing exceptionable about it? Mr Woodhouse, for example, seems to be a very properly-minded gentleman, with many a scruple as to behaviour and manners.'

'He is properly careful of his own well-being. Which reminds me, Mama, at Mr Knightley's Christmas party Mr Woodhouse requested a basin of gruel and would take nothing else. Do we have any gruel we can offer him?'

'Good heavens, I shouldn't think so, but I can ask Martha to make some. Gruel? I never heard of such a thing except for an invalid! But Mr Woodhouse is a fine gentleman, to be sure. I suppose he must be humoured. I do not think it an altogether bad thing for a gentleman to be of steady, regular, decided habits, even if they are a little odd. A lady could do much worse than ally herself to such a man. Foremost amongst all his good qualities, however, is the prospect of him settling locally. For a local girl wishing to stay in Highbury, this would be an attractive proposition. Do you not think so, Hetty?'

Hetty had been in the passageway while Mrs Bates made these observations, trying to find something— an umbrella stand, a jardinière—which would at one and the same time disguise the awkwardness of the sudden stair at the turn while at the same time alert any unsuspecting visitor to its presence, 'For,' she mumbled to herself, 'I am sure I have tripped up it a hundred times myself, and I know it's there.' But on hearing her name she re-entered the room. 'Mama? Did you say something?'

'Mama wants you to set your cap at Mr Woodhouse,'

Jane replied. She had been dusting their few belongings and plumping cushions and had heard all her mother had said.

'Jane!' Mrs Bates cried, 'I would never conceive of such a disgusting and disgraceful notion! Go downstairs and speak to Martha about the gruel.'

But when Jane had gone Mrs Bates stepped up to Hetty and took her hand. 'I was simply saying, dear, because I know it is not an idea that would occur to you without a little prompting, that you might take the opportunity to get to know Mr Woodhouse a little better. Find out his character, and let him see what a kind-hearted and gentle person you are, how excellently you would support and tend your husband—for that, I believe, is what he most requires. Humour him, Hetty. That is my advice. And I would have you wear your good gown, the one with the lace trim, and I shall arrange your hair. For, if you were inclined to like Mr Woodhouse, and he to like you, a match between you would secure you in Highbury permanently. He is building a house. He intends to settle. And what better for me, than to have you constantly by me? Jane, I do not expect to keep always. But you, Hetty, dear, are rooted in Highbury. I place the possibility before you, dear, and leave it to your good judgement to decide whether you might pursue it.'

Hetty, who, as her mother guessed, had harboured no thoughts of matrimony in relation to Mr Woodhouse or any other person, considered the matter doubtfully. Mr Woodhouse was not an ill-looking man in one sense—he had a pleasant countenance and gentle eyes. In another sense he was very ill-looking—a furrowed, anxious expression, a stooped figure and a penchant for multitudinous layers of clothing that quite obscured his form. He was superlatively fastidiousness in the matters of dirt and disease, which gave him an air of being in permanent recoil or repugnance. He was old beyond his years—that was certain. But, Hetty decided, that was no bad thing in itself. It would make him stable and dependable. His situation in life had much to recommend it—wealth and a readiness to settle. And her mama was quite correct—his choosing to settle in Highbury was a highly appealing circumstance. The Hartfield property was but half a mile from the village and, she speculated, might be

large enough to accommodate her mama as well as the
new Mrs Woodhouse. Altogether she found the idea
of marrying Mr Woodhouse not wholly disagreeable
and she determined to follow her mother's advice and
use the occasion of the evening gathering to get better
acquainted with him.

To Jane, Mrs Bates only observed, 'Lieutenant Weston
is a very handsome man, is he not? And very dashing,
in his uniform? I heard Miss Ursula say she thought
him the handsomest man at the dance last night, and
the best dancer in the room, and boast that he had
told her she was a fine girl.'

Jane shook her curls airily. 'It pains me to agree with
anything Ursula Winwood thinks, but Lieutenant
Weston was by far the handsomest and the best
dancer. As for her being a fine girl, I believe that was
only good manners, for he told George Knightley,
who told me, that she was lumpen and graceless and
had trodden on his foot a dozen times. They both
agreed that I was far prettier. George told me that,
most particularly.'

'Did he? Well, that was chivalrous of him.'

'Oh Mama,' Jane said, climbing down from her high

horse, 'he is very dashing. But that is the least of his charms. He has travelled, and today he told me such a lot about the places he has been. If only girls could join the militia!'

'A militiaman's life is very unsettled, I believe. They move from place to place with hardly a day's warning. Battle, you know, is not a walk in the park. I surmise there is much tedious routine between military postings—boots to be polished, uniforms kept spruce and endless marching up and down.'

'You do not in the least discourage me, Mama. But do not worry. I will not disguise myself as a boy and run off to join the Hampshires!'

'I am pleased to hear it, dear Jane. Now, what news of the gruel? Can Martha supply some?'

The three ladies ate a hasty dinner and repaired to their rooms to change. In spite of protracted attention to their toilet they were ready a full hour before the tea tray was due. At last they heard a knock at the door. Jane flew to the casement in time to see two gentlemen waiting below and a third—Mr Knightley—in the shadow of the Crown's porch in close conversation with Mrs Stokes. 'They are here!'

she cried. 'Mr Knightley in his usual drab—he is talking to Mrs Stokes. I wonder what they can have to talk about in so clandestine a manner. And Mr Woodhouse is so smothered in a greatcoat and shawl I can barely make him out, and Lieutenant Weston is in his uniform.'

'Jane, come away from the window and seat yourself. Here, take this sewing in your hands. Occupy yourself, while Martha takes their coats and shows them up.' Outwardly, Marie was all composure, but inwardly she too wondered what business Mr Knightley could have with Mrs Stokes twice in one day. They had danced together often on Christmas night—indeed she believed he had stood up with Mrs Stokes more than any other lady. Mrs Weston had remarked on their compatibility and Mrs Winwood likewise. And all in all, Marie cautioned herself, it wasn't an impossible match. Mrs Stokes was relatively young and quite pretty. As a lady in trade, she danced on the line of respectability but Highbury forgave her—she had been badly treated by her husband and saddled with his debts on his death. The Crown had been her only means of discharging these, an unenviable task she had set about with determination and dignity and not a small measure of business acumen. From an unpromising situation she had made remarkably good. The squire might admire that. On the other hand, there were rumours of late-night carousing in the bar. Mrs Ford, whose shop abutted the Crown, spoke darkly of 'goings on'. Mrs Stokes had a son—a wastrel of a lad who had found himself more than once on the wrong side of the law. He was too fond of keeping company in the bar and not fond enough of helping his mama. If Mrs Bates' memory served her correctly he was currently awaiting trial, charged with some misdemeanour involving racehorses. It was no part of Marie Bates' character to dwell upon—much less to spread—unsubstantiated gossip, but when a gentleman of such eminent respectability as Mr Knightley risked being besmirched by association, it did concern her. And she did instinctively feel that Mr Knightley would be tainted by connection with Mrs Stokes.

The gentlemen could be heard below. Hetty shot out of her seat and looked as though she would bolt out of the room, quite like a hind at bay. 'Oh my,' she fluttered. 'How my heart beats. Whatever is the matter with me? Is everything in readiness? I hope Martha has the kettle on to boil. There mustn't be any delay. We promised the gentlemen tea at six and it wants but five before now. I should go and help her. But who will warn them about the step at the turn? Oh! I am quite in a fright unless one of them trips.'

'Hetty, dear. Martha has everything prepared and will show our guests upstairs,' Marie soothed. 'She will be sure to point out the step to them. Sit down by the fire and take up a book. Here is William Buchan's *Domestic Medicine,* a treasure trove of medical knowledge. It will calm your nerves, and if conversation between you and Mr Woodhouse falters, you can look at it together. I conjecture it is just the kind of book to interest him.'

Heavy footsteps without and Martha's soft and deferential voice could be heard, and then the gentlemen were announced. First to enter was Mr Knightley, keen to look about him and see the accommodations which his pounds and shillings had provided. Lieutenant Weston followed closely behind, smiling and holding his hand out to each lady in turn. 'Good evening to ye, I hope I find you well,' and 'a delightful walk. Knightley sets up a bracing pace, I must say. He was anxious to get to the Crown to discuss something of moment with the lady there but would not have us be tardy here. Well, as it turns out, we are here ahead of our hour, but we thought it would not signify,' and 'by my word, Miss Bates, what a vision you are, and Miss Jane too … Quite the … that is to say … 'with a look of extreme approbation, 'upon my word … the firelight and the glow of the candles … Well, it is a pleasure, indeed.'

Mr Woodhouse was somewhat behind-hand in following, divesting himself of his wraps and taking the stairs and passageway with extreme caution for fear of the notorious step. By the time he made his appearance, Mrs Bates was engaged in showing the squire her late husband's volumes on the alcove shelves and Jane was endeavouring to follow Lieutenant Weston's description of a new card game, so it fell to Hetty to greet him and usher him to a comfortable chair by the fire.

'Oh, Mr Woodhouse,' she began, 'what a pleasure it is! And how good of you to come! I hope you did not find the journey too onerous. To be sure, the Crown is but across the street, but one can never be too careful. I have known the High Street to be icy, or intolerably muddy. The horses, you know, tend to leave … and, in short, such a small distance it is but yet fraught with inconvenience, and so Mama and Jane and I are all the more grateful to you. Tea will be here upon the instant. And we have gruel, you will be pleased to hear. I know how you prefer it, in the evenings, and Martha went to her mother's today especially to get the receipt, for she has never made it before, and although Mama has made it, that was for little Tommy Hackett, who could keep nothing down three winters ago, nothing but Mama's gruel, and, indeed, Mrs Hackett said that Mama had saved him, for it was only after she started sending gruel down to him that he rallied. But that receipt, she was convinced, would not serve in this case, and so she sent Martha to her mother's especially to get the receipt, for she has never made it before … but there I am repeating myself, and I have not asked you how you are.'

It happened, happily, that no question could have been preferable for Mr Woodhouse, who liked nothing better than to enumerate his various ailments, some real—or almost real—but mainly imagined. He proceeded to give a full history in each case with an account of the treatments suggested by various physicians. This recitation lasted while tea (and gruel) was brought in and served. Tinctures tried and restoratives sampled, their success, or, more usually, their failure, took them through bread and butter (sparingly spread). Various watering places—Bath, of course, but also Leamington and even Buxton—were compared, the benefits (doubtful) of sea-bathing explored while the others made up a four for cards.

For her part, Miss Bates entered fully into the liturgy of ailments, expressing as much concurrence in Mr Woodhouse's alarms and apprehensions as he could possibly wish, and perhaps a little more. If Mr Woodhouse wanted gentle sympathy and calm reassurance, someone to allay his fears, Miss Bates increased, rather than diminished, his disquiet. 'A sore throat? Oh, to be sure, a bad throat is a very serious thing, especially when tending to the putrid. I do hope yours does not tend to turn putrid. My own dear papa, in fact, had, towards the end …The surgeon really feared, and so indeed … Oh dear! A congested chest should never be ignored. It is so often a harbinger of pneumonia. I do hope yours may be nothing like. Old Mrs Larkins, Mr Knightley's steward's mother actually succumbed, you know, not two years ago, and pneumonia was quite certainly cited … Ah! Now I have heard Dr Watson's Specific often recommended. You find it efficacious? But it is reported to be extremely bitter. Mrs Snell tried it, and the reaction was so violent it turned into veritable stomach convulsions. But she has a weak constitution, generally, and is sick at anything … Oh my! Creakings in the neck you say? Aches in the spine? Swelling of the lower limbs? Spasms and tinglings? All most lamentable. I am amazed at your fortitude, Mr Woodhouse, so very debilitating as it must be. What it must be for you just to get out of bed in the mornings! I know of no other person so afflicted except, perhaps …' But Mr Woodhouse had little interest in the health or sickness of others, rapt, as he was, in his own peculiar and absorbing symptoms, and the conversation faltered.

Miss Bates tried another topic. 'You travelled to Highbury by public conveyance?' Happily, this was another subject of awful interest to Mr Woodhouse and Miss Bates was able to affirm and escalate his apprehensions. He mentioned the execrable quality of the roads. Miss Bates supplied harrowing detail— snow, mud, ice, ruts and potholes—and added, for good measure, the idea that contagion, in the close confines of a carriage, from persons who were unwashed, infected, infested, scrofulous or generally degenerate, was a real danger.

'Miss Bates you quite frighten me,' Mr Woodhouse interrupted, and while his eye displayed a decided wildness, his lip actually trembled. 'Perhaps I will hire the Crown's conveyance to take me on my onward journey, when I embark on it,' he said, in a voice which was tight and rasping. 'To be sure, the dangers of the road will be the same, but at least I can be sure of not encountering any pernicious infection.'

'Sir, consider, you will have to stop at *coaching inns*,' Hetty re-joined, implying dens of iniquity, vice and contamination, 'and run the risk of their scrupulousness in the matter of linens. Not to mention vermin. The Crown, I know, is free of such nuisance, but one cannot speak for others. One hears such tales—places alive with lice and flies, cockroaches, rats …'

Mr Woodhouse turned so pale that Hetty thought he might swoon. She looked at him aghast. She had no real fear of such things—had never encountered them and probably never would. Her remarks, as usual, had been wanton hyperbole, delicious because baseless. But *he* seemed genuinely disturbed.

'Let us look at this book together,' she said, quickly, pulling Mr Buchan's compendium onto her lap, 'it will distract us from such distressing thoughts.'

The game Lieutenant Weston taught them was merry indeed, and spirits were high around the card table. Mr Knightley, not usually a man with much time for games or frivolity, unbent himself to join in, keeping one eye on his hand of cards but the other pretty fixed on Mrs Bates. In the firelight, she looked lovely indeed, not a trace of grey in her hair, her skin blooming with health, a proper, motherly concern as she regarded her two daughters and monitored what passed between them and the two younger gentleman. There was a certain becoming sadness in her eye, from time to time, when the conversation touched on what

Reverend Bates might have said or done on any given occasion, and when Lieutenant Weston offered his condolences, which he did with sincerity and gentleness, but the sadness was soft and accepting. Did she still suffer pangs of grief? Were her wounds less grievous than they had been? No one knew better than he the sharp stab of bereavement but he had found that, in time, the pain eased.

Presently Lieutenant Weston showed Jane another game, a two-handed one, and Mr Knightley and Mrs Bates withdrew to another part of the room.

'You seem to have settled comfortably, here,' Mr Knightley observed. 'Of course, it is not the vicarage …'

'The vicarage was a pleasant home,' Mrs Bates replied. 'Some think it too close to the road, I know, and others have *recently* observed that the dining room is rather small. Of course, it was built before people entertained regularly, and, in any case, it was not supposed that a country parson would hold dinners. But we were very happy there. I do not know if you are aware, Mr Knightley, but before we came to Highbury, Frederick and I ministered in the metropolis. We had two rooms. After that, Highbury vicarage was a palace.'

'You do not feel that these rooms have taken you a backward step?'

'These rooms are a boon and a blessing, sir. Without their provision I do not know what we would have done. They do not compare in any degree to the lodgings we had in Curzon Street. Of course, one needs shelter and warmth—what creature does not? But I fancy I am the kind of woman who can adapt to my surroundings. If we had been offered a humble cottage, I think I could have gone there cheerfully, and swept it out and collected fallen wood for a fire if necessary.'

'I believe you could, Mrs Bates,' said the squire, sincerely, 'and if you had found yourself in a substantial house—such as Clayton Park, for example—you could as easily have adapted yourself to that. You are a lady—and a lady always knows how to behave, wherever she may find herself, in whatever company, regardless of the circumstances.'

'You are very kind, sir.'

The squire threw her a look which penetrated her so

thoroughly that she could not meet his eye. The fact
that it came so hard on her curiosity about Mrs Stokes
added considerably to her confusion. She sought a
change of topic lest she betray herself. 'Tell me that
George and William Larkins were not too
disappointed to miss their dip in the mill pond today. I
was shocked to hear they intended such an adventure.

Mr Knightley smiled. 'Boys will be boys,' he said, 'and
I have swum in the mill pond on many an occasion
myself, but at this time of year it was a foolhardy plan.
I told George that, come the summer, there will be
opportunity enough, for I have agreed with Hopley
that we shall have a new water wheel for the mill. I
have an engineer working on the drawings now, and
we will need all hands to remove the old one and
install the new.'

'I am glad about the boys. George is a strong lad but
William Larkins is prone to bronchitis. I cannot
imagine he would have escaped unscathed.'

'George must stay well. He goes to school in the new
year and I would not have him behind the other boys
in his lessons.'

'Little danger of that,' Mrs Bates said. 'Frederick

thought him many months ahead of most eight-year-olds. You will miss him, I daresay, when he is gone.'

'Of course, I shall, and so will John, but,' with a sigh, 'so it must be. He will go away a boy and come back a man.'

Marie hesitated a moment before saying, 'I hope you will not think me impertinent, Mr Knightley, but if you wished for some help in preparing George's things for school … I am sure Mrs Lemming will not object to the help, for she is busy enough, and, if you will forgive me, there is something in a mother's hand which cannot be supplied even by the kindest of servants. If your dear wife had been alive, of course she would have known better than anyone which of his books and toys he would wish to have with him, which cakes and treats would most cheer him. But since she is not able to do it, and if you have not any other lady ready to offer her help, I will do so, if you will permit it. There may be some mending or alterations to make about his clothing. *That*, at the very least, I can do.'

The squire's eye looked a little glassy. He reached for Marie's hand and pressed it in his. 'Madam,' he said, his voice low and laden with emotion, 'you are so good. I conjecture there is no one more considerate or kind in the county or beyond. If you would come to Donwell and see to George's boxes, nothing would give me—or him—greater pleasure.'

The heat and pressure of the squire's hand revived in Marie discomposure of the most alarming and also of a peculiarly pleasant kind but the image of Mrs Stokes came powerfully to her mind. She withdrew her hand, saying, 'Mrs Stokes danced with great elegance last night. I fear she gets few opportunities for such enjoyment. None of us can quite know what her life has been, heretofore. I suspect Mr Stokes was far from being an easy husband and she has that wayward son of hers to manage. I ought to call on her. I should encourage her into society more than I have done. I feel quite ashamed that I have neglected her. I will invite her to attend the Ladies' Benevolent Knitting and Sewing Circle. Do you think she would attend if I asked her?'

'I cannot say, ma'am,' the squire said. 'But as regards the son …'

'Oh, *he* would not be welcome at the Ladies'

Benevolent Knitting and Sewing Circle!' Marie interrupted, shrilly. Having introduced the topic of Mrs Stokes she found it was the last one she wished to pursue.

Mr Knightley frowned and turned back to study the books on the shelves.

The lieutenant and Jane had abandoned their game. Weston was telling her about his travels in Europe, their various encampments, getting lost in the Dordogne, eating snails in garlic at an inn near Cognac. 'Of course, I did not know, until I had eaten them, what was in the bowl, but I must say they were tasty enough—slightly rubbery—but the garlic, you know, predominates.'

'I have never eaten either,' Jane said, wistfully.

'I *would* never eat either,' Hetty put in, from across the room.

'I commend you for your sense, Madam. Neither would I, on any account,' Mr Woodhouse agreed, 'although William Buchan, here, in this interesting volume Miss Bates and I have been perusing together, does agree that garlic has some healthful benefits. It balances the humours, he thinks.'

'And isn't it reputed to keep evil spirits away?' Lieutenant Weston laughed. 'I think a peasant woman in France said so, but my French was hardly adequate to the task of translating. I may have misunderstood.'

'Let me ring for the supper tray,' Marie said. 'We have that cheese you were so good as to send, Mr Knightley …'

'Oh no, madam, not on my account,' Mr Woodhouse interrupted, rising with difficulty to his feet. 'Your hospitality has overwhelmed me as it is, but cheese I certainly cannot take so late in the evening and I do not recommend any of you partake of it either. The digestion, you know, cannot support it.'

'You will not break up our party so early, Woodhouse?' Lieutenant Weston cried, 'it is scarcely gone eight.'

'Is it as late as that?' Mr Woodhouse asked, fumbling to get his watch from his waistcoat pocket. 'My word, it is! What an enjoyable and edifying evening I have had,' looking significantly at Miss Bates, 'and indeed I am loath to leave you all. But I am supposed to take my medicine at eight prompt. A quarter of an hour later and I assure you the repercussions … well, I shall not elucidate, but a sleepless night will be the least of them. I must say that for some reason this evening I feel in additional need. A little breathlessness, some agitation in the lungs, flutterings in the stomach. You say there is not an apothecary in Highbury?'

'No, sir, the nearest is Mr Wilcox, in Kingston.'

'It is the one flaw I have found in Highbury's amenities,' Mr Woodhouse said, layering himself with an extra woollen waistcoat and two scarves. 'We must see if we cannot find one who will come and set up practice here, when my house is built. But, in the meantime, madam, if you would be so good as to call for your maid. She took my coat and umbrella ...'

With that, Mr Woodhouse took his leave. The rest of the party watched him from the casement window as he scurried across the street and disappeared into the Crown. In spite of his warning, Mrs Bates called for supper to be brought in and it was eaten with great enjoyment, cheese and all.

'This is the last of our Madeira, Mama,' Hetty said, as she poured some into tiny glasses. 'I believe it is very good, although I am no judge myself.'

'It is excellent,' said Lieutenant Weston. 'We touched

on Madeira, you know, en-route to the Canaries. A very beautiful island indeed. You can taste the sunshine in the wine, I find. Have you travelled much, Knightley?'

'Not so widely as you, Weston. In this country I have toured extensively—Scotland, Wales, the West Country. The Peak District was quite breath-taking, as regards scenery. I have been to Ireland but I would not recommend it to anyone who enjoys civilised society. But I have not been abroad.'

'I long to travel,' Jane said, 'even so far as London—which is only sixteen miles distant—but better still I would like to see the sea.'

'I have no desire to go anywhere,' Hetty said, with a sniff, 'and Mr Woodhouse agrees with me. Indeed, he tells me that he has postponed his journey to Oxfordshire. Even that, he finds beyond his current capacity. And I told him I thought him most judicious. Travel at any time is uncomfortable and tiresome, but in winter, no one but a fool would attempt it.'

'Call me a fool then, Miss Bates,' Lieutenant Weston said, 'for I am due in Brighton today fortnight. My Colonel calls, and I must answer.'

'So, Mr Woodhouse stays on in Highbury, does he?' Marie said quickly, to mask Jane's cry of dismay.

'Yes, indeed. He wishes to finalise the purchase of Hartfield, and to better acquaint himself with the area. I suggested that tomorrow, if the weather is clement, and if he is well enough, he might walk to the vicarage. We might get as far as Randalls.'

'There is a property I would like to own, one day,' Lieutenant Weston said warmly. 'I have admired it since I was a boy and I used to go scrumping in the orchard. Such a woebegone, forlorn looking place and yet what beauty of architecture; the symmetry of the wings, the quiet, sheltered nature of that little courtyard, the jaunty character of the gabled attic windows.'

'You warned Mr Woodhouse off it very strongly. An east wind and prone to snow, I think you told him!' Mrs Bates said, a smile in her lips.

'Of course, I did,' Lieutenant Weston replied with a grin. 'I did not want him to buy it from under me!'

Chapter 9

The following day, being Sunday, Mrs Bates and her daughters naturally attended church. The predicted snow had arrived overnight and lay two or three inches thick along the High Street. It had ceased to fall by the time breakfast was over, and from their parlour window the Bateses had an excellent view of the Highbury roofs all swathed in snow and the white countryside beyond.

'I long to go to Donwell,' Jane said. 'George Knightley and William Larkins are sure to be tobogganing. The mill pond may be frozen enough for skating.'

'You are too old for that now, Jane, and George and William are not fit companions for you. I wish you would make friends with one of the Winwoods.'

'I have told you, I can never meet Ursula but she must tell me about the 'improvements' they are making at the vicarage. I am sure she does it to wound me. There are alterations afoot in the old morning room. She was anxious to give me chapter and verse. You saw how Sophia behaved at Donwell. Surely you would not have me associate with such a girl.'

'Befriend Cordelia, then. She is only two years younger than you. I do not mind. But do make an effort. Hetty, you too should make a point of engaging the Winwoods in conversation after church. I would not have the slightest suspicion of resentment taint our relations with them. They have not returned our call but we will not give them the satisfaction of thinking we care. Jane, have you got your thick stockings on? Hetty, be sure to wear an extra spencer. I do not wish you to catch cold.'

'Oh, I am happy to talk to anyone, you know that, Mama, and I have tried to converse with Miss Hermia Winwood. But she is so very bookish and I am all at a loss,' Hetty replied, tying the laces of her thickest boots.

'You might ask Miss Winwood if she has joined the circulating library in Kingston. I have two volumes I would like you to return there and she might like to accompany you.'

'Hetty is not a member of the circulating library,' Jane exclaimed. 'She never picks up a book and would not know one author from another.'

'She will be so good as to return my books, though, and, in doing so, could introduce Miss Winwood.'

'I enjoy the walk to Kingston on a pleasant day,' Hetty said, 'for I often meet with several acquaintance. Mrs Cropley is often on the road in her gig, and bids me ride with her. She takes her eggs to the poultry market, you know, three times a week. Mr Coxe goes on horseback almost daily and is always very civil. Abel Larkins goes on Donwell business …'

'We do not need an inventory of every person who goes to Kingston, Hetty,' Jane said, testily. 'It will take all day and we will be late for church.'

'I will happily take your books, Mama,' Hetty said, quietly, 'and invite Hermia Winwood if it pleases you. I suppose this snow will not lie long.'

'I do not think that it is our place to make advances to the Winwoods,' Jane observed, haughtily. 'You called on them, when they arrived—horrible as it was for you to see their nasty pictures on our walls and their innumerable gewgaws cluttering every surface and their insufferable draperies hung around everything— so our duty is done. They ought to return the call. Mama, I think you should wear your green shawl. It is thicker than the black one. I will fetch it for you.'

'I hope they do not call,' Hetty cried. 'There will not be room! Five girls and their mama as well! How would we accommodate them? I do not suppose we have enough teacups. Jane, I cannot find my other glove. One was in my pocket but the other cannot be located. Have you seen it?'

'Surely, they would not come en masse,' Mrs Bates said, settling her bonnet. 'I will invite Mrs Winwood and the two oldest girls. She can hardly refuse. We must establish acquaintance somehow. Your glove is on the floor, Hetty, under the chair. Thank you, Jane, the green shawl is much warmer, and it is not such a very bright green as to be inappropriate. Let me tie your bonnet. There, we are done and it is time we set out.'

'In times gone by we could have run across the garden and been in our pew before a moment had elapsed,' lamented Hetty as she put on her glove.

'Those days are gone and it is useless to grieve over them,' said Jane.

They descended the stair and stepped out onto the street. Other Highbury townsfolk were already making their way toward the church, where the bell tolled steadily.

Miss Bates forgot her melancholy and greeted all and sundry as they walked. 'Oh Mrs Ford!' she called, 'how are you? Mr Ford, good morning, sir. And Mr Obadiah Ford also. What a pleasure! Good morning to you all. How do you? How do you like the snow, Mr Obadiah? I must say I like it excessively—so pretty, before it has been trampled by our feet or soiled by the horses, do you not agree? Oh! I think he does not hear me. Never mind. Mrs Stokes! How are you? The pump is frozen? That is very inconvenient. The poor horses! You will be able to draw no water for their mash. Martha said that, but she had drawn ours last night, we should have had to go without our morning tea! Mrs Coxe! How the little Coxes are enjoying the snow! How warmly you have them all wrapped up. Yes indeed, a warm chemise and thick stockings—Mama insisted! Hello Miss Fanny. Your bonnet is very becoming, I must say. Did you trim it yourself? Oh dear, little William Coxe has slipped. I hope he has come to no harm. No, see, he is up and running again. How delightful it is to walk with our neighbours. And here is the lych gate. No, please, Mrs Weston, after you. No, really, I insist. Oh, well, if you really are adamant, thank you very much. You are very kind. Oh, Reverend Winwood. Good morning, sir. How do you do? I hope you wrapped the azaleas last night for this snow will certainly scorch the buds. The vicarage azaleas are a delight in the spring, you know—they are quite a blaze of colour but they are susceptible to cold. Oh, you did not? Oh. Well … that is to say … Let us hope they have come to no harm. Yes, Mama, I know I must go in. Quite a queue waiting to shake the reverend's hand. Where is my prayer book? Oh here, in the pocket of my pelisse. Hush. The organist is playing … something. I do not quite recognise. Oh, it is Miss Ursula who plays. Well, I had not known her to be accomp … that is to say, I did not know she played the organ. A very spirited attempt indeed. Yes, Jane, I know. I must be quiet now. Very well. But,' in a somewhat lowered tone, 'what an execrable mess she is making of the voluntary. Is it supposed to be the Prelude in C? I should not have recognised it.'

Mrs Bates and her girls slid into seats behind a pillar in

the shadow of an unlit side chapel where they could worship without reminding the congregation of the pastor they had loved and lost. Mr Knightley sat with George in the Donwell pew beneath the pulpit. The many Winwood women pressed into the vicarage pew below the lectern. Lieutenant Weston sat with his mother and father and one of his sisters a row behind. The Fords, Snells, Coxes and Larkins filled in seats behind them, the Hopleys, Cropleys and lesser tenant farmers arranged themselves in rough precedence beyond. The simple peasants and such household servants as could be spared from the preparation of the Sunday repast, the making of beds and cleaning of grates took the seats in the draught from the ill-fitting door.

They stood and sang the first hymn. The oldest Miss Winwood lisped the lesson and Reverend Winwood ascended the pulpit to preach.

After the service the citizenry of Highbury gathered about the porch and along the gravel path. A few more fat flakes of snow were beginning to fall but it did not deter them from this, their weekly opportunity to mingle and exchange news.

As directed, Hetty sought out Miss Hermia Winwood. She was tidying hassocks in the gloom of the empty church. Hermia was a young woman of something over average height, rather thin, with a long nose and a receding chin. But her eyes had a gentle, almost sad expression which compensated for the unfortunate aspect of the other features and her hair was a pretty shade of brown, thick and lustrous. Her complexion was pale, but very fine. She was a sober, thoughtful girl given to the contemplation of deeply intellectual matters. As such she was no very likely friend for Hetty but the two were within a year or two of being the same age and it seemed that so far she had seen no significant success in forming friendships in Highbury.

'Such a surprise to hear you read the lesson, Miss Winwood,' Hetty began. 'Papa would never have contemplated Jane or I doing such a thing. To be sure, I could not have done it anyway—would have been sure to have read the wrong passage or mis-pronounced one of the prophets' names—but Jane could, I am certain, if she had been given the opportunity. And your sister played the organ. My, my. Quite a family affair!'

'John Abdy was to have read the lesson, but he slipped in the snow and so was unable to come,' Miss Winwood said. 'I did not want to do it, I assure you, but Mama insisted. I would not put myself forward for the world. As for Ursula's murdering the music—I have no excuse for that. Once she heard I was to read she was determined to exhibit herself. She held her breath until she went quite purple and Mama said that Papa must allow it or she would give herself an apoplexy.'

'Dear me. I can imagine the scene,' Hetty said, with genuine sympathy, 'as much as one loves one's sisters, they can be …'

'Oh! Ursula's histrionics were as nothing compared to Sophia's,' Miss Winwood went on. 'Such fuss over frills and trimmings and having to have Bolton all to herself for the arrangement of her hair. She refused point blank to wear her fur tippet—declared the chill of the church and the draught from the vestry (which blows into the vicarage pew with a vengeance, as I am sure you remember) nothing to her. Did you see her? Her shoulders exposed like a showgirl! I am ashamed of her. All because she knew Lieu … That is to say, she expected a certain gentleman to be in church, and she wanted to be taken notice of. As if that is appropriate, in the house of God.'

'No, indeed. So, Miss Sophia feels herself developing an attachment to … a certain military gentleman, does she? Well, I am not surprised. He is so very pleasant. I suppose these things do rather creep upon one.'

'They would not creep upon me,' Miss Winwood said, stoutly, tweaking the blooms of an arrangement in a niche. 'I would only attach myself on the basis of thoroughgoing knowledge and understanding of a man's character. Only a long acquaintance, I am convinced, can really establish the basis for a genuine attachment.'

'Oh, but one does not always have the luxury of a long acquaintance,' Hetty said, thinking of Mr Woodhouse, whom she had met precisely three times.

'Then, in my opinion, one had better not commit oneself,' Miss Winwood pronounced.

'I do not know if I share your opinion,' said Hetty, feeling rather confused. 'Usually, I can call to mind some example or other. A successful match formed on short acquaintance, or an unhappy one entered into

after a long, or vice versa, you know—I am quite
disinterested. But I cannot think of an example of
either one or the other, so I had better not pronounce.
Miss Winwood, I wondered if you would like to
accompany me to the circulating library in Kingston
one day this week. Assuming the snow clears, of
course. It can be a pleasant walk—hardly four miles
each way. And it occurs to me, if you feel your sisters'
company somewhat irksome on occasion, the
opportunity to be away from them might be
beneficial.'

Miss Winwood almost smiled. 'To Kingston? Oh! I
should like that, very much Miss Bates. Thank you.'

Mrs Bates found herself next to Mrs Winwood. 'An
edifying sermon from Reverend Winwood this
morning, ma'am,' she began. 'That passage in
Lamentations is so often neglected. And Miss
Winwood read the lesson very well. I have been
meaning to ask you to do us the honour of calling, one
day. We would be so delighted. Perhaps you might
bring Miss Winwood and Miss Sophia with you. My
girls are avid to improve their acquaintance.'

Mrs Winwood looked about her, but there was no

escape. 'I should be delighted to wait on you—
perhaps on Wednesday? I will see if I am disengaged.
One is so caught up, you know, in the improvements.
I find the builders cannot be left unsupervised and the
joiner is scarcely more reliable.'

'It is Christmas,' Mrs Bates said. 'Gideon Mortimer,
the builder, is away visiting his mother and father in
Buckinghamshire. John Joiner will be ensconced in the
Crown until twelfth night.'

Mrs Winwood bridled and prepared herself for a
cutting repost. But the church path was crowded—no
place for her to lose her temper. 'Such a charming
evening that we had at Donwell Abbey,' she said,
through gritted teeth, 'I declare the squire quite
overwhelmed us with his generosity. Sophia in
particular enjoyed the dancing—and here is Lieutenant
Weston, who was so good as to partner her for—
oh!—Ever so many dances. I quite lost count. Good
morning Lieutenant Weston.'

Lieutenant Weston made his bow. 'Good morning
Mrs Winwood. I hope you are quite well. Mrs Bates,
let me thank you once more for a delightful evening.
Have you heard from Mr Woodhouse this morning?'

Mrs Winwood sniffed. 'You dined with Mrs Bates yesterday? No wonder you were unable to accept our invitation.'

'Your kind card awaited me when I returned from my morning business,' Lieutenant Weston said, with another bow. 'But I was already engaged. I dined with Mr Knightley and Mrs Bates had been so good as to ask us to drink tea with her in the evening.'

'You and Squire Knightley both?'

'Yes, indeed, and my friend Woodhouse. I don't know if you have met Mr Woodhouse?'

'The invalid gentleman who sat by the fire at Donwell and did not mingle? No. I have not had the pleasure.'

'Speaking for myself, I would be happy, on another occasion …'

'I am not sure when we next have an evening at leisure,' Mrs Winwood said, haughtily. 'Indeed, any entertaining at present is almost impossible, I was loath to extend hospitality but Sophia … well. That is by the bye.' She bent her eye back upon Mrs Bates. 'Upon my word, Mrs Bates, three unattached gentlemen! I am astonished. I had not suspected

Highbury to be so dissipated. Good morning to you.'

She turned away and was lost in the crowd. 'Oh dear,' Lieutenant Weston said, with half a smile upon his lips, 'I believe we have somewhat descended in that lady's good opinion, Mrs Bates. My mother, ma'am, presents her respects, and requests the pleasure of your daughter Jane's company for dinner today, if she is at liberty. Do I have your permission to deliver the invitation? The carriage will be sent, naturally.'

'Dear Lieutenant Weston, James, if I may call you so—I have known you since you were in swaddling bands—you are very proper to ask me first. And your dear Mama is very good to ask Jane. It will be the first dinner she has attended alone. She is,' with a slight but significant frown, 'but seventeen years old, you know.'

Lieutenant Weston returned her look with frank understanding before taking his leave to find Jane. As luck would have it she was conversing with Miss Ursula Winwood and Miss Sophia Winwood.

'Good morning, Miss Jane,' Lieutenant Weston cried, hailing from along the path.

All three girls bobbed curtseys. The Misses Winwood chorused, 'Lieutenant Weston.' Miss Sophia regarded him from beneath her eyelashes before saying, 'How do you like my ribbons, Lieutenant Weston? They are the colour of your regimental insignia. I chose them especially.'

Miss Ursula said, 'You promised to call, Lieutenant Weston, and did not. Mama invited you—Sophia had no end of trouble securing you an invitation. Mama was adamantly against it, I assure you. In the end Sophia threatened to throw herself down the stairs— and your reply came unconscionably late.'

Weston laughed. 'Her invitation came somewhat tardy, Miss Ursula. I was out and about all morning on business with Mr Woodhouse and only returned in time to change to dine at Donwell. Next time your boy should find me with his message, not leave it at my mother's.'

'Ursula is very surly, Lieutenant Weston,' Sophia Winwood put in, with a simper. 'I know that surliness will not answer where beaux are concerned. I shall make sure that Mama invites you again—I shall throw myself down the stairs, if necessary. I shall not care if I break both my legs if it means I get my own way—for we long to have you dine with us at the vicarage.'

Lieutenant Weston bowed.

'Mama does not long to have anyone to dine until she can double the size of the dining room and get the drawing room fireplace to stop smoking,' Miss Ursula remarked, 'although the dining room is unconscionably small. There is scarce room for us, when the whole family is gathered, let alone any guests. Mama wonders that the previous incumbent managed to entertain on any scale worth mentioning. She quite despairs of it, indeed.'

'We were not so numerous,' Jane said, coldly. 'In addition to ourselves we could easily accommodate six guests. Mama's dinners were celebrated as amongst the best in Highbury and the Bishop, who came once or twice, remarked there was no better hostess in the Diocese.'

'However, if you do come,' Miss Ursula went on, as though Jane had not spoken, 'I shall play for you. For we have a pianoforte. The old morning room has been made over and is now our music room. Double doors will open from it into the drawing room, you know, so it will easily be incorporated into our evening entertainments. Mama says she cannot conceive how it was ever managed before. An evening party without music is no party at all, in her opinion. In fact it is not impossible that we may not have dancing there—the two rooms together are quite large enough, when the door between is opened right up, to accommodate six or even eight couple.'

'We shall have dancing, I am determined,' Miss Sophia gushed, 'when you come to us.'

'Your broken legs notwithstanding,' Jane muttered.

'We shall invite some other gentlemen to meet you,' Miss Sophia forged on, '(we have quite enough ladies in the house, you know, Lieutenant Weston—we shall not need to invite more),' this with a mischievous glance at Jane, 'and we shall dance until our feet bleed.'

'Dear me, Miss Sophia! I hope I shall not exercise you so far as that!' Lieutenant Weston cried.

'You shall exercise me as much as you like, sir,' Miss Sophia replied, with a very coquettish look upon her face.

'Sophia!' Miss Ursula remonstrated with her sister, 'you go too far. And in any case, I do not know which other gentlemen we could invite. Squire Knightley is too old. Young Mr Ford is too miserable. The Snell boys are away—we have yet to get a glimpse of either of them. I do not suppose the Claytons would condescend. So who else is there?'

'Perhaps Lieutenant Weston has some friends in the militia who would oblige. Do you, sir? Are there any brother officers in the vicinity?'

Before he could answer, Mrs Winwood could be seen hurrying down the path towards them.

'Sophia! Ursula! It is time we went home. You know we must dine early, if papa is to be ready for the afternoon service. Good day, Miss Jane. I did not see you there. But seeing you reminds me to tell Sophia that she is invited to call upon Mrs Bates on Wednesday, with Hermia and me. You are disengaged, Sophia?'

'I do not know,' Sophia looked shifty.

'I am engaged,' Ursula announced, with a triumphant look at Jane. 'I am engaged to visit my very good friend Miss Lavinia Snell on Wednesday. We are to make an inventory of the contents of her trinket box.'

'That will be no very long affair,' Jane remarked. 'Last

time she showed it to me it had but three things in it, and one of those was broken.'

'You were not invited, Ursula,' Mrs Winwood said. 'I daresay Mrs Bates does not have room.'

'She probably cannot afford the cake,' Sophia added, 'everyone knows she can barely keep the wolf from the door. But you are such a greedy pig, Ursula; you would eat her out of house and home.'

'Miss Jane,' Lieutenant Weston put in, quickly, offering his arm to that young lady and drawing her away, 'I beg you will walk with me a little. Good day, ladies.' The two strolled but a step or two away before Lieutenant Weston said in a voice quite loud enough to be heard by the Winwoods, 'My mother invites you to dine with us. I hope I may tell her that we are to have the honour of your company?'

There was a muted shriek from Sophia Winwood, and a sound which may have been her mama giving her a slap, but neither Lieutenant Weston nor Jane Bates turned round to look.

The snow began to fall again in earnest and the residents of Highbury began to say their farewells. Lieutenant Weston walked back to the Bates' house with Jane on his arm. 'This snow shall not deter us,' he said as they parted. 'The carriage will call for you, do not fear.'

But when three o'clock came the knock at the door was not the Westons' coachman but Lieutenant Weston himself, dressed in his army greatcoat, the collar turned up and a hat pulled well down. Jane, who had been dressed and ready for the past hour, full of excitement at the prospect of her first dinner engagement and anxiety that the weather might put paid to her expectations, ran down the stairs to open the door herself. The High Street was deserted, inches deep in thick snow. Flakes still fell fast from a laden sky, making the afternoon prematurely dark. Gladness at seeing the lieutenant and fear that he had come to tell her that the dinner was to be abandoned made tears shine in Jane's eyes. With the fresh bloom on her cheek, her hair curled and piled upon her head and wearing her best gown, she looked quite beautiful, and Lieutenant Weston's greeting died on his lips as he looked at her.

Then he recollected himself and stepped into the shelter of the little hallway. It was impossible, in such confinement, for the two not to stand in very close proximity. Lieutenant Weston drew off his gloves and took Jane's hand. 'It is too bad for the horses,' he said, 'but see, I have brought you my cape.' He drew it, now, from beneath his coat. It was long, thick and lined with silk—very warm. 'It will cover you entirely—there is no danger of your dress being spoiled, and it has a hood to protect your hair. If you put your outdoor boots on now, you can easily change into your evening shoes when we get to my mother's house. It is less than two minutes' walk—I timed it as I came. We need not deny ourselves the pleasure— that is, the pleasure will be mine—if you will trust me, and not be afraid.' He pressed her hand. 'You are not afraid, are you Jane?'

'Oh no,' Jane replied, looking up at the lieutenant with eyes that were bright and brave, 'I am not at all afraid.'

Hetty, standing at the casement above, said, 'I do not see the Westons' carriage, Mama. There is not a soul in the street. Do you suppose that was the Westons' man with a message to say the dinner is cancelled? Surely that is the case, for no one would expect anyone to set out in such weather as this. The treacherous surfaces underfoot, to begin with, will be hazardous, and then the cold and damp. And even supposing Jane were foolish enough to set out—not that you would sanction such a thing, Mama, how would she get home? She could be at the Westons for days. To be sure, the snow falls so very thickly, I could not make out who came to the door but I am sure it is their man to tell Jane that she will go to no dinner today.'

Mrs Bates, whose eyes were keener than Hetty's, had discerned very well who had come, and what his intention might be. She went to the parlour door and opened it enough to call, 'Have a delightful evening, Jane dear, and give my respects to Mr and Mrs Weston. I will wait up for you.'

Then she closed the door firmly and rang the bell for their own dinner to be brought up.

Jane changed her shoes and Lieutenant Weston put the cloak around her shoulders, drawing the hood carefully over her coiffure. He tucked her silk slippers into his pocket and then opened the door. The two of them stepped out, into the blur of snowflakes.

Lieutenant Weston said, 'You will allow me?' and placed his arm around Jane in such a way that he drew her closely to his side and almost lifted her from her feet, and the two set off through the snow, along the High Street and down the lane which would bring them to the Westons' substantial villa.

Chapter 10

Jane thoroughly enjoyed her evening at the Westons and came home with no worse consequences than a hem drenched in snow and the arrangement of her hair somewhat disordered by the hood of Lieutenant Weston's cloak. She had hardly felt the cold—declared herself quite unaware of it—and the storm had been no inconvenience whatsoever. She elaborated on the cosiness of Mrs Weston's drawing room, the hugeness of the fire both there and in the dining room, the succession of courses designed to nourish and warm. Mr Weston had been generosity itself, kind and welcoming, Mrs Weston attentive and motherly. Both the married sons had been there to meet her, with their wives, and the unmarried sister. The friendliness of the whole family had been marked; they seemed disposed to like her and she had been allowed to hold the baby. Mrs John Weston had played the harp after dinner, and Jane had sung, there had been cards and charades and then tea. All this she regaled her mother and sister with at breakfast the following morning. What she did not describe—although she thought about it a great deal—was the strength of the Lieutenant's arm on the walk homeward, the way he had borne all of her weight and carried her bodily over the deepest drifts, sweeping her quite off her feet in every way.

While Hetty might exercise herself over the likelihood of Jane's catching a cold, or pneumonia, chilblains or frostbite, the needless spoiling of an evening gown and what was to be done with the Lieutenant's cloak which still hung on a peg in the hall and dripped on the floor of the passageway and smelt damp, Mrs Bates kept her counsel. Jane might only now be forming her knowledge of Lieutenant Weston's mind and character, but she had known the family for many years, and knew them to be unexceptionable people. That James Weston was an open, frank and honourable man she had no doubt—he would not toy with Jane's feelings. To be sure, he was a military man, and his life was unsettled. But that might exactly suit Jane, who would be adaptable and resourceful enough to suit herself to whatever circumstances might arise. It would satisfy her yen to travel, but eventually, Marie Bates felt sure, Lieutenant Weston would quit the militia and return to Highbury, perhaps to settle in his family business but more likely to have no need of additional income. He had spoken of Randalls as his future home. Even if she married Lieutenant Weston and went away, one day, Jane would come home. On the whole she was content to allow the liaison to progress.

The ladies stayed indoors all that day. The snow fell without ceasing, and a keen east wind had developed, blowing the snow into drifts against the houses, obscuring the pavements. The usually busy High Street was all but deserted; only the hardiest person venturing along it, well-muffled against the wind and weather. Ford's and the post office opened. Other shops stayed firmly shut.

Out in the country the snow blew across the fields and billowed out through the hedgerows so that the lanes were all but impassable. They were impassable indeed for the gentlefolk, of course, who kept themselves indoors, warm by their fires. But they were not considered to be impassable for the boys and men who were sent out to deliver messages between the houses, enquiring after health, sending compliments and altering and cancelling plans. The farmers struggled on, finding stock buried under snow drifts, spreading out extra feed and breaking the ice on drinking troughs.

Squire Knightley was not to be kept indoors. He set off to inspect his cottages, to make notes of repairs needed to slipped slates and damaged guttering, to give orders for fallen boughs to be cleared and the wood to be delivered to widows and the needy. George went with him, the snow up to his thighs but keeping up nonetheless with his father's long, loping stride.

Mrs Winwood looked out on the snowstorm, the blanketed vicarage garden and the unfamiliar contours of Vicarage Lane and doubted she would be able to keep her engagement to call on Mrs Bates. She was glad of the excuse, to be truthful. The obligatory return call was a politeness which had been neglected because Mrs Bates' status was rather moot. Mrs Bates was now almost (but not quite) at that rank which must be viewed with benevolence. She was poor. Whilst flasks of hot soup and charitable blankets would be insulting they were not far off being necessary. But she was also respectable—something was due to her, it was just that Mrs Winwood did not know what. She had formerly been a person of note in Highbury, but she could not now be considered an equal. But then who could? Mrs Winwood considered herself, in the absence of a Mrs Knightley, the first lady of Highbury. She must be very judicious in the matter of establishing acquaintance. Highbury society must acknowledge her pre-eminence as a matter of course. She might condescend to association with them but they should not presume to connexion with her. It would reflect well on Mrs Winwood's magnanimity to notice Mrs Bates; it would be gracious, but it would not necessarily be generous. It would not ultimately be kind to encourage Mrs Bates to think of herself as still equal to the new vicar's wife. No, she must be helped to establish herself in her new, lesser sphere, escorted to the respectable shadows of retirement and left there. But she very much feared Mrs Bates was not the kind of woman to know her place.

It would be a kindness to allow the Winwood daughters to befriend the Bates girls but it would not necessarily be a pleasure and it would not inevitably be beneficial if it meant they sank to the Bates' level. The Bates girls were portionless—everybody knew that. They could not aspire to any kind of respectable match. Miss Jane had personal qualities which would take her a degree or two higher than her natural level but Miss Henrietta's oddness would in all likelihood drag her back down again.

Nevertheless, one had one's duty. That should never be neglected. Therefore, at last Mrs Winwood wrote a note to say she very much hoped to have the pleasure of calling on Mrs Bates on Wednesday, but she feared the weather would make it impossible. Regardless of her being able to call, Sophia would have to decline, having caught a severe chill in church. They would have to see what the next two days brought. Hermia enclosed her own note to Miss Bates lamenting most sincerely that their walk to Kingston would have to be postponed. Their man set off through the penetrating wind and driving blizzard to deliver the message, very much resentful of being taken away from the warmth of the servants' fire.

Mr Woodhouse sat alone in the private parlour of the

Crown, glad to have put off his journey to
Oxfordshire, happy that he had avoided being caught
in the storm and entertaining himself with thoughts of
the perils he had avoided—the coach over-turning, the
contagious ailments of other travellers, the freezing
temperatures and the doubtful hospitality of wayside
inns. He played out a fanciful scenario in his mind—
the coach losing a wheel, the horses bolting, being
caught in a terrible squall of snow and sleet with only a
rough animal shelter between him and a slow death
from exposure. The grim smell of animal ordure, the
piercing chill of draughts between the ramshackle
stones, the cold and damp … It all upset him so much
he had to ring the bell and ask for brandy and an extra
bucket of coals.

When he was calmer, he dwelt instead upon the
unutterable relief he felt at having delayed the ordeal at
Mr O'Brien's in Oxfordshire. He had slept the better
knowing he had placed it at a distance which
significantly lessened its ability to frighten and appal
him. At the same time the ennui of being confined to
his rooms began to oppress him. The storm rendered
it absolutely impossible that he should stir outside. He

was not a great reader of books and those things that did while away his leisure hours—he was a collector of buttons, having a sizeable compendium in various designs that he liked to catalogue, compare and contrast—he did not have with him. He had sat alone all day on Sunday and Monday likewise looked like being a day in which he would be denied company. Weston had sent a note to say he would be closeted with his father and brothers on business that day. He had considered and rejected the notion of inviting the squire to dine with him. He paced the room and looked often out of his window at the barren street, the empty shops and the occasional struggling journeyman, and found his eye drawn again and again to the windows of Mrs Bates and her daughters. They were pleasantly lighted and bright. A plume of smoke rose from their chimneys. From time to time he saw one of the ladies passing the casement. There would be company, agreeable conversation, weak tea and dry toast. He was tempted. Surely he could cross the street in safety? It was but a step or two. If he wore his thickest coat and his sturdiest boots, there could be no harm. The cold, of course, would be considerable, but he would not be kept waiting on the step more than a moment. Miss Bates' effect on him was quite singular—such a meeting of minds! Such a peculiar concord of opinion! And yet her concurrence did not quite reassure him. She feared, if anything, more than he did, her apprehension out-stripped even his. The previous evening he had needed two doses of medicine to calm his agitated humours. The very thought of them eating cheese so late had put him entirely out of sorts. He looked out of the window again. Those drifts were so deceiving. Anything could lie beneath the surface to trip or ensnare him. There would be ice. The pavement outside Mrs Bates' house was uneven. The wind blew very fierce. No, he thought he had better not venture.

The day wore on. Mrs Stokes came in to make up the fire and to discover his requirements for dinner. A poached chicken breast with boiled potatoes. A very few greens. A stewed apple. A glass of Madeira.

An idea occurred to him. 'Mrs Stokes, be so good as to send to Mrs Bates with my compliments and ask if she and her daughters will be so good as to step across after dinner. You will serve us tea, at the appropriate hour? And do you have cards, or backgammon?

Excellent. Please to explain that I am a little indisposed—too unwell to go out, but quite well enough for company here. I thank you, Mrs Stokes, I am most obliged to you.'

Mrs Stokes carried the message herself. She knocked on Mrs Bates' door, was greeted by Martha and shown into the upstairs parlour where the three ladies were busy at needlework.

'Mrs Stokes,' cried Marie Bates, putting her knitting to one side and rising to her feet. 'What an unexpected pleasure. Won't you sit down? Hetty, give your seat up to Mrs Stokes if you please, and tell Martha to bring refreshment.' In truth Marie was more discomposed than she liked to admit by the presence of Mrs Stokes. That lady had been a good deal in her thoughts— much more than was beneficial to Marie's peace of mind. She found she was extremely desirous of knowing exactly how relations between Mrs Stokes and Mr Knightley stood but could on no account satisfy her curiosity. She was well known for her disapproval of gossip.

'On no account,' Mrs Stokes replied. 'This is no social call. I have but come to deliver a message. Mr

Woodhouse invites you to take tea with him this evening.'

'That is most gracious of him,' Mrs Bates said, 'and we shall be delighted to accept. We have been within doors all day. I believe we are as fond of each other as any family but a variation of society will be most welcome.'

'Indeed, it will,' Jane agreed, 'for Hetty's interminable ponderings have driven me distracted.'

'You have had enough to say about a certain military gentleman,' Hetty replied, 'and I have not complained.'

'Girls,' their mother enjoined them, 'Good Mrs Stokes has no interest in your petty squabbles. But since you are here,' turning to that lady, 'won't you stay a few moments? I was only saying to Mr Knightley a couple of evenings past …'

'Mr Knightley?' Mrs Stokes looked alarmed, her face quite white, 'what did he have to say concerning our private business?'

'Nothing but …' Marie found idea of Mr Knightley and Mrs Stokes having private business surprisingly upsetting, and now she thought of it, Mr Knightley had determinedly expressed no opinion about Mrs Stokes at all, had quite refused to be drawn on the subject. 'Nothing at all, dear Mrs Stokes,' Marie went on. 'I was only saying that I wished to encourage you to join the Ladies' Benevolent Knitting and Sewing Circle and I asked him his opinion of the scheme. Would you consider it?'

'I don't think so,' Mrs Stokes said, with a decided shake of the head. 'I am so busy at the Crown I have scarcely any leisure for needlework or for society. I am a poor seamstress. I fear I would make no addition whatsoever.'

'I am a poor seamstress also,' said Hetty, holding up the crochet-work in her hands. It was impossible to identify, a mass of holes and knots. 'I have been working on this for weeks and make no progress whatsoever. But the meetings are pleasant, nonetheless, except Mrs Winwood threatens to take charge, and proposes reading her husband's sermons aloud as we work.'

'That will make no very strong inducement for Mrs Stokes to join us,' Jane observed, dryly.

'As I mentioned, I have no strong inclination to join,

and, if I had, no time to dedicate to such a project,' Mrs Stokes repeated, 'although I am sure it is very altruistic. Unfortunately, I cannot linger here, much as I might like to do so—your fire looks very inviting. But I have rooms to turn and a slatternly cook to chivvy. I heartily wish it were not so, I assure you, but so, at present, it must be.'

'At present?' Mrs Bates said, in spite of herself. 'You hope, then, for some respite in the future?' She thought of Donwell Abbey, a house crying out for a woman's touch, of Mr Knightley, similarly in need. Had he given Mrs Stokes cause to hope? Or, more? Grounds to expect such an outcome? It seemed impossible to her that Mr Knightley would engage in any manner of clandestine courtship but how else to explain that from nowhere, out of nothing, such a level of intimacy had sprung which encompassed two visits in one day, and the several dances she had witnessed at Donwell?

Mrs Stokes blushed, adding fuel to the fire of Mrs Bates' suspicion. 'I shall inform Mr Woodhouse that he should expect you at six, and I will have everything in readiness. He occupies a private parlour—quite comfortable. Good day, ladies.'

Mrs Stokes left them and the two girls returned to their labours. But Mrs Bates' hands lay idle, and she stared into the flames of the fire. She had no right—none whatsoever—to judge Mr Knightley's conduct or his choices. He was free and would choose his own path. That he should wish for a new wife was no very wonderful thing. He was strong and virile. He had boys who needed a mother—they would be a strong incentive for him to consider selecting a new helpmeet. Mrs Stokes was respectably widowed and of good character—that is, Mrs Bates knew no positive ill of her. She was beautiful, or she could be, with a little rest, better sleep, some fresh air, more time to give to her person and dress. She was not elegant, to be sure, and she did not have that grace of manner one would wish of the lady of Donwell, but her present station in life did not call for it. In fact, a certain roughness, a hard-edged pragmatism was essential to her, who must deal with pot-men and coachmen and stable lads. Who was to say that, given a change in her circumstances, an elevation of the kind that marriage to Mr Knightley would certainly be, she would not develop all the elegance and excellent manners one could wish?

And yet Marie found she revolted at the very idea—
felt so strongly against it that she feared she might
weep. She must examine herself, she decided, must
come to an understanding of her feelings and once she
was mistress of them, she would be more rational.

'I shall go to my room and lie down,' she told the girls.
'I have a headache.'

'Oh Mama,' Jane exclaimed. 'Would you like a cool
cloth for your head?'

'No, Jane dear. I fear I have strained my eyes with this
knitting—the pattern is so complex and the stitches
dance before my eyes. A little rest and I will be quite
well.'

But when she got to her room she did not lie down on
the bed. She stood at the window and stared over the
jostle of roofs and sheds, yards and alleys which lay
below.

Her feelings for Mr Knightley were all confusion.
There was an attraction—a powerful attraction—
which threatened to dominate all the old, friendly and
comfortable associations she had had for him these

many years past. His touch, her sense of his eye upon her—they wrought in her vibrations of a most shocking and yet unmistakable kind. Had these base sensations been isolated they would have been disgusting indeed, but they were not. Mr Knightley's manners, his intellect, his character were all equally attractive. He was often—almost constantly—in her thoughts. Rather than thinking of Frederick—what he might have thought or done—she found that George—what he might think or do—came more quickly to her. She was in love with Mr Knightley! The first feeling that this realisation brought was guilt—she was too recently widowed, it was not seemly or respectable. How could her feelings betray her so, not five months a widow! How poorly it reflected on dear Frederick, so soon usurped in her affection! The second was sadness—he was almost certainly engaged to Mrs Stokes. What a treacherous path she was preparing to tread, leading only to heartbreak and disappointment. The third was resolve; she must master these traitorous feelings. And with this resolution firmly in her mind and her heart, she knelt down to pray.

Chapter 11

Just before six Mrs Bates and her daughters crossed the High Street and entered the Crown. Mrs Stokes showed them into the private parlour where Mr Woodhouse rose stiffly from his seat to bid them welcome.

'Mrs Stokes will take your wraps and hang them where they can thoroughly dry and air. I would not have you put on damp things to go home in. What about your boots? Your feet are not wet? Ah! What forethought. Galoshes! Who would have imagined? I am astonished at your resourcefulness. Come and sit here, Mrs Bates. You need not fear a draught from the window—I have had them all stopped up. See the cloths there? That was my idea. A terrible draught, formerly, but I fancy Mrs Stokes is so impressed she will leave the cloths in place after I depart. Miss Bates. What a pleasure to see you again. You have not caught cold? I saw you all going to church yesterday. I thought it a little foolhardy, I must say. But the snow did not begin to fall in earnest until later. I was glad of that, at least. I was not sorry to see that you did not venture out for

Evensong. Miss Jane, how delightful. I have cards, you see, all prepared for you, and tea will be served directly. Mrs Bates, I pray you will be so good as to pour when it arrives. It is a lady's role, you know, to officiate at the tea table and nothing gives me more pleasure than to see a lady presiding at tea, even though I do not take it myself.'

Mr Woodhouse's solitude of the previous days made him loquacious and anxious to please. It seemed that nothing was too much trouble for him, nothing left wanting that could add to their comfort. He settled the ladies and then took his own seat, only to rise from it a moment later to adjust the coals on the fire, and again, to pull the curtain more tightly across the door.

'Please do not exercise yourself on our account,' Mrs Bates cried. 'The room is perfectly warm and snug and we are delighted to bear you company.'

'I have been anxious that you would begin to find your visit to Highbury very dull,' Hetty said, 'particularly after extending its duration. What bad luck that the snow should begin to fall now, to keep you indoors and prevent you from getting to know the neighbourhood. How disappointed you must be! I conjecture you have been quite down-hearted, and after postponing your trip to Oxfordshire on Highbury's account.' Mr Woodhouse nodded. He had been a little downhearted. Miss Bates had correctly inferred and perhaps even increased by a degree or two his dismay. 'And I have never known it to stick before! Well, not above a couple of days. Frosts we have, quite hard frosts. And rain, of course, sometimes a deluge that goes on for days and days. But snow is almost unknown, I am sure. At least, I am almost certain. And never much. It does not usually signify. But this! Quite unprecedented.'

'My own thoughts exactly,' Mr Woodhouse said. 'I cannot believe that such weather has been known before. It is alarming in the extreme.'

'Quite frightening, the severity of it.'

'Hazardous to all.'

'I recall several periods of snow like this,' Jane said, levelly, to arrest the catalogue of agitation. 'I have tobogganed three or four days in a row at Donwell, more than once. I would have gone today, only Mama said I mustn't. One of their meadows has just the right degree of slope.'

'You are past the age when it would be seemly,' Mrs Bates said.

'I am not past the age of finding the prospect exciting, however,' Jane replied. 'And I do not think this is so very bad. Lieutenant Weston says that in Germany they have drifts up to the roof tops, and people employed to clear the roofs lest they collapse under the weight. Snow is the last thing to keep me indoors. I went out to dinner last night, Mr Woodhouse. Lieutenant Weston came and escorted me. The inconvenience was insignificant.'

'Mrs Weston was so good as to invite me,' Mr Woodhouse replied, with a startled look at Mrs Bates, 'but I did not consider accepting. I do not understand why people should send out invitations when the weather is so inclement, and, solely for their own entertainment, expect others to leave the warmth and comfort of their hearths. I had imagined Mrs Weston to be a more considerate woman. I am surprised that you sanctioned your daughter's attending, ma'am.'

'I was surprised too,' Hetty said, oblivious to the irony of Mr Woodhouse's remark. 'It seemed the height of foolishness to me. And I said so to you, Mama, did I not?'

'Several times,' Mrs Bates acknowledged.

'How alike you two think on every topic!' Jane laughed. 'But it is no different from us coming here. Mrs Weston's house is but a few dozen yards further than the Crown. Physician, heal thyself!'

'Have you received many cards?' Mrs Bates asked, quickly, to prevent a squabble breaking out between her girls. 'For I assure you Highbury is avid to make your acquaintance. Word has got out about your settling here. There was much discussion about it, after church.'

'You have had many enquiries, I am sure,' Hetty put in, before Mr Woodhouse had a chance to reply. 'You will have been quite inundated, for Highbury is a sociable, friendly place. Mr Weston, I am sure, will call on you soon if he has not done so already. He is never behind hand in the duties of a neighbour. Reverend Winwood, I presume, will call in due course. I suppose,' with a sniff, 'parish duties occupy him and prevent him from being quite so alacritous as one would wish … Papa would never have neglected so important a courtesy—that I do know. Mr and Mrs

Bittern are from home, or they would be sure to seek your acquaintance. Mr Snell you know already. Mr Coxe is a good neighbour, Mr and Mrs Ford …'

'Are you going to list the entire parish register?' Jane said, cuttingly.

'Here is the tea,' Mrs Bates said.

The evening passed off very pleasantly. While out in society Mr Woodhouse tended to nerves and agitation, on his home ground he was all ease and generosity— no trouble was too great for him to ensure their comfort. Quiet chat, a warm fire, a bowl of thin gruel and selection of bland accompaniments were what he liked above anything and he was delighted with the company of Mrs Bates and her daughters. After tea they played whist, and then Mr Woodhouse was persuaded to tell them a little more about his family and history and it was at the conclusion of this that something very extraordinary occurred.

He was the elder of two children, he told them. His sister was well married but lived abroad due to her ill health. His mother had been dead ten years, his father had passed away the previous year leaving Mr Woodhouse himself in sole possession of a sizeable fortune and some property. The family home, however, was not conducive to his idea of comfort or convenience, a mausoleum of a place, rambling and draughty, bought by his father without proper consideration in the early years of his marriage. It was situated in a county neither beautiful not fashionable, quite a wilderness in every way. The family had no particular connexion to the place or the area, and Mr Woodhouse had sold it without a moment's hesitation. 'My father and grandfather had spoken of this county with such warmth,' he told them, 'and I know the family name is still prevalent here. I passed The Woodhouse Arms on the coaching road, and Weston says there is a village called Woodhouses on the other side of Kingston. Our original property must be lost, now—I do not know where it was. But in building Hartfield I shall feel that I am coming home.'

'You could not do better,' Hetty assured him. 'If I am to give my opinion it is that nowhere other than here is fit for human habitation. The cities are too dirty and crowded, the coasts too damp, the northern counties too wild and inhospitable. The midlands are void of any kind of appeal whatsoever—flat and featureless I believe, a dearth of culture, society quite wanting. So where else is there? Everybody, I think, should live in Highbury and go no further than Kingston under any circumstances.'

'Your thesis has a flaw,' Jane pointed out, with a smile. 'If all of England comes to Highbury we should be homeless, for accommodation would be at a premium and our little apartments would certainly be taken away from us and given to someone who could pay.'

'*You* would never be homeless, Miss Bates, while I had the power to prevent it,' said Mr Woodhouse, gallantly. 'There would always be a home for you at Hartfield when I have built it.'

The import of his words seemed to strike them all. Whose shock was greater, it is hard to say. Mrs Bates looked from her daughter to Mr Woodhouse. Hetty was all confusion and blushes; unusually silent. Mr Woodhouse looked self-conscious and awkward. If he were going to say more—to declare himself, to offer his hand—now was the moment, embarrassing as it was, with the other ladies present. If he wished to retract, to smooth over his avowal as mere chivalry and empty oratory, that, too, ought to be done immediately. But Mr Woodhouse said nothing, just toyed aimlessly with the cards which lay strewn on the table. Perhaps he did not know how far he wished to commit himself.

Mrs Bates took charge of the situation. 'I think it is time we took our leave,' she said, standing, and picking up her reticule. 'Jane, you will be so good as to go and find Mrs Stokes and ask for our wraps. I will collect our galoshes from the passageway. Goodnight, Mr Woodhouse, and thank you for a most agreeable evening.'

She and Jane left the room, leaving Hetty and Mr Woodhouse together. For once in her life, Miss Bates was unable to conjure a single syllable. She was not sure what had just occurred. Had Mr Woodhouse proposed to her? His meaning ought to be made clearer, before she made any response. But she did not know what her reply should be, even then. Under the guise of arranging her shawl, she regarded him narrowly. Mr Woodhouse seemed equally at a loss. He stood by the fire and looked down at his hands, which rested on the head of his walking stick. A coal shifted in the grate. From beyond the doorway the quiet voices of Mama and Jane could be heard as they donned their cloaks and put on their galoshes. Hermia Winwood's words came to her with some force. 'Only a long acquaintance can really establish the basis for a genuine attachment.' Too true. But then, at her age, and in her situation, she could not afford to be too particular. If only he would speak, spell out his meaning, step forward, or step back. But he only got out his handkerchief and dabbed at his nose.

'Mama is waiting and I must take my leave,' Hetty said at last, 'if … I suppose … if you have nothing more to say to me? Or, if you do not require to hear anything further from me?'

Mr Woodhouse knew he had as nearly as possible pledged himself. It may be that he *had* pledged himself, without quite meaning to. If he had, of course, he would stand by it. On the whole he thought he could do much worse. Stumbling into marriage, almost at the slip of the tongue, was not the same as stepping boldly and deliberately into it. But it was the way Mr Woodhouse did most important things—passively, along the line of least resistance, falling in, for easiness, with what other people expected. Like many ineffectual people he made up in the little things for his incompetence in the large—insisting that servants walked quietly about the house and turned the handle just so to prevent doors ever slamming, but permitting them to walk roughshod over him in the matter of viands for the servants' table and coals for the servants' fire. So now—Miss Bates' understanding of the situation, therefore, would determine his position. He needed her to clarify it before he said more. He must give her the opportunity—it was impossible now, with the mother and sister outside the door, and in any case, it was time for his medicine—tomorrow would have to do. Chief among the merits of this plan was that it put off, until a future time, the necessity to bring the matter to a climax. If there was one thing Mr Woodhouse liked more than another it was procrastination. Making decisions was such an arduous thing, acting on them even worse—in this case, very frightening indeed. There would be hands to clasp, waists to encircle, lips to kiss. He made it a point always to put off until tomorrow things that could be done today and so he said now, with relative cheerfulness, 'I hope that tomorrow—if the snow has ceased and the ways are navigable—you will walk with me. You promised to show me the vicarage, you know.' That at least, he thought, with some satisfaction at his clever handling of the case, would give him the opportunity to see how the land lay. In a far corner of his mind, he conjectured that the storm would continue, or the drifts be too deep. Another day, or two, would pass before he would have to meet Miss Bates again. By then, they would each have considered, they would know their own minds. Or the moment might have passed altogether, which might be better still.

Miss Bates curtseyed. 'We generally walk at eleven. Good night, Mr Woodhouse.'

Chapter 12

The morrow, however, brought two occurrences not calculated to add to Mr Woodhouse's comfort. The day dawned bright and clear. A high blue cloudless sky declared that no more snow would fall. The temperature, to be sure, was low, but the air was pure and pleasing. The wind had dropped leaving Highbury calm and sparkling with brightness. A thick covering of snow lay draped over the fields but the roads, trodden by early feet eager to resume the mercantile operation of Highbury, were safe; clearly delineated, firm underfoot and not at all icy. The shops in Highbury were open, the street busy with people impatient to be out after their enforced confinement. From his window Mr Woodhouse saw Lieutenant Weston walking with some purpose in the direction of Donwell, Mr Snell opening up the door to his chambers, Mrs Pellins arranging vegetables on a table to one side of the shop doorway. There could be no possible reason why Mr Woodhouse should not keep his engagement to walk with Miss Bates. Accordingly, after breakfast, he dressed himself with care and prepared to meet his fate.

The clock wanted a quarter of an hour of eleven when Mrs Stokes knocked at the parlour door and presented him with a letter. 'The post has got through,' she announced, 'and this came for you, sir. It is postmarked Oxford.'

The letter was from Mr O'Brien. Mr Woodhouse broke the seal and affixed his eyeglass so as to be able to read the page, which was crossed and difficult to decipher. Its tone, however, was easy to interpret. Mr O'Brien was in high dudgeon. Mr Woodhouse had been expected for Christmas, accommodations made ready for him and neighbours invited to meet him. His failure to arrive had caused consternation at first— they had feared for his safety. Then they had received his letter. Consternation had turned to anger. Mrs O'Brien was most aggrieved. The O'Brien girls were very disappointed. Mr O'Brien himself, while wounded, was ready to hear that insuperable obstacles had prevented Mr Woodhouse's keeping his engagement—a crisis in business, severe ill-health, a family bereavement. Mr Woodhouse's letter had not entered into particulars; it had simply announced that his visit would be delayed until the New Year. If the delay was simply a whim—it was not good enough. It would not do. It would not do at all. More was due to him, as old Mr Woodhouse's lifelong friend. More was due to the promise the two men had made each other, that a union between their children would cement their friendship for perpetuity. It was Henry Woodhouse's duty to accede to his father's most cherished desire and to do so without delay. If he did not, then the wider Woodhouse family would hear of it; Uncle Jeremiah Woodhouse and Aunt Adelaide Woodhouse of a certainty should be informed. Doubtless Lord Woodhouse of Heathcote, the Viscount and all the Honourable Ladies would get wind of it too. In conclusion, Mr O'Brien expected to hear by return that Mr Henry Woodhouse was *en route* to Oxfordshire, or a very compelling explanation as to why he was not.

Naturally this missive upset Mr Woodhouse a great deal. He sank down onto his chair and put his hand to his chest—a sudden tightness there was quite painful. At the same time, a spasm in the lower abdomen presaged drama in the chamber pot.

Across the road, Miss Bates and Jane stepped through their little doorway. Eleven o'clock had arrived. They spent some time arranging their gloves and bonnets and re-tying their boot laces, craning every now and again to see the clock on the church tower, just visible above the rooflines of Highbury High Street. Clearly, they were waiting for Mr Woodhouse to emerge from the Crown, but he sat on, oblivious to them, slumped in his chair, woebegone and agitated, despairing, angry and afraid. Miss Bates looked as though she would step across to the Crown to call, but Jane stayed her with a decided shake of the head. At last they linked arms and walked off together.

In half an hour, Mr Woodhouse had collected himself. Languishing here did no good. He needed someone to tell him what to do. He finished dressing, adding a topcoat and a wide-brimmed hat to his existing layers, and stepped out into the crystal brightness of the day. He would follow Weston in the direction of Donwell, he decided. Weston was a practical man who would give decided advice. He would see Mr Woodhouse's dilemma in a clear, uncomplicated light and would know what should be done. He would walk all the way to Donwell, if necessary, heedless of drifts, of frostbite or sheet ice. Miss Bates, no doubt, would have added avalanches, crevasses and wolf packs to the list of perils between the Crown and Donwell, but she was not there to supply them and Mr Woodhouse's present and urgent trouble had put her entirely out of his head. He only thought to himself, as he stepped gingerly along the High Street, that if he were to fall and break a leg, perhaps that would be sufficient reason to assuage Mr O'Brien.

Now it happened that the road out of Highbury leading to Donwell went past the top of Vicarage Lane. Hetty and Jane had walked that way, partly because it was the route Miss Bates was to have gone with Mr Woodhouse and she half wondered if he had gone on ahead of her, and partly because Hetty was charged to deliver a message to Mrs Winwood. The message was written down, in avoidance of the inevitable garbling and irrelevant superfluities that Hetty's verbal deliverance would have entailed. It presented Mrs Bates' compliments and assured Mrs Winwood that, the storm having blown over and the roads being quite safe, Mrs Bates continued in the pleasurable expectation that Mrs Winwood would call the following day. Jane was to walk further. She was to go to Donwell in pursuance of Mrs Bates' promise to help George Knightley pack his trunk for school. Jane had memorised this message which went: Mama's compliments, and she begs to do herself the honour of calling tomorrow to be of any assistance required to Mr George, if still required. That final clause 'if still required' had been adamantly insisted upon. Jane was to discern, if possible from Mr Knightley, if not from Mrs Lemming, the housekeeper, or even from George himself, whether any alternative person had offered— or been invited—to undertake the task. Mrs Bates would not presume—she certainly would not usurp— the natural and rightful claim of a Mrs Knightley in waiting. This was her intention—of course she did not share it with Jane who was to deliver the message and bring back the reply all unknowing of its import.

The girls parted at the top of Vicarage Lane, Jane to continue the quarter mile to Donwell's gates and the quarter mile more of driveway to the Abbey itself, Hetty to accomplish the shorter walk—two furlongs, no more—to the vicarage door. She walked rather slowly, stopping to watch birds busy in the depths of the hedgerow and to speak to a donkey which put its head over a field gate.

She and her mother had had some conversation the previous evening, trying to agree upon Mr Woodhouse's exact words and to fathom their meaning. On the whole, Hetty thought that Mr Woodhouse had meant nothing more than noble civility by his declaration. A man like him would not commit himself on so slight an acquaintance, would he? And as for herself, she would never have suspected any particularity in his behaviour if her mama had not suggested it. She had never thought much about marriage, she owned, had not especially desired it for herself nor expected it. Mrs Bates believed that Mr Woodhouse had spoken without premeditation and yet impulsively, sincerely, from the heart. He had been as surprised as the rest of them by his words, but he had meant them. Both women agreed that Mr Woodhouse would have to say more, to make his meaning much plainer, before Hetty should be induced to examine her own heart.

'If he does not,' Mrs Bates had concluded, 'I shall have

to go to him myself and ask him what he is about. Or I shall ask Mr Knightley to do so, on my behalf, as a family friend. He is Jane's god-father, you know, so it would be quite proper.'

With all these thoughts churning and swirling in her mind, bumping into each other and getting mixed up with the burned kedgeree Martha had served up for breakfast and her piece of crochet which refused to resolve itself into the desired muffler, Hetty gained the vicarage and handed her message to the maid who opened the door, and had turned to walk back up towards the High Street when she met with Mr Woodhouse. He had taken a wrong turn, having had the idea that Donwell was reached via Vicarage Lane and, not recognising the road he had taken in the coach on Christmas night, had been on the point of turning back when he had spied Miss Bates walking slowly, distractedly up towards him. And so Mr Woodhouse and Miss Bates met within view of the vicarage windows, hard by the withered buds of the prize azaleas and close to the stump of the beloved apple tree.

'Mr Woodhouse! How do you do?' Miss Bates'

greeting was polite, but a little guarded. 'So, you decided to walk after all?'

'Oh yes.' Mr Woodhouse recalled, now, his engagement to walk with Miss Bates and his ambivalent declaration the evening before. But this, the newer crisis, utterly overshadowed it. 'I must apologise. I was tardy and … in short, I find myself quite discomposed this morning. I had thought to find Weston—but I do not know where he might be. I am in need of a friend, to talk things over.'

'Mr Weston is engaged to spend the morning with Mr Knightley,' Miss Bates said. 'They are to go over the plans for the new water wheel together. Jane has gone to Donwell, to deliver a message for Mama. Let us walk in that direction together. I will happily show you the way. I anticipate we shall meet Jane on her way back and if Lieutenant Weston is not with her—well, I shall be very surprised indeed. To be truthful, I will be glad of an opportunity to talk, also. I too have spent a restless night. I think, in circumstances such as these, a quiet chat between friends is the only remedy, don't you?'

'Oh yes, Miss Bates. I am obliged to you.'

They began the walk to the top of Vicarage Lane and, once at the junction, turned left towards Donwell. Judicious, inviting silence did not come easily to Miss Bates and as Mr Woodhouse seemed unable to broach the topic which must be uppermost in his mind, she made a few general observations about the weather and the scenery to give him the opportunity to compose and open his mind. But Mr Woodhouse was unreceptive, too caught up in their delicate situation to find the right way of raising it. At last she said, 'Mr Woodhouse, I am a great talker to no particular purpose but, I assure you, I can listen too, and when necessary—if I really concentrate—I can speak concisely and plainly. Let us be plain now, and understand one another.'

'You do not know how it will relieve me,' Mr Woodhouse cried, the insulted O'Briens and the heavy burden of his promise to his father at the very forefront of his mind. 'The facts are these: I made a promise without quite understanding the import of it, and now I am called to honour it.'

Miss Bates had no inkling of the letter received that morning, no notion of any O'Briens or of any solemn undertaking made in callow youth. She only had the memory of Mr Woodhouse's avowal vivid in her mind. She was alive to the angst it had caused her and could think of no other source for his suffering. That he did suffer was obvious to her, and it moved her. She was, perhaps, closer at that moment to being in love with Mr Woodhouse than she had ever been hereto. So it was with great compassion that she asked him, 'And you do not wish to?'

'No. Yes. I hardly know—that is the truth. I do not know.'

Miss Bates took a moment to consider this. It was not flattering, to have provoked only feelings of confusion and doubt in a gentleman. But she suppressed her feelings of disappointment before saying, 'If I am to give my opinion, Mr Woodhouse, if you are not sure, you had better not keep your promise. If you made it in haste, without due consideration …'

'I did not make it in haste,' Mr Woodhouse said.

'Did you not? But you made it … perhaps you felt … obliged to make it?'

Hetty rehearsed in her mind the conversation the evening before. She had spoken warmly of Highbury, her preference for it against any other place. Jane had teased her, and said if the whole country took notice the Bateses would find themselves without a roof. Then Mr Woodhouse had said … Had such inconsequential banter caused him to feel obligated?

'I certainly did,' Mr Woodhouse asserted.

Hetty stopped walking. How powerful, then, was the human tongue, how prone to being misinterpreted! All these years her mama had been quite right. If such a slight, jesting insinuation could be taken so seriously, how much more could the wild exaggerations and spontaneous flights of fancy so common to her speech lead to error?

Much chastened, Hetty turned to look at her companion. 'Mr Woodhouse,' she said, 'I do not presume to know much about the world. I have lived quietly. Probably I am very ignorant and silly, and I know I often speak out of turn. It is a failing of mine—I quite acknowledge it. I am sorry for it. But if I ever said anything—thoughtlessly, unconsciously— which compelled a person to make a promise he had no desire to make, well, I would hate myself. I would bite my tongue off rather than hold him to it.' Hetty found there were tears upon her cheeks. She sought in vain for a handkerchief, dropping her glove in the process.

Mr Woodhouse picked up her glove, and drew forth his own handkerchief. Hetty pressed it to her eyes.

'Dear lady,' Mr Woodhouse said, gently, stepping close, 'you would never do such a thing.'

'Not knowingly,' Hetty sniffed. 'Not knowingly, ever, in the world.'

'Of course not,' Mr Woodhouse soothed. Somehow, in the distraction of the moment, Hetty's glove found its way into Mr Woodhouse's pocket, and his handkerchief got into hers, and Hetty's hand remained pressed in Mr Woodhouse's hand most earnestly. He was only a moment behind her in tears. Another instant and they would be on his cheeks as clearly as they were on hers. His terrible dilemma, his critical want of decision weighed heavily on his heart and in his mind. Her kindness and apparent understanding were a balm almost too much—they would undo him.

'You are too good,' he said, with heart-felt sincerity. 'I wish I were half so good.'

For Hetty's part she was beginning to think that perhaps she would like to be his wife—but not because he felt honour bound. Not because she had noosed him with her impetuous tongue.

Presently they carried on along the road, close together, their shoulders touching, her hand still in his, until the gates of Donwell came into view. Jane and Lieutenant Weston were walking along the driveway towards them, still at some distance. They were engaging in horseplay, jumping into drifts at the side of the road, throwing snowballs at one another. Jane's bonnet was off and her hair was becomingly awry. Across the intervening parkland their shrieks of laughter could be heard. In spite of the recklessness of such behaviour—Jane could turn her ankle at any moment. Walking without a bonnet would surely give her a head-cold—Hetty almost envied them their carelessness.

Mr Woodhouse looked on too. 'And yet,' he said with a heartfelt sigh, thinking of his papa, how earnestly he had desired to be allied to Mr O'Brien through their children, how actively he had promoted the match, 'one has one's duty. A promise is a matter of honour.'

'Of honour?' Hetty faltered. 'Yes, I suppose so, where one is disinterested. But it is not honourable to go against a decided inclination. That is sacrifice.'

Mr Woodhouse looked at her. 'I do not know that it would be a sacrifice,' he said, so quietly that Hetty could hardly hear him, 'but I am beginning to think …' In the brisk morning air Hetty's cheeks were flushed and pink. Her eyes sparkled with tears that hovered unshed on her lashes. She was almost beautiful, he thought to himself, and Weston had been quite right, she was very kind-hearted. Her reticence, her discretion spoke volumes in her favour. She would have been within her rights, he thought, to have thrust aside all discussion of his worries and insisted upon a clarification of his ill-considered declaration. She could have held him to it—told him that she considered herself engaged. And he would have stuck to it. He would have had to bear the imprecations of Mr O'Brien, the condemnation of Uncle Jeremiah and Aunt Adelaide, the reproaches of the Lord Woodhouse, the Viscount and all the Honourable Ladies and that would have been very disagreeable. But she had been all gentleness and patience; she had not even referred to his gaffe. It was forgotten. A night of worry—over nothing. And yet, would it have been such a bad thing?

'You are beginning to think ..?' Hetty prompted him.

But Mr Woodhouse shook his head. He did not know. He just did not know. He was the last person to know, without being told. He knew he feared the anger of Mr O'Brien and the censure of his elevated relations. He knew he had the right and the faculty to marry for love, if he chose. He knew he ought to do the right, the honourable thing; the thing his father had so dearly wished. But he knew also that if he did not he would not be materially, socially inconvenienced. No one had the power to make him marry an O'Brien girl. But Mr O'Brien's letter had been very compelling— very forceful indeed.

If only somebody would just tell him.

Jane and the lieutenant were almost upon them.

'Your patience with my predicament does you great credit, ma'am,' Mr Woodhouse said, with a deal of anguish in his voice. 'No one else, I am sure,' he went on, with equal feeling, thinking of the irascible Mr O'Brien, 'would be so good as to just give a man time.'

Hetty recognised Mr Woodhouse's profound irresolution—his quandary was written large across his face, in his glassy eye and trembling lip—but, of course, she entirely mistook its source. The advice she decided to give him was calculated to serve what she perceived to be his happiness as well as her own—she would not press him, but neither would she close the door on what was just beginning to look to her like an appealing prospect. She could not know—how could she—that the words she spoke would blot out that panorama for good.

'I think you should be able to presume upon a person's patience' she said, in a low voice, 'in such a case as this. You can certainly depend on mine, if it helps at all.' She retrieved her hand but with a smile she hoped was warm and encouraging without being flirtatious. 'I think that the recipient of any promise would not hold you to it unless they knew you were sure. That might take time and patience, and longer acquaintance. If there is no hurry, why should you rush? You must be sure of your own mind before you commit yourself.'

'Commit yourself to what, Woodhouse,' said

Lieutenant Weston, giving Mr Woodhouse a hearty slap on the back. 'What a splendid day! What a simply marvellous day, isn't it?' He beamed at Jane, at them all, his happiness clear upon his face. Jane too looked radiant.

The four of them began to stroll back towards the village. 'We have been discussing duty,' Miss Bates said, 'and under what circumstances a promise is not a promise.'

'Oh,' Lieutenant Weston said, 'as to that, a promise is always a promise.' He looked, significantly, at Jane. 'Mine is, anyway. Knightley bids me invite you to dine, by the way, Woodhouse, if you are at liberty, tomorrow. And you, Miss Bates, and your mama.'

But Mr Woodhouse had turned rather pale. 'I am not sure,' he muttered. 'I think I may have to continue my journey to Oxfordshire.'

And indeed, the following morning, Mr Woodhouse departed in the Crown's closed conveyance, looking every inch the lamb to the slaughter. Hetty watched him go in confusion and distress. She could not say how things stood between them, how things had been resolved. She thought she had encouraged him to think of themselves as not engaged but ready to discover if they might become so. But his leaving— without a word of explanation, with no mention of when—or if—he might return gave her little confidence that he shared her understanding. His departure was a conundrum she could not fathom. He bid her neither au revoir nor adieu. He did not ask permission to write. He kept his counsel. But he also kept her glove.

Chapter 13

The following day Mrs Winwood's call on Mrs Bates was made, with great ceremony and fuss, but to the satisfaction of both. Mrs Winwood came with Miss Winwood and two liveried footmen to assist them—quite unnecessarily—along the snow-covered lane. Mrs Winwood made a performance of removing her shawl and pelisse in the confined hallway and exclaimed loudly enough for her hostess to hear in the apartment above that the stairs were so dark she could barely see to put one foot in front of the other. But once she had stepped into the parlour the welcome awaiting her there was extremely gracious. Everything declared the Bates' consciousness of the great favour she conferred and her ruffled feathers were soon smoothed. She was led to the most comfortable chair—a little threadbare, perhaps, around the cushion, the arm somewhat worn—but of undoubted pedigree and superior quality. The chair was at the exact distance from the fire that one would wish, a screen placed behind her to protect her from draughts, a footstool for her feet. Refreshments were brought speedily to hand—excellent Madeira, most warming on a cold day—and some very good cake. Mrs Winwood had the satisfaction of being made quite as much of as even she could wish.

For Mrs Bates' part she felt the gratification of having forced Mrs Winwood to do her duty—the call was overdue and every day that went by without its being paid added to the snub. The precedent had been set—Mrs Winwood was demonstrably on calling terms with Mrs Bates. Everyone in Highbury had seen her enter and whether she did so voluntarily or under duress did not signify. She had crossed the Rubicon. Mrs Bates, though a widow and poor, was no crone in a hovel to be pitied and patronised; she was in every way Mrs Winwood's equal and in some ways decidedly her superior; it was insupportable that she should be slighted. Certainly, in the matter of good taste and excellent manners Mrs Bates could not be surpassed. She was determined that Mrs Winwood should come away from her visit with nothing to criticise or lament. Thankfully Mr Knightley had sent with his compliments an exceptional bottle of Madeira to replace the one which had been finished on Boxing

Day evening, and Mrs Cropley had sent a seedcake rich and yellow with the yolks of her flock. Both passed Mrs Winwood's lips and her exacting standards without her having a suspicion of them being of charitable origin—otherwise they might well have choked her.

'The snow we have had for the past few days is quite unprecedented in Highbury,' Mrs Bates remarked, when the wine and the cake had been consumed. 'I assure you, it is not at all normal for the area.'

'Oh, as to bad weather,' Mrs Winwood replied with an airy wave of her hand, 'when we were in Derbyshire we had feet of snow quite regularly, and it lay for weeks and weeks. This was nothing. A mere flurry.'

'Reverend Winwood's parish in Derbyshire was large?'

'Geographically large, encompassing several large farms and two country houses of note as well as the village. Numerically it was not so large as Highbury. Perhaps I should say the congregations were not so large, at any rate. Derbyshire is almost heathen, you know.'

'Their hearts were hardened perhaps,' Mrs Bates said with a sigh. 'That must have been very discouraging.

The congregation was small here too, at first. I know Frederick despaired at times. But somehow he enlarged it. The Lord convicted them.'

'I hope you do not tend towards low-church evangelism,' Mrs Winwood retorted, tartly. 'You will draw no 'hallelujah' from me, I assure you.'

Mrs Bates did not dignify this remark with a reply. 'Your daughters have settled, I hope?' she asked.

'My girls are resourceful; they make themselves at home wherever they find themselves.' Mrs Winwood said, 'as do I. Hermia, in particular, takes great pleasure in books. I believe Miss Bates has offered to introduce her to the circulating library? That is most kind, but I think Reverend Winwood will take her, and pay her subscription. Miss Henrietta need not trouble herself. Ursula has her music—she is proficient, but it takes practice—that occupies many hours. Sophia will go to town. My sister will be there with her daughter, who will come out this season. My sister is married to Archdeacon Bland, you know.'

'I did not know.'

'Oh yes, and the Archdeacon is soon to become Suffragan Bishop of Pimlico—that is between ourselves you know, it is yet to become public knowledge—with apartments in the Palace. He will be Venerable, then. We do not call Suffragan bishops Reverend, you know. Sophia will be presented.'

'Indeed?'

'Cordelia and Arabella return to the schoolroom next week; their governess will take them back in hand so the house will see a little more peace, I hope. Five girls, you know, Mrs Bates, and two more in the nursery—you cannot imagine the difficulties. To get them all safely married and settled … But perhaps you can. Your daughters—I suppose they are in search of husbands? I saw Miss Henrietta yesterday with a gentleman—unchaperoned. If I might venture a word of caution, from a position of pastoral responsibility; it is unwise, unless there is to be an engagement? Is there? And Miss Jane has been seen on numerous occasions with Lieutenant Weston. I hear he escorted her—alone—to dinner and home again, through the blizzard, at night. Sophia thinks him a charming young man but Sophia is no judge. I found him very tardy in the common civilities. Militiamen, in my opinion, are unstable, given to wildness. I wouldn't trust my daughter within a dozen feet of one.'

Mrs Bates bridled at the notion of Mrs Winwood's assuming any 'pastoral responsibility' over her, the implied slur on Hetty and Jane's integrity not to mention the slanderous stain on Lieutenant Weston's character. She replied, 'My girls are in mourning. They are not thinking of matrimony at present. Hetty met Mr Woodhouse quite by accident—he was lost, having taken the wrong turning for Donwell. Frederick and I have been intimate with the Westons for many years. Our families are close friends. I find Lieutenant Weston a gentlemanlike man with unexceptionable manners. I have no hesitation in committing either of my daughters to his care.'

Mrs Winwood stiffened in her chair but did not offer a riposte.

Presently, Mrs Bates went on, 'I think it healthy for young people to be out and about.' She glanced at Miss Winwood and Hetty who were seated on the window seat together. 'Confinement in the house and a tendency to solitary pursuits can lead to introspection and depressed spirits. Unless you have specific reason to be very decidedly against it, I would suggest you allow the young ladies to visit the library together.'

Mrs Winwood sniffed, but let the challenge pass. 'Ursula is out with Miss Lavinia Snell, or she would have been delighted to call today. The Snells are very genteel people, I find. The law has not tainted them. They have two sons at Oxford I understand. Two very eligible, gentlemanlike young men. They have not come home for the vacation—too busy studying, I presume. Up to their necks in Virgil and Pythagoras.'

'Studying?' Mrs Bates repeated, with a lifted eyebrow. She thought it more likely the two Snell boys were up to their necks in dissipation and debauchery, but did not voice her opinion. Neither did she say that Miss Lavinia was a girl of small intellect and no conversation, contenting herself with, 'Miss Lavinia is a sweet, simple girl, an ideal companion for Miss Ursula, I am sure.'

'The Snells have asked for the honour of our company at dinner next week,' Mrs Winwood said, 'and we are invited to the Westons the week afterwards. Of course, one does not expect elegance on any significant scale. Homely entertainments can be very pleasant, in their way but I hope, in due course, to set the standard. Where I set the example, people are sure to follow, I think. Do you dine from home very often?'

'Remarkably often. This evening we dine at Donwell. We dine with the Westons, the Coxes and the Snells, and with the Bitterns, too, when they are at home. You will not be acquainted with Mr and Mrs Bittern, I think? They live at Grange Spinney, down by the river. But Mrs Bittern's health is very uncertain, and they go to Europe for the winter where the climate agrees with her constitution. Formerly we dined with a number of Kingston families but that has had to be given up, since Frederick's death. We have no carriage, now.'

'You dine at Donwell? Well,' with a shake of the head, 'we have not been so honoured, as yet.'

'The squire rarely holds formal dinners. He entertains only his oldest friends and the occasion is very easy-going, I assure you, without ceremony of any kind. I surmise that he waits until he can secure company from the first circles—perhaps the family from Clayton Park, or the Rawlings from Kingston—before inviting you. The Rawlings are a very superior family, you know. Mr Rawling's brother takes his seat in the upper chamber. Archbishop Rawling. I am sure you have heard of him.'

'Certainly, I have,' Mrs Winwood said, much mollified. 'It is very good of Mr Knightley to wish to secure the proper guests to meet us.'

'Mr Knightley *is* very good,' Mrs Bates agreed.

'His plan is remarkably similar to my own,' Mrs Winwood observed. 'Naturally I am avid to return such hospitality as we have received but until the improvements at the vicarage are complete … Of course, we have no airs. None whatsoever. We will sit down with anyone. But people seem to feel keenly that something is due to us. It is most gratifying, and naturally one wishes to return the compliment.'

Miss Bates and Miss Hermia Winwood sat together on the window seat of the casement window while their mamas conversed. The casement was deep and at some distance from the fire. The two young women could speak with some privacy. Miss Bates, however, was less garrulous than usual. The danger of unregulated chatter to be misconstrued, to frighten or mislead had been powerfully impressed upon her. The result of her comparative reticence was to draw Miss Winwood out.

'I long for our visit to Kingston,' she confessed. 'Papa has promised to pay my subscription. Mama says that he must take me. She feels that it would not be seemly for us to go together. I shall prevail, however.'

'I shall be happy to introduce you,' Hetty replied. 'Oh, look, there is Mrs Coxe in the street below. I expect she is going … but it would be wrong to speculate. What a pleasant day for a walk. She has all the little Coxes with her—they look quite like a gaggle of goslings, walking behind her like that, do they not?'

Miss Winwood, finding no productive rejoinder to this observation, went on, 'And when you go to Kingston, do you visit the circulating library only, or do you have other errands?'

'It depends. Sometimes Mama has commissions for me. I like to look in the shop windows. Ford's, you know, is a very superior haberdasher, and one wouldn't dream of buying one's requisites from anywhere else. But there is more variety in Kingston.'

'It is not unusual, I suppose, to meet acquaintance in Kingston?'

'Oh, not at all unusual. I seem always to be bumping into people I know, and it always delightful to exchange news. Although, one must be careful. It is wrong to gossip of course. And one must be sure not to pass along mere impressions or ideas, as if they were truths.'

Miss Winwood nodded sagely, but went on, 'There can be no harm at all in genteel, civil conversation between social equals pursuant on an accidental meeting.'

'Oh no. Of course not.'

'And do you,' Miss Winwood lowered her voice just a decibel or two, 'do you ever walk along by the river, or near the college, or in the precincts of St Luke's church?'

St Luke's was a large church which encompassed a seminary for the training of impecunious ordinands, known locally as 'the college', located some small distance outside of Kingston, hard by the river.

'No,' Hetty said, with a frown, 'that is, I have never had occasion to walk that way. But I believe it is a very pleasant walk. Jane has been. She used to accompany papa when he went to deliver lectures to the collegians. He would sneak her in at the back so that she might benefit from his teaching and the incisive questions of the students afterwards. She says the bluebells in the grounds are lovely. We will have to wait until April to see those.'

Miss Winwood sighed, heavily. 'I should love to see them,' she said.

'Then of course we will walk that way,' Hetty said. 'I dare say we will be in no danger from the trainee curates and clerical underlings.'

'Not the least in the world,' Miss Winwood agreed.

Chapter 14

The New Year came in and on the appointed day
Lieutenant Weston left Highbury to join his regiment
in Brighton. His leaving was an alteration which
touched almost everyone in Highbury and marked the
end of the sociable Christmas season. Highbury's
opinion was that Lieutenant Weston was a charming
and lively young man and that parties without him
would certainly be duller. His going without any
engagement being announced was a disappointment.
He and Jane had exchanged sufficient significant looks
across Highbury's tea tables for it to be generally
suspected that there was at least an attachment
between them; their failure to consummate this
impression with an acknowledged engagement left
onlookers feeling strangely cheated. Jane was closely
watched for signs that she would faint away from
lovesickness, but watched in vain. She waved
Lieutenant Weston off from the parlour window
which overlooked the street, and spent the rest of the
day in tears, but she was not a girl to be undone by
romantic notions, to sigh and lose the bloom from her

cheeks or to languish away for want of her lover, and she soon composed herself.

She did speak of Lieutenant Weston very often, in glowing and affectionate terms, but she did not own to an engagement, nor even to an understanding. What words had been spoken, what promises exchanged, remained private. However things had been left, she seemed content.

There was a significant change at Donwell: George Knightley went away to school. He went with his clothes properly mended and packed and his favourite books stowed in his trunk alongside a selection of treats to share with the other boys in his dormitory. Mrs Bates, being 'still required' had overseen his mending and packing as well as the provision of additional things necessary to an eight-year-old boy. During the course of her endeavours at the Abbey she had watched Mr Knightley closely to ascertain if there were any signs about him of a man in love—and she had seen them, too. She caught him sitting abstracted at his desk leaving letters unwritten. He walked a good deal around the shrubberies and gardens of the Abbey with his hands clasped behind his back, apparently in deep contemplation of some weighty matter. At other times he stood stock still and stared seemingly into space. None of these actions was habitual to him, a man generally so active, so engaged, so eager to make progress and do good. The housekeeper made dark reports of meals barely tasted or sometimes missed altogether.

'There is somethin' very much on 'is mind,' Mrs Lemming told Marie. 'Even Abel Larkins says 'e can get no sense out the master. I know 'e does not sleep at night for when I comes down in the mornin' the fire is still burnin' like 'e 'as been sat by it all night long, and the bed scarce rumpled.'

'Perhaps he is anxious about Master George going away?' Marie ventured.

'There is that,' the housekeeper agreed, 'but I suspicion somethin' more troubles 'im.'

Regardless of her private feelings for Mr Knightley—which perplexed and shamed her very much—as his long-standing friend, Marie was extremely concerned for him. She yearned for him to confide in her, but would make no move to invite him to do so. She did not trust herself not to reveal to him something of her own inner turmoil. That she held him in the highest esteem—that need be no secret. That she respected and admired him as a gentleman and squire—she would be proud to own it. But those warmer, more personal feelings, of fondness, of affection, of attraction—those must be kept strictly in check. She did try to tame them—as often as they bubbled to the surface she pressed them down again. As frequently as he came into her thoughts, she ushered him out. But they would keep coming, subjecting her to guilty pangs. These were all dangers to herself, but there was danger for him, also. How it would destroy the precious bonds of established friendship if he were but to suspect her inclination! She flattered herself this far: that to distance himself from her as a friend and supporter around the parish—which he would surely do, once he divined her inner heart; he would shrink from her in embarrassment and revulsion—would be a blow to him, and one she would die rather than inflict.

If Squire Knightley found the halls of Donwell quiet without his elder son, he did not say so; he was resolutely silent about all his troubles. John was not so reticent, bawling heartily at the absence of his brother and patient playmate. It seemed that only Jane Bates could comfort him, and Jane took to going to Donwell almost daily. She was often accompanied at least part way by her mama, who adopted once more her role of visitor to the sick and needy, delivering such succour as she was able. She quite threw herself into it, indeed, seeking respite from her jangled nerves and wayward feelings by immersing herself in the troubles of others.

In this she had no fear of stepping on Mrs Winwood's toes. Clearly, she had no intention of taking up the mantle. She baulked at such charitable visits—could not abide a hovel and would not dirty her skirts crossing a muddy farmyard to get to one. Her scruples did not earn her favour amongst the common people of the parish. This was a significant sea-change—unvoiced yet powerfully felt. From being broadly welcomed, the Winwoods were becoming less popular. There were mutterings. The Bates' ministry had led the people of the parish to expect and enjoy a certain level of pastoral care from their spiritual leaders. They relied on and delighted in it. Reverend Winwood visited the dying when called upon to do so but the serene presence of Mrs Bates near a death bed, the soothing timbre of her voice as she recited the twenty third psalm and the comfort of her hand meant that she, more often than he, was summoned.

As it was amongst the lower orders of Highbury society, so it was also amongst the higher. They had accorded the Winwoods due ceremony—dinners had been provided and eaten in their honour, tea poured, cards played—but no one had, as yet, received the honour of an invitation in return. That wholesale alterations were afoot inside the vicarage was no secret. The builder and his men were there daily. The place was alive with hammering and sawing, thatch was repaired and glazing renewed. Mrs Winwood spoke loudly after church of a cabinet maker being brought from London. A French polisher was despaired of. Where oh where were velvet drapes and Turkish rugs to be got? In a declaration as close to blasphemy as made no difference, Ford's was declared to be too provincial—sufficient for the everyday needs of the hoi polloi but for her—no choice at all, no quality to speak of—oh no. She would have to go to Kingston or very likely to town. Her sister Mrs Bland (the Venerable Bishop's wife, you know) would have to be commissioned. Her taste could be relied on. In spite of the affront to their precious haberdashers—Mrs Ford, on hearing an account of Mrs Winwood's opinion, burst into tears—the Highbury appetite to see the improvements at the vicarage was thoroughly whetted. But nobody managed to set foot inside the vicarage on any pretext whatsoever; not a sniff, not a peek was to be had.

When February came William Larkins turned fourteen and began his apprenticeship under Mr Hopley the miller. A boy taking up an apprenticeship raised few eyebrows in the village but it constituted an enormous step for him and sealed the prosperity and wellbeing of the Larkins family for the next generation. Mr Knightley had paid his indenture, the fee being beyond Abel Larkins' purse, and secured for William a role in the mill at a time of innovation and modernisation. The new wheel and ancillary machinery were under construction at the forge and would be installed at summer's end so that it could be commissioned after harvest home. There was much to be learnt in the meantime. William accustomed himself to the rattle and shake of the mill as the machinery turned. He grew nimble—easily scaling the ladders from the granary floor to the loft—and strong, hauling sacks of grain and flour. After seven years at the mill he would familiarise himself with the workings of the forge and of the farm. By the time he was twenty-five he would be as competent in all aspects of the Donwell estate as his father, ready to assist George when his time as squire should come.

Chapter 15

March brought with it a deep depression that settled over Highbury and deluged it with rain without let up for a period of two weeks. The High Street was awash, gutters poured and fires smoked from damp wood and wet coals. Farmers despaired of their crops—the fields were quagmires and seed would not germinate. A sheep and several new-born lambs drowned in the river, which burst its banks and swamped a pasture, sweeping them quite away, before the farmer could bring them to higher ground.

A brown patch on the ceiling of Mrs Bates' bedroom got darker and larger and eventually started to ooze so much moisture that she had to place a pot on the rug beneath it to catch the drips.

'I must speak to Mr Pellins,' she said one morning, as the family took their breakfast. 'I assume he owns the building and therefore the responsibility for the repair is his.'

'Hardly anyone ventures out today,' Hetty observed. She sat on the seat in the casement and from that vantage point had a clear view of the street in both directions. 'I doubt there will be many customers so Mr Pellins will be quite at liberty to assist you. You might go as far as there, but you will not go further will you Mama? It is too wet.'

'I had promised to call on poor Uriah Nidd. He has ulcers which need dressing, and Mrs Tremble's new baby has colic. But you are right, it hardly seems sensible, in this rain.'

'Mr Snell hazarded the walk,' Hetty went on, craning to see up the street. 'I saw him half an hour ago opening his office door, his umbrella pouring rain. And Mrs Stokes is out and about also; she has just come from his chambers. But Ford's is still closed. Mr Obadiah Ford is within—I saw him through the window—but the sign on the door hasn't been turned. The puddle outside our door has turned into a lake. Any visitors will need a boat to get to us, but,' with a sigh, 'I do not expect there will be any.'

'I believe the drain by the step is blocked,' Marie said. 'I will mention that to Mr Pellins also. It is embarrassing, since we live here rent-free. I would not wish him to think I find fault. Perhaps I ought to offer to pay a contribution towards repairs but I hesitate. One never knows what a builder will find. What if the entire roof needs to be replaced? That could not by any means be afforded.'

'Someone must pay the rent,' Jane said, practically. 'That committee or guild or whatever it was John Abdy told us about. The Pellinses are not the losers by having us as their tenants. But Gideon Mortimer is too occupied at the vicarage to attend to any other property,' she went on. 'Unless you know of another tradesman, we will have to fill up all our jugs and teacups with water from the leak until the vicarage is completed!'

'Everywhere is so damp, and I cannot get my pelisse dry,' Hetty complained. 'I envy the Bitterns, in the warmth of southern France.'

'In fact, they are on their way home,' Mrs Bates said, indicating a letter by her breakfast plate. 'I have been re-reading the last letter I received and it is quite certain that they will be home again by the beginning of April at the latest. They stop *en route* in Paris, she says. There is a new specialist she wants to consult.'

'Paris!' Jane sighed.

'Here comes the squire,' cried Hetty. 'Well, I declare, he is an early bird. I wonder what his business can be at this hour of the morning. He will not call here, surely?'

'I will ring the bell and ask Martha to clear the breakfast things,' Jane said, getting to her feet. 'It is rare that he comes to Highbury without calling.'

'Hitherto Mr Knightley was seen but rarely in Highbury,' Hetty observed. 'He had so much business about his estate or on the Magistrates' bench in Kingston. I have often known him go to London for two weeks or more. Yet it seems these days he often has reason to visit the village. I would not be so rude as to pass comment upon it—the squire's comings and goings being nobody's business but his—but it does set one's mind a-wondering. Oh, he goes into the Crown. Perhaps he goes to reserve a seat on the London coach.'

'I expect he has business with Mrs Stokes,' Marie said through pursed lips. 'It seems to me that recently he has often had reason to visit the Crown.'

'I can't imagine why,' Hetty replied.

'As you properly say, Hetty, it is none of our concern.

234

Now I will find my galoshes and go down and speak to Mr Pellins.'

'But you will miss Mr Knightley, if he comes.'

'That cannot be helped.'

Marie thought in fact it might rather be wished. It was true that Mr Knightley was more frequently in Highbury and naturally he would never pass the Bates' door without paying his respects. He would not stay long—a quarter hour in the Bates' parlour was usually sufficient for them to assure him that they did well and lacked nothing. Nevertheless, a steady supply of Donwell butter, cream, root vegetables and game birds did stubbornly find their way there. This necessitated notes of thanks to be delivered, usually by hand. It was not infrequent that if Mrs Bates was visiting old acquaintance amongst the poorer members of Highbury or Donwell parishes, it happened that the squire had thought to visit there also. Sunday church, of course, was attended by both and a meeting was unavoidable. It had come to be known—as these things do in small, rural communities—that the squire's former reluctance to mingle with his neighbours at dinners and so on had relented, and the honour of his company begun to be sought for them. It was not at all infrequent that his friend Mrs Bates was invited to meet him, she being the ideal antidote to that anathema to hostesses everywhere—the single gentleman. A single gentleman—or lady—disrupts the seating plan, but one of each readily to hand and generally at liberty is a remedy impossible to pass over. She had therefore encountered him at Mrs Weston's house twice and once at Mr and Mrs Snell's.

All in all, Mrs Bates had found herself in Mr Knightley's company with disturbing regularity, and consequently fought a battle in the privacy of her heart on an almost daily basis. She endeavoured to maintain the appearance of cordial relations with him, to be as much herself as it was possible to be. But preventing expressions of a warmer kind from manifesting themselves inevitably resulted in a coolness of manner, a reserve, which she was powerless to prevent. His feelings were impossible to fathom. That he noticed— and lamented—an alteration in their relations was evident. He greeted her with more than his usual courtesy and a sort of hesitant deference which increased, rather than diminished his attraction. He sought her out and engaged her in conversation, seemingly as eager to break down the barrier between them as she was to maintain it. He mentioned Frederick often, commiserating on her loss and offering the hopeful balm that time would lessen the pain. But he spoke to her also of other things—his tenants, his news from George, his pleasure in John's progress—walking and talking and not yet two years old. He spoke naturally, directly, as he always had done, and yet there was something in his air which was not as usual. As strongly as she was holding something back, so too was he. He was a man with a secret; with a private tribulation and Marie was convinced it centred on Mrs Stokes. Much as she had tried not to keep watch Hetty was an inveterate looker-out of the window and reporter of all that passed on the street below. There had been frequent accounts of him going in to the Crown or coming out of it. Mrs Stokes had visited the squire at the Abbey on at least one occasion (Mrs Hopley had told Mrs Larkins, who had mentioned it to Mrs Weston who had informed Mrs Bates of it.) He had been seen on horseback in company with Mrs Stokes' son, Simon. It saddened her that he could not share whatever was afoot, and it surprised her too—he was not a man to engage in subterfuge of any kind. Why should he conceal a preference for Mrs Stokes? This hole-in-corner behaviour was very far from his character. But it frightened her that he might confess his attachment to Mrs Stokes.

So, dinners and evening entertainments a-plenty she had had to suffer in Mr Knightley's company but the one redeeming factor had been this: the Winwoods had been included in none of them. General feeling in the parish had by now turned thoroughly against the new incumbent and his wife. He was declared morose and taciturn, she was called proud. Rumours that they were waiting for some august company—titled relatives or some other very superior connection—to display to Highbury at their debut buttered no parsnips. If residents were meant to be flattered by boasts of entertainment in a style entirely new, the lavish provision of food and drink, elegance and éclat unseen in Highbury before, they were left singularly unimpressed. Their eagerness and curiosity turned to frustration and affront. The insult offered to Mrs Ford injured them all, but the implication that the social intercourse they had so long enjoyed had been in some way lacking cut them more deeply still. Their cosy dinners and friendly, unpretentious suppers had always satisfied in the past, what need had they of anything more? A little music, a song, a hand of cards had always sufficed. Natural good manners, the warmth of genuine friendship, companionship without airs or affectations—this was what Highbury delighted in. They came to think that dinner at the vicarage would not be so very good a thing. She would be sure to lord it over them, to simper and fuss over her draperies and bagatelles. He could not be supposed to have a liberal hand with the wine, miserable old curmudgeon that he was.

On the day of which we now speak, Mrs Bates was delayed in the Pellins' shop by a protracted tirade of complaint from Mrs Pellins on the subject of Reverend Winwood. He had declined—positively refused—to christen their latest grandchild on the pretext that Mrs Pellins' daughter lived in a different parish. No matter that she had been baptised and married in Highbury church, or that her grandparents were buried there. Her father's service on the

Parochial Church Council counted for nothing. Mrs Pellins' provision of flowers for the altar and years of flower arranging were trodden underfoot. Here was yet another serious breech by the Winwoods of Highbury etiquette: it was a thoroughly established fact that Highbury children remained Highbury parishioners wherever they may roam.

'I shall think twice before I set foot in that church again, and so shall Pellins,' the aggrieved lady had concluded, 'and as for flowers for the altar—they are at an end. But as to your original enquiry, Mrs Bates, I must inform you that Pellins and I are no more owners of this property than you are. Mr Knightley owns the whole row this side, from the butcher's shop right along to Mrs Grace the seamstress' cottage at the other end.'

Marie imparted the news to Jane she removed her shawl. 'The squire owns this property as well as several other properties on the other side. Ford's, Mr Snell's chambers. I do not recall the others. I was too overcome with surprise to take in the details.'

'Half the village! More than half! I was never so surprised in my life,' Hetty declared. 'I had no idea of him owning so much property in the village. Land, of course, I know he has in countless acres, but bricks and mortar? He must be richer than we thought.'

'Hetty, it is vulgar to contemplate such things,' Marie said. However, the news made her feel more wrathful toward Mrs Stokes than ever. She must know of the squire's wealth. No wonder she had set her cap at him. It made Marie's blood boil, that Mr Knightley should be so taken in. The woman was mercenary—there was no doubt of it.

But she brought the subject to safer ground by reporting, 'Mr Pellins says the drain by the step has been blocked since last winter. Mrs Pellins declares she has asked him to clear it out more times than she can recall, but he has never got round to it. It is some while since the roof was looked at, he says, but she says that now we are tenants of the upper floors it is up to us to notify the landlord.'

'Well, that is easily done,' said Jane, 'for here he comes.'

A knock at the door, Mr Knightley's voice in the vestibule below, his quick steps on the stair and he was in the room. Marie scarcely had time to glance in the mirror to check her hair was tidy.

'Good morning ladies,' he said, with his usual cheer. 'A sorry, soggy day. I do not think you will get your exercise this morning.'

'*You* are out, regardless of the weather,' Mrs Bates remarked with more asperity than she had perhaps intended. Even more, now, did she feel revolted at the idea of him coming straight from the Crown to her. 'Something very pressing, I conjecture, prevents *you* from staying in the dry.'

'Why yes,' the squire replied, with a puzzled frown, 'it does.'

Marie felt quite angry with him. Her knowing it was unreasonable could not suppress it. She found she could not meet his eye so she turned and busied herself about her writing desk.

'How does John?' Jane enquired. 'Is his tooth through?'

'At last it is, but a night of howling we had because of it,' Mr Knightley said with a smile, turning to Jane. 'Oil of cloves did not seem to ease him at all, but he was sleeping when I left, so we hope that is the end of it.'

'Until the next one comes,' Marie added, tartly.

The squire turned to her again, his confusion at her tone plain upon his face. 'You are right to temper my optimism,' he said, quietly. 'Of course, every stage of childhood has its difficulties.'

'Mama has been out today,' Hetty put in. 'See, there are her galoshes drying on the hearth. She had occasion to visit Mr Pellins but he tells her that …'

'Hetty!' Marie cut in, brusquely. 'We will not trouble Mr Knightley with that business at present.'

The squire looked from one to the other. 'Anything I can oblige you with, you know I would be more than happy,' he said.

'It is nothing at all, and Hetty was wrong to mention it,' Mrs Bates snapped. Her feelings were in utter disorder. She was jealous, she realised; she revolted at the idea that he was fresh from Mrs Stokes' arms. Her dismay that he had been so taken in was beyond description. This was a terrible impropriety—she knew it. She had no right whatsoever, no claim on him. But her feelings made her angry and she could not, in this state, ask anything of him. It felt wrong to be beholden to him as much as she was; she was ungrateful, wanting more. That she should be no more than the object of his philanthropy wounded her heart and her pride, both.

'Very well,' the squire said, after a pause. 'If you are sure there is no service I can render you I will say good morning.'

'Good morning, Mr Knightley.'

The squire took up his hat and had his hand on the door when he turned back to say, 'Except, I have quite forgot the reason for my call, the 'pressing business' you perceived. Have you collected your post?'

Marie shook her head. 'I meant to call for it while I was out, but something … it went out of my head.'

'No matter. You will hear today or tomorrow, to be sure. Our friends the Bitterns are back on English soil and will be home at the end of the week. We are asked to dine a week from today. I came to offer you the carriage. It is too far to walk and impossible anyway in this weather. May I call for you?'

His face held all the eagerness and openness she loved in him, a genuine desire to be useful, his old familiar generosity. Marie's heart almost burst. Indeed, she felt tears pressing behind her eyes. She had been so cold and cruel to him! She longed to see her friend Mrs Bittern once more. It would be a joy to dine at Grange Spinney in such comfortable company and to spend the drive there in private communion with Mr Knightley—but she must control these feelings. It occurred to her that he might also have offered to collect Mrs Stokes although that lady was rarely included in dinner invitations.

'Well,' she said, falteringly. 'I must not presume to be included in the invitations. I have not heard …'

'Oh! It is certainly the case for Bittern mentioned it specifically in his letter to me,' Mr Knightley said. 'But if you wish to wait until your own letter arrives, so be it. My carriage is at your disposal.'

'I suppose the Winwoods are to be honoured?'

Mr Knightley laughed. 'I doubt it. They are not acquainted. No, *that* pleasure will be postponed until the Bitterns have been home for a while and,' with a sly grin, 'you never know our luck, we may not be invited.'

The Hartfield pasture remained undisturbed. No news came of Mr Woodhouse. But Hetty had opportunity to spend a considerable amount of time analysing her own conduct in relation to that gentleman. During the first weeks of January her mama had been at Donwell preparing George's trunks for school and Jane had gone with her, leaving Hetty to solitary contemplation. Then, when the weather had cleared and the roads were once again walkable, she had gone with Miss Winwood to Kingston. Their first expedition meeting with success, they had repeated it on several subsequent occasions. Miss Winwood was zealous in her delight at the town's shops, parks and amusements and could not go there often enough. Their conversation on the way there and home again had been enjoyable but Miss Winwood had chanced each time upon an old acquaintance—a Mr Paling, collegian at St. Luke's—which had distracted her attention in the town itself. They had met him first on St Luke's fields, then as they strolled along the river footpath and on the final occasion by the market cross. It had been the merest coincidence, of course. They had exclaimed a great deal about the slim probability of their meeting in such a bustling town, of their both happening to have business in the same locale on the same day. The two having much news to exchange and many associates in common, Hetty had fallen behind while they talked, and given the hours of their communion over to her own private contemplations.

The more she went over in her mind the conversation she had had with Mr Woodhouse, the more uncertain she became as to what had been actually said, or just inferred. He had seemed in some considerable doubt as to his feelings for her. 'I do not know,' he had said, more than once. There had been a palpable air of reluctance in his demeanour but this had caused him pain, as though he had wished to love her, but could not. He had spoken of honour—but as Daniel might have spoken of the lions' den—that to hold to his word would be all bitterness and sacrifice. She understood him to be a man of independent means, free from obligation, and yet in this it looked as if he were not at liberty. Hetty's limited understanding of these things was that, generally, a person weighed obligation on one side of the scales against the heart on the other, duty against desire. But Mr Woodhouse had seemed to find one as unappealing as the other. It was a conundrum.

She continued to see her casual remark at the Crown as thoughtless but harmless—she could not in all honesty upbraid herself for it too harshly. But she recognised that there was much—very much—in the rest of her discourse of which she ought to be ashamed. There were elements of Mr Woodhouse's fears and alarums which were on the excessive side of normal for a relatively well-travelled gentleman used to the world. His many little ailments and complaints did not really signify; his fancy that he was ill had been much stronger than any actual indisposition. These things she owned—the fault was not all on her side. But she had taken his concerns and compounded them. The small things he had feared, she had made large. Histrionic exaggeration, a ghoulish tendency to purple melodrama, she had turned drama to crisis with every ill-considered anecdote. People in Highbury knew her ways, and made allowances for them, discounting one half of what she said and taking the rest with a large pinch of salt. This in itself was no source of pride to her—to be an object of pity, even of ridicule. But Mr Woodhouse had taken all her silly embroidering and gothic gloom as gospel. She had seriously disturbed him, she knew she had. In the end, it seemed likely to her that that had been at the root of his indecision. He had seen good in her—he had said she was kind and patient. But she had frightened him with her ungoverned tongue. So far, she decided, she had been the author of her own failure.

This bitter lesson did not teach her to still her tongue—that would have been impossible—but to control it. In this there was a palpable alteration in conduct. She taught herself to look around for safe, uncontentious topics of conversation: the weather, the landscape, their daily comings and goings. She learned to count her blessings and to describe them with exhaustive diligence. She still talked as much as ever but her subjects were always general and generally positive. Whatever her interlocutor said, she agreed with, thoroughly, but went no further than they did. When initiating conversation, she became adept at arguing two sides of every case, the pros and the cons, which had the effect of taking up a great deal of conversational space without advancing any discussion forward an iota from its starting point. But she found, as her speech was occupied less with panic and alarm, disaster and dire outcomes, her mind was likewise less engaged with them. She found less to fault and more to praise and was generally much happier, outwardly at least.

The skill of generalised, observational conversation was one which Hetty Bates was to perfect and demonstrate all the rest of her days; she became mistress of the obvious, an expert describer of everything that was apparent to everyone. She spoke in lists: what had been done or said, remarked on or pondered; a perpetual, unabridged narrative of the commonplace. Mrs Bates was to find herself developing a convenient deafness to Hetty's interminable, mild but ultimately pointless exegesis of every topic.

Chapter 17

For the following week Mrs Bates remained at home feigning indisposition, that she might not need to meet Mr Knightley. Her letter from Mrs Bittern arrived and the Bitterns themselves followed hard on its heels. The dinner was to take place, Marie was certainly invited. As much as she trembled at the idea of being in company with Mr Knightley she could not deny herself the great pleasure and relief of a reunion with Mrs Bittern and when the day of their dinner arrived she was ready to enter the Donwell coach when it called. Mr Knightley handed her into his carriage and they drove together through the village, down the lane towards the river. Marie succeeded in keeping up an artificially bright stream of inconsequential conversation to avoid the dangerous waters which threatened to engulf them.

Grange Spinney was a large, very ancient house, stone-built and swathed with creepers. Welcoming lights shone in every window as they rode up the gravelled drive.

'Ah,' breathed Mr Knightley, when Marie's soliloquy had come to an end. 'How good it is to see the house occupied once more. How glad I am to have them home.'

Mr and Mrs Bittern were as ideal a couple as it would be possible to meet. Equal in rank and understanding, perfectly suited in manner and temper, they were devoted to one another even after over forty years of marriage. They had sought acquaintance with Frederick and Marie immediately upon their arrival at the vicarage. Mr Bittern was a long-standing friend of Mr Knightley. They were of an age and occupied an equal station in society; with no brother to turn to, William Bittern was the squire's natural and preferred confidant. The two were as active as one another in local matters, both sat as magistrate at the assizes in Kingston. The Bitterns, Mr Knightley and the Bateses had formed a close-knit and exclusive social circle in Highbury which had endured over many years. Mrs Knightley had been eagerly encompassed into it as soon as her engagement to the squire had been announced. Marie and the late Mrs Knightley had both found solace in the good advice and experience of Mrs

Bittern over the years; she was an extremely sagacious and intelligent lady, well-travelled, well-versed in human foibles with a wealth of experience to call on.

Mr Bittern's business was now managed by his son, leaving him at leisure to pursue his private interests. Chief of these was his wife, a lady perhaps ten or eleven years his senior and encumbered, in recent years, with ill-health to such a degree that European travel and sojourns at a number of watering places had been their lot these five or six years past. These extended stays in sanatoria and spas meant that the four remaining members of the close-knit circle had scarcely been together since the demise of the departed affiliates. While there was much joy at the reunion, there was sadness also for those who had been lost.

Marie Bates found the dinner and the evening which followed to be an oasis of good taste, understated excellence, warm friendship and fond reminiscence. Old associations, the easiness of the company, the happy memories they called on all served to overcome her front of coolness toward Mr Knightley. She was almost able to forget that such a person as Mrs Stokes existed. Mr Knightley seemed all his habitual self once more, attentive, open-mannered and with an excess of good-humour she had not seen in him for many weeks, and she was powerless to resist it.

The Bitterns' travels and events in Highbury were all the talk during soup and fish. The Winwoods occupied the whole of the roast and most of the dessert—Mr Knightley lamenting very bitterly his ever having offered the living to them. Hartfield and the probability of it being the site of a new house took them through cheese and then the ladies left the gentlemen to their wine.

'I am so happy that we decided to be just four today,' Mrs Bittern remarked as she led Marie into the drawing room. 'I invited no one to meet you. Isn't that shocking? But we wished to be as informal as possible. I did not want to mar our reunion with superfluous guests to whom things would have to be explained, connections unravelled, histories filled in. We have been through so much together. We instinctively know the path of each other's thoughts and I didn't want mere politeness or etiquette to interfere with our conversation. It was selfish of me, I know. There are those whose arrival ought to be honoured. But they can wait. Now I have you all to myself at last.'

'Dearest Josephine,' Marie sighed, squeezing that lady's hand, 'you do not know how I have missed your calm good sense.'

'You have had a vast deal to endure, Marie,' Mrs Bittern said, pressing her friend into a sofa by the fire and taking a seat beside her. 'Poor Frederick. I was mortified to be away from Highbury when you needed me the most. Your letter waited for me at Avignon. William was all for travelling straight home again I assure you, but that he would not leave me behind without his protection, and it would have been impossible for me …'

'Dear friend, I would not have wanted it. The journey would have been too much for you. And by the time you had got here, Frederick would have been buried. What could you have done?'

'I could have comforted you, which I wanted with all my heart to do. And I could have eased your anxieties.' She lowered her voice, 'William says you were left quite penniless and practically without a roof over your head. He shows me all his letters, you know.

There are no secrets between us, so what Knightley tells him, I am sure to find out.'

A footman approached with a salver. Mrs Bittern took two glasses and handed one to Marie. 'A little *digestif*,' she said. 'I have quite got into the habit of it, abroad.' When the man was out of earshot she went on, 'You should have come here. It ought to have been your first thought. Grange Spinney was empty—begging to be occupied. Biddulph would have admitted you without a moment's hesitation and Mrs Craythorne would have had beds made up in a trice, the covers off the furniture in the small drawing room—everything for your comfort and convenience.'

'I can honestly say the idea never crossed my mind. But, in the event, I was well provided for. The justification is some convoluted clause in the parish annals but of course I am not fooled. I know my friends have rescued me. I expect Mr Bittern has been amongst my benefactors. I am more grateful than I can say.'

'By no means,' Mrs Bittern declared. 'We have had no part in it. It is the work of another.' She allowed her eyes to flicker towards the dining room. 'No doubt those two are deep in conversation over some parish map or other. Six or seven months asunder and yet the matter of premier interest is blocked culverts.'

'I suppose Mr Knightley has missed his friend as much as I have missed mine,' Marie replied.

'My poor girl. Are you still grieving?'

Marie shook her head. 'I miss Frederick of course. But he was so very ill at the end. There would have been no coming back from it and if he had—he could not have been my Frederick. His mind, you know, was quite gone, his brain destroyed by the seizure, the doctor said. I find myself thankful he did not have to endure that. That *I* did not. Given his condition, it was a mercy. And so, although, if I could pray him back into life—fully sensible, as he always used to be—I would do, it cannot be so. In short, I have my girls, I have my little abode and I am content. I find ...' with a little hesitation, 'I find I look to the future. As often as I feel I ought to have my mind fixed on what has been, I find it is drawn to what might be.' She looked down at her mourning gown. 'I am in mourning, but I do not mourn. Is that very hypocritical of me? Does it make me shallow? I fear it makes me very shallow indeed.'

'Not at all, Marie, it shows your strength of character. It shows God's grace.'

'It is only seven months since Frederick died! Can I have recovered so soon? I thought one was supposed to wait a year until one could even contemplate …'

'Oh Marie! What are society's norms? Just empty protocol! What has convention to do with the heart? We cannot make ourselves feel sad, any more than we can make ourselves love—or prevent it, come to that. Of course, we can control our actions—but our feelings are a law unto themselves. It takes honesty and courage to acknowledge them. I knew Frederick well, I think. He would not have wanted you to languish. He would want you to be happy. I know that when I die—no my dear, do not protest, for it must be so one day—William will need another wife. We are not designed to live alone. William is no older than Knightley and he looks to the future, I think.' Mrs Bittern gave Marie a narrow look. 'Do you not think so?'

Marie found she could not meet her friend's eye. Mr Knightley, then, must have written to his friend about his intentions. 'I … I have suspected a partiality.'

'Of course you have. And what more natural a thing could there be?'

Marie sipped her wine. It was sweet but very strong. 'You think, then ..? I mean, you have no reservations? You perceive no impropriety in the match?'

'None whatsoever, my dear. On the contrary, Bittern and I think it would be a very good thing. But we will talk of other things—I see this subject distresses you. I hear you have resumed your old duties about the parish—that must be a comfort.'

'It is always a comfort, to comfort others.'

Mrs Bittern took a deep breath. 'I am glad you are comforted, my dear, for I have news to impart which, I flatter myself, will disappoint you. Bittern and I are to leave Highbury. We have bought a villa in Vichy and I will see out my days there. The doctors all agree the climate here aggravates my condition and so we must go. Grange Spinney is to be sold. A young widow has been left with enough money to buy it and open a school for girls. You know we lost our little girl and so the idea appeals to us. She is called Mrs Goddard. I know I can rely on you to welcome her into Highbury society. Oh, do not cry, my dear, you will set me off and Bittern will worry. Here, dry your tears. I hear the gentlemen stirring. We shall have tea.'

The evening concluded with merriment which, for Marie's part, was somewhat forced. They spoke of the Bitterns' new abode—the exotic plants and strange foods, the treatments which were to improve and extend Mrs Bittern's life. They agreed wholeheartedly on the excellence of the notion of a school. Jane, Marie thought, might apply for a teaching position. She certainly would do all she could to support and encourage young Mrs Goddard in her endeavour. Mr Knightley lamented the necessity of finding a man to replace Mr Bittern on the bench. 'If I am not careful Lord Clayton will have his man appointed,' he said, 'and then there will be no justice done in Kingston at all, for Clayton has a cruel streak and goes by the letter of the law, instead of its spirit. Between us, Bittern, you and I have kept him in check but now …'

'I will sit at the assizes in April,' Mr Bittern said. 'After that the ne'er-do-wells will have to take their chance.'

'You are home in the nick of time for that, at least,' Mr Knightley said with a resigned sigh, 'and heartily glad I am of it.'

To begin with the journey home was quiet, Mr Knightley and Mrs Bates both in deep thought as the carriage traversed the gravel of Grange Spinney's wide sweep and began the ascent of the lane.

'A pleasant evening,' Mr Knightley remarked presently, his voice low and gentle. 'You had enjoyable conversation with Mrs Bittern?'

'Oh yes,' Marie said.

'She had … news to impart?'

Marie nodded. 'Much news. Their son is to be a father again. They hope for a girl, this time. Continental ladies are wearing much more satin; Mrs Ford will have to look to her stocks.'

'Ha!' Mr Knightley laughed, 'I shall be sure to inform my housekeeper! But I meant, really …'

'I know what you meant,' Marie burst out. The carriage, at that moment, came out from under a canopy of trees and moonlight flooded the interior. She lifted her face to his and her tears were clear to behold, trembling on her lashes. 'It seems that all those I … I care for are to be taken from me.'

Mr Knightley took her hand and bent his head until it was close to hers. 'The Bitterns' departure is a blow we must both endure, Marie. And coming so soon after the death of your dear Frederick, his loss still so raw … You must be patient. Other friends will come in the Bitterns' stead. And, one day perhaps, your heart will admit another … For my part, I have found …'

But Marie could not endure it. Would he now confess his engagement to Mrs Stokes as evidence that as his grief had healed, so too would hers? Who did he think she would ever love, if not him? It was too bitter, and the temptation to spill out all she felt was too strong. She must contain it. As her friend had told her, to feel these things was one thing, to act on them quite another. She withdrew her hand and moved away from him, to where a whiff of fresh air came through the carriage window, and the houses of Highbury could be seen along the lane.

'Mr Knightley,' she said at last. 'Please forgive me. I am very tired.'

Chapter 18

Bitter indeed were Marie's thoughts the following day, a dark pall on a day which was very fine, the epitome of spring. A strong breeze had cleared away the rain, bright sun glinted off the daffodils and fresh green pastures. Accordingly, both girls were from home; Hetty had set off to Kingston with Hermia Winwood, Jane had gone to call on Lieutenant Weston's sister, the two having formed, after the dinner there, a strong friendship. Usually, Marie herself would be out and about, but the day found her listless and unable to stir. She sat in Hetty's usual seat—the window casement—and stared vacantly down upon the comings and goings of Highbury.

So an engagement between Mr Knightley and Mrs Stokes was a certainty. Mrs Bittern had all but declared it. His calls would cease. Invitations to Donwell would stop and there would be no need for Marie Bates to interest herself in the tenants and cottagers there—the new Mrs Knightley would take them under her wing. What a loss would all this be to her—who had lost so much already. But she supposed she must be happy for Mrs Stokes, who had known such unhappiness and tribulation in her life. She would find safe harbour at last. Presumably the Crown would be sold, or perhaps Mrs Stokes' son would take over the running of it. But Simon Stokes was an indolent young man, lazy and given to drink—a fault manifestly passed on by his drunken father. He gambled and was frequently away at race meetings where he mixed with a very dubious crowd. Perhaps, under Mr Knightley's influence, he could be improved; Marie very much hoped so. The opportunity to be guided by a man like Mr Knightley would be a boon for any young man. She only prayed young Stokes would seize the opportunity he had been handed.

And then the news of the Bitterns' departure; blow upon blow. Certainly, Mrs Bates wished her friend improved health. The idea of a villa in Vichy was quite delightful. The doctors there seemed excellent in every way. No one who called themselves a friend would put any obstacle in the way of Mrs Bittern's enjoying to the full all the advantages of health and society that the continent could offer, and Mrs Bates was a genuinely good friend. But she would be bereft! To be sure Mrs Weston was a close confidante—an excellent woman—but there was neither that easiness nor that equality between them that existed between Josephine Bittern and herself. To whom would she turn for disinterested advice? Certainly not to Mrs Winwood! She had enjoyed close acquaintance with families in Kingston but she had let them drop since Frederick's death. How intensely did she lament, now, the lack of a sister or a sister-in-law. Marie was almost at the age when she might begin to look at least to her elder daughter for support, but alas Hetty would always be on the needful side of that equation. Thank heavens that Jane would one day be a sensible, dependable young woman. Indeed, she was almost so now! That was a blessing, Marie told herself, she must count very dearly indeed.

Her reveries were interrupted by Martha, who brought the post. A letter in a hand she did not recognise intrigued her very much and she broke the seal without delay. The letter was from Frederick's brother, Captain Jeremy Bates (Retired), then resident in Brighton

It had come to his attention (he wrote) that on the

decease of his brother, Frederick's widow and daughters had been left in some want. Being unmarried and consequently childless himself, and living on a Navy pension, he had seen no opportunity of being of use, but it had lately occurred that a comrade of his, Admiral Sealy, had passed away leaving a wife much in need of ladylike companionship and cheerful company. Mrs Sealy was an invalid but a thoroughgoing lady. Her house was in the very best, most respectable quarter of Brighton, comfortable and very well appointed. The Admiral had left Mrs Sealy excellently provided for. If Mrs Bates would write to Mrs Sealy offering the services of one of her daughters to act as companion, and enclose a letter of recommendation from some disinterested but reliable person, Mrs Sealy would look upon the application most favourably and offer terms.

Mrs Bates' immediate response was to give way to the tears which had been threatening all morning. She was to lose Jane, too! (For Jane it must be. Hetty she would not trust to a situation such as Mrs Sealy's promised to be; she had not the temper or the good sense for it, and Marie could not inflict Hetty's garrulousness on a woman who was unable to quit the room.) Of course, there was the natural anxiety of a mother in the contemplation of a daughter's removal, sadness and anxiety mixed. But in fact there was a good measure of gratitude in Marie's tears. Here was just the opportunity she had wanted for Jane. Here in her hand was the ticket Jane herself had longed for—an opportunity to see more of the world, to go out on her own account, to be useful, to travel, to encounter new people and experience new places. Marie blessed Captain Bates for thinking of them. Here, in all the morass of dismay and heartache, was a shining light of positivity. She would focus on it with all her strength. The situation sounded eminently respectable and genteel. Mrs Sealy—an elderly lady, Mrs Bates surmised, well-travelled, informed, interesting and intellectually active—wanted someone to keep her company, to read to her and to bring her news of the outside world. Perhaps she required someone to act as hostess occasionally. Mrs Sealy's companion would have the run of the house, perhaps even be called upon to undertake the housekeeping, managing the servants and domestic arrangements. It would be a far superior situation to that of a governess; there would not be a blush in fulfilling it.

And Jane would be admirably suited to the role. She was confident, intelligent and quick-witted. She could hold her own in any circle. It would satisfy Jane's desire to leave Highbury and experience the wider world but she would exercise her independence within the safe confines of a widow lady's home and under her good supervision. If marriage were not to take Jane away from her, this seemed to be the next best thing. But it was not outside of the bounds of possibility, Marie acknowledged, that in this case, the one would lead to the other. Lieutenant Weston, after all, was stationed in Brighton.

Mrs Bates read the letter again, and in spite of her resolve only moments before, her heart sank. Who could she ask for the letter of recommendation Mrs Sealy required but Mr Knightley—exactly the person to whom she would rather not request any favour at present. She had yet to mention the leak in the bedroom ceiling, so strained had their relations become. She knew that formerly, even if he had not been the landlord, she would have consulted him. Mr Knightley, she realised, was her first recourse, her preferred advisor, her preeminent friend in every situation. How she was going to miss him. As much as she wanted this opportunity for Jane she did not feel she could proceed without taking some advice, so she wrote an acknowledgement to Captain Bates and put the letter away in her bureau.

A few more minutes saw her back on the casement seat. A group of young girls comprising the Misses Sophia and Ursula Winwood, Lavinia Snell and two of the Miss Coxes came into view from the direction of the vicarage. Miss Sophia carried a basket which seemed to contain a good many envelopes—carried it with much importance and ceremony, tossing of curls and self-satisfied smiles. Every so often she stopped, knocked on a door and handed over an envelope with a short speech and an elaborate curtsey. The other girls hung around her, consulted the addresses on the remaining missives and pointed out the correct doors to Sophia but she clearly was the only one permitted to discharge the responsibility of delivery. Presently the girls came to Mrs Bates' door, knocked, and handed one of the notes to Martha. Marie shrank back within the recess of the casement. Sophia's fluting voice could be heard but no words distinctly made out. Then they continued on their way down the High Street.

'A note from Mrs Winwood, ma'am,' said Martha, puffing from lack of breath at the top of the stairs. 'A lot of folderol in the delivering, but that's what it is.'

Marie opened the note, which was written in a bold but richly ornamented hand, with many flounces and curlicues. 'Reverend and Mrs Winwood respectfully request the pleasure of the company of Mrs Bates, Miss Bates and Miss Jane Bates at a musical soiree and supper to be held at Highbury Vicarage ...' A date two weeks hence, in the middle of April, was named.

So, the much-vaunted party was to take place!

Down in the street the girls had reached Ford's window and had been instantly distracted by it as all young women tended to be. Ford's was the next building along from the Crown and Simon Stokes could be seen there, leaning idly against the door to the coaching yard, smoking a cheroot and watching the young women as they pointed out the ribbons and hat trimmings displayed. After a while he approached, bowed, and indicated by a gesture that he wondered what the notes in Miss Sophia's basket concerned. The young ladies embarked on protracted explanation. Sophia's curl-tossing and simpering increased. The Coxe girls dissolved into fits of giggles. Lavinia Snell went such a bright shade of scarlet that Mrs Bates wondered if she might swoon. Miss Sophia rummaged in her basket and located the invitation which was addressed to the Stokeses. Simon Stokes took it, kissed it, and pressed it to his heart. The girls' reaction was affected in the extreme—moans, shrieks, cries, bosoms clutched, palpitations strongly indicated, ringlets provocatively preened. Miss Sophia looked as though she might melt into a puddle. The little party remained in pleasant, animated conversation for some minutes before it was clear that Simon Stokes was offering to accompany the ladies, holding out one arm to take possession of the basket, extending the other to take possession of Miss Sophia.

As the little scene played itself out, Marie became increasingly concerned. The girls were young. Simon Stokes was unreliable, barely respectable. He was not a fit companion for them. She half rose from her seat, considering going down, hurrying after them, suggesting with as much authority as she could muster that they should return home. But at that moment Mr Knightley came along the street on horseback. He dismounted outside the Crown and was on the point of going in when he saw Simon Stokes and the young ladies. He threw his reins to a stable lad and strode quickly up the street, apprehending young Stokes with a word, separating him from the girls and accompanying him back to the inn. Stokes' face was creased into a sullen scowl, Mr Knightley looked extremely angry. The young women's disappointment was clear to see but they walked on and continued with their errand without assistance.

'We met with Sophia Winwood and her entourage of harpies,' Jane reported when she returned from her call. 'They were delivering invitations. Mrs Weston got one, Mrs Snell, the Coxes and I don't know how many others. Highbury is agog with it. Gideon Mortimer must have worked some kind of miracle with the vicarage if it is to contain all those who are summoned to attend.'

'Here is ours,' Mrs Bates replied, indicating the card on the table. 'I suppose we shall have to go.'

'We certainly shall,' Jane cried, 'for Sophia declares that there will never have been such an elegant and superior party in all of Highbury ever before. We are to have all things French: canapés, hors d'oeuvres and champagne to name but three. She spoke as though she had swallowed a French dictionary. She is to sing and Ursula is to play.'

'The Lord help us,' Marie muttered.

'Indeed. I shall take screws of cotton for my ears. But I long to taste champagne. Sophia is in high dudgeon with Mr Knightley. Apparently, he deprived her of her beau. Who does she mean? Are the Snell boys home from Oxford?'

'I fear she refers to Simon Stokes,' Marie said. 'He greeted them earlier in the street and would have walked with them, but Mr Knightley intervened.'

Jane gave a shudder. 'Simon Stokes is no beau. Not one that I would choose, anyway.'

'You are too sensible, my dear.'

'Now I must go and look for my pencils. Miss Weston and I have decided to begin sketching Highbury's wildflowers and pressing them, to make an illustrated compendium month by month. The primroses in Donwell woods are nearly over so I said I would go there this afternoon and gather some.'

'An excellent and lady-like scheme,' Marie said.

The following day Marie Bates took her morning walk to the church. She stood for a long while by the grave of her late husband before entering the church by a side door to spend some time in prayer. That she needed some assistance in enduring her situation was clear to her—her nerves were worn thin, she barely slept. Her inner conflict was taking its toll and she could see no end to it. To whom could she turn? If she had hoped for comfort from Mrs Bittern that hope was at an end—she was all approbation and delight at the match between Mr Knightley and Mrs Stokes. She wished with all her heart to feel the consolation of Frederick's presence and ardently prayed for a still, small voice, but both were denied her.

Presently, she went on her way to a little group of humble cottages, to see how Mrs Tremble's baby did.

Chapter 19

Mrs Winwood had picked the choicest cherry of her family and also of her acquaintance to display before Highbury's great and good. The dinner was to be small—very select indeed, the dining chamber, despite Mrs Winwood's most ardent desire, having proved resistant to being doubled in size. As well as the Blands and Mr Knightley only a Mr Paling, a young protégé of Reverend Winwood's currently preparing to take orders at St Luke's were to dine, with one of the Winwood girls and the Blands' daughter making up the numbers. But the evening party was to be grand—all of Highbury's first circle (and some of the second) were invited to take tea at a musical soiree. Miss Ursula Winwood was to exhibit her prowess on pianoforte and harp. Miss Sophia Winwood and Miss Beatrice Bland were to sing. Highbury was abuzz with the event. Even those who had declared themselves disgusted by the Winwoods and determined to refuse the blandishments of any invitation found their curiosity sufficiently piqued to relent. Those who had been invited couldn't help crowing over those who had not. Those who had not affected not to care, but did, very much.

The Winwood's cook was joined by a French pâtissier who sent orders daily to the butcher and the baker and further afield—the details of these were widely discussed. The culinary delicacies formed all of Highbury's conversation for a week before the event was due. Extra maids and footmen were hired—they were pumped for information. A marquee was ordered from town and two days before the party a team of men arrived to erect it over the spot where the apple tree had stood. Village boys and girls scrambled onto the vicarage wall to watch proceedings with avid interest. General expectation was very high, equalled only by the level of cynicism. April, after all, was not an ideal time for outdoor entertainment. High winds were likely, a storm not beyond the realms of possibility. Weather-wise eyes scanned the horizon and read the clouds. It was hard to say if Mrs Winwood's triumph or utter humiliation were more eagerly anticipated.

The squire of course received one of Mrs Winwood's invitations but his summoned him to dine, as well as to the evening entertainment. Mrs Winwood enclosed a note—the Venerable Bishop Bland and Mrs Bland were to be present, having come to collect Sophia on their way to town, she very much hoped Mr Knightley would do them the honour & c. Mr Knightley thought the dinner would be dreary—he rather disliked ecclesiastical types and expected the Venerable Bishop Bland to be dull company. The dinner was to take place the day before the April assizes, an occasion which loomed large in Mr Knightley's calendar, but it could not be avoided and so on the day before he called at Mrs Bates' house to offer her the use of his carriage. She declined, speaking of the enjoyment of a walk after dinner, the lighter evenings, the possibility of hearing a cuckoo, the 14th being almost upon them.

'Well, the carriage will be at your disposal,' he said with a shrug. 'I would not use it myself, but Mrs Stokes has turned her ankle in a fall down the cellar steps, so I have offered it to her. She does not want to miss the Winwood's party—she has so little opportunity to enjoy herself. So you see it will be right outside your door and can easily accommodate the whole party. Think on it, and use it if you wish. I shall tell the coachman to call in any case.'

'I thank you most kindly, Mr Knightley,' Mrs Bates replied. 'But the girls and I will walk.'

'As you please,' he said.

Mr Knightley arrived at the vicarage a few moments before three o'clock on the appointed day. The daffodils were in full bloom all along the hedgerow, their heads dancing and nodding in the stiff breeze. The vicarage garden was ablaze with primroses and crocuses but the swathe of lawn where they were usually particularly thickly strewn was obscured by the marquee, the flowers presumably crushed beneath the rush matting floor. The azaleas flanking the short-flagged pathway to the door were brown and wizened. Mr Knightley regarded them sadly before raising his hand to knock, and sighed as he thought about the letters he had left half written in his study, the new engineering drawings of the mill machinery he had left un-examined, the winter wheat in the high pasture which ought to be looked at for signs of blight. He had other matters on his mind—very weighty, pressing matters he would very much have liked to mull over in the calm sanctuary of his study—but they, like all the rest, would have to wait.

He was greeted by a bobbing maid—farmer Cropley's youngest girl. The squire knew her well and they exchanged a few words while she took his hat and gloves. Then he was shown into the parlour where the remainder of the company was already assembled. Conversation within that room had been animated— he had heard it as he had spoken to Sarah Hopley— but it came to an abrupt halt as he entered. He had the fleeting but distinct impression that they had been discussing something of interest to them but which was to be kept secret from him. This was not a happy notion and it both annoyed and piqued the squire as he made his entrance to a party which, on the whole, he would rather have avoided.

'Forgive me,' he said, pointedly, 'I do not wish to intrude. You have private business to discuss?'

'My dear Squire,' Mrs Winwood began. She was sumptuously arrayed in a manner far beyond the purse and somewhat beyond what was tasteful for the wife of a country parson. 'We are honoured. Let me …'

But before she could utter a syllable of introduction the Venerable Bishop Bland stepped forward, absolutely blocking her path and drowning out her words with a homily of his own. This was highly irritating to the squire. Good manners dictated that other guests hung back until the host had greeted each new arrival; this upstart did not know his place and the squire was not inclined to notice him. Mr Knightley looked left and right for Reverend Winwood, giving scant attention to the bishop's protracted greeting, eventually locating that gentleman pressed into a small chair towards the back of the room. As soon as—or rather before—the bishop had done, the squire crossed to greet his host, making more of the business than was perhaps necessary but doing so to make a decided point: he would not accede to the bishop's dominion. Reverend Winwood hardly rose in acknowledgement before hurriedly sitting again. Behind him, even more in awe of the occasion in general and the bishop in particular, Mr Paling, the young candidate for curacy looked as though he wished he could melt into the new-papered wall, but the squire acknowledged him with his usual disinterested civility and in pointed preference to giving the bishop any cognisance whatsoever.

The Venerable Bishop stubbornly held the centre ground of the room; he would by no means give way. The two young ladies sat with their eyes downcast and their lips sealed—they would not challenge the bishop on any account. Mrs Winwood regarded her brother-in-law with awe-struck complacency—while she was delighted to be able to call such a noteworthy personage brother, his determination to preside as de facto host was appalling—she was aghast at his overbearing self-importance. She threw occasional, withering looks across the room at her husband; why would he not intervene? Her sister, the Venerable Bishop's wife, remained seated, taking up most of a seat designed for two, and barely lifted her bejewelled hand in recognition of the squire.

The Venerable Bishop Bland was everything Mr Knightley had feared—superlatively conscious of his standing, resplendent in purple, the insignia of his office prominently displayed. He had the advantage of being tall—the low ceiling of the vicarage hardly accommodated his height—and looked down on everyone and everything as though it was very small and unimportant indeed. Reverend Winwood's shrinking manner indicated that the bishop would have his way. His resignation left only Mrs Winwood, who girded herself for battle. She simmered, she positively trembled with frustrated vanity. As disappointed as Mr Knightley was with Reverend Winwood—he had failed to fill even one of Reverend Bates' shoes—and as disgusted as he was with Mrs Winwood—her refusal to visit the poorer members of the parish was shameful—Mr Knightley found Bishop Bland's determination to ride roughshod over the Winwoods insupportable. Even a family member had no right to take such liberties with his host and hostess. Since no one else was prepared to slap down the bishop, it was left to him. When Mr Bland pressed him to take a glass of Reverend Winwood's Madeira wine, Mr Knightley refused it. He deflected likewise the bishop's repeated attempts to interrogate him on the extent and value of his lands, his family connections and his political leanings, but the man would not be deterred.

'I refuse to be drawn, my Lord, on these or any other topics. They are not designed to appeal to the general company,' he cried at last. 'Let us remember where we are, and what is due to our hosts. Here are some delightful ladies who have no interest in my acreage or my barley yield. Here is also Reverend Winwood's domicile, newly improved—I fancy *that* will be a topic of far more appeal. You are quite satisfied with the renovations, Mrs Winwood,' he enquired, turning towards his hostess, which had the pleasing corollary of turning his back to the bishop. 'Gideon Mortimer has presented his bill and I do not wish to pay it until I know you are happy. I hope there will be time for me to inspect the improvements.'

'This is *your* property, Mr Knightley?' the bishop boomed before Mrs Winwood could answer.

Mr Knightley rolled his eyes. 'Indeed sir,' he replied through gritted teeth, 'and the living of Highbury is within my gift.'

The bishop cast a sharp look at Reverend Winwood which said as clearly as any words, 'You should have told me this,' but dinner then being announced the matter was left in abeyance.

Bishop Bland stalked alone into the dining room, stopping only to call over his shoulder, 'Knightley, you will be so good as to escort Mrs Bland.' The squire was all-but dumb-founded; the bishop's order countermanded all etiquette. Reverend Winwood ought to take Mrs Bland. The bishop should have held back and taken Mrs Winwood in last. He—the squire—should have taken one of the young ladies and Mr Paling the other. The bishop's instruction denied everyone their due precedence and left one lady without an escort—Mr Knightley almost felt sorry for Mrs Winwood—her vexation was quite palpable. He offered his arm to her and indicated that Reverend Winwood should do the honours with Mrs Bland. That left Mr Paling to escort both girls, a task he was so alacritous to perform that he almost dislodged a tray of baubles from a small side table.

Things did not improve over dinner. The bishop intoned an overly protracted grace and then gave his attention wholly to his dinner, taking no notice of anything that was not on his plate. His wife and Mrs Winwood embarked on an exchange of barbed repartee. Reverend Winwood, whose place at the foot of the table had been wrested from him by Bishop Bland, remained almost silent throughout the meal, the squire's attempts to draw him out on matters of parish business meeting with only mumbled responses. Miss Winwood, on the other hand, was more animated than Mr Knightley had ever seen her before. When it was her turn to be conversed by Mr Paling, next to whom she was seated, she seemed to have a good deal to say and be very zealous to listen, but they spoke quietly and did not contribute to the discussion at large. Miss Bland said almost nothing; the squire's conversational gambits producing monosyllabic replies and platitudes.

'You are newly arrived at Highbury, I believe?' he tried.

She simply nodded.

'And do you stay long?'

'I do not know,' was all her reply.

'You find society in London most entertaining, I think.'

'Yes, sir.'

Mrs Winwood had been brought low by the bishop's usurpation of the proper ceremony of the dinner procession and his interference with the seating plan at least had the advantage of allowing her to fulminate at him from her end of the table. She retaliated with, 'I am the last person to stand on ceremony, my Lord Bishop. I would have people sit where they choose, only let there be no doubt, I do know the protocol and can apply it, when the occasion demands, and you can be sure I will do,' with a very significant look at her husband, 'very rigorously, when our circumstances alter.'

Bishop Bland addressed himself to a glass of wine, which prevented him making any reply. Reverend Winwood avoided her eye by finding something very much amiss with the state of his soup spoon.

Mrs Bland drawled, 'Dear Emily, it is hardly necessary here, in so rustic and homely a setting, to uphold the ceremonies of high society. To be sure, I was surprised to hear the dressing bell. I do not imagine your parishioners dress for dinner, do they?'

'The lower orders would not dream of it, of course,' Mrs Winwood sniffed, 'but we are not so reduced.'

'I had imagined you quite pastoral and bucolic, here. I expected the girls to be barefoot.'

'You quite shock me,' Mrs Winwood cried. 'Mr Knightley will concur, for the provinces, we are very refined in Highbury, are we not?'

'I do not dress for dinner, unless I am invited out,' the squire admitted, 'but when I am invited, whether it be to Clayton Park or to my good friend Mr Hopley the miller's, I always dress. It is common courtesy—mere good manners. I think,' with heavy inference, 'that whatever one's status, they should always be applied.'

If Mrs Bland felt his implied rebuke, she did not show it, but she struck back with, 'Sister I am sure you have worked wonders with this unpromising little cottage. Your improvements are to be commended in every aspect. What we will have to endure at the Palace will not be so easy to remedy.' She went on to enumerate the deficiencies of the accommodations provided for them at the Archbishop's Palace—the rooms so small and awkward, barely space for them, let alone the servants, the entrance unremarkable and so hidden away that it might have been mistaken for a tradesmen's access—while soup and the fish were served and eaten. Mrs Winwood—forgetting perhaps what was due to the squire—parried with her own experience at Highbury vicarage—this dining room as a case in point—so very confined, she was almost ashamed of it; the parlour fire—inclined to smoke; their improvements re the morning room; the general décor quite deplorable; a want of elegance in every room. The joint was brought in and the bishop carved it, reserving the choicest portions for himself. Mrs Bland entertained the company with her regrets at leaving the Archdeaconry—the circle of acquaintance she had propagated there, the musical evenings and cultural lectures they had enjoyed. 'Whoever replaces us,' she said, with a complacent glance at her sister, 'will be most fortunate, whereas I shall have to start over. Pimlico, you know, is a cultural desert.'

'You will not often have to visit Pimlico, my dear,' his Lordship broke his silence to say. 'I daresay you will find something to appeal to your intellect in Lambeth. The archbishop's wife, you know, will introduce you. She is intimate with a great many very superior ladies. You there,' to the servant, 'bring me more potatoes.'

'Yes, indeed my Lord. I do not wish to seem to complain, only, you know,' with a covert glance at Mr Knightley, 'one cannot speak so plain as one would wish, but what is gain for one is sacrifice for another, that is really all I want to make clear.'

'I do not think being a Bishop's wife will be such a sacrifice, sister,' Mrs Winwood observed. 'And, remember, for dear Beatrice here, it will provide unrivalled opportunities. She will move in the first circles. For her sake, if not for your own …'

'*Your* daughters will not be the losers by it, either,' Mrs Bland retorted. 'You will find your own opportunities considerably enhanced, I can assure you.' She cast a supercilious glance around the dining chamber, 'This little chamber is a world away from the dining room at the Archde …'

'Listen to the wind!' Mrs Winwood exclaimed shrilly. 'I fear excessively for the drawing room fire. Gideon Mortimer's chimney boy has been able to do nothing with it; the least gust seems to unsettle it. I have told the girls on no account to allow anyone to put any fuel on it or we will be deluged with smoke and soot. But here is the syllabub,' Mrs Winwood concluded, 'I do hope cook has whipped it sufficiently.'

'Our cook refuses to accompany us to Lambeth,' Mrs Bland lamented. 'That, too,' again, with a look at Mrs Winwood heavy with import, 'is a boon our successor will inherit.'

The significance of the conversation was soon clear to Mr Knightley. He had not spent forty years running an estate, serving as a magistrate and overseeing parish affairs without being able to hear what was unsaid quite as loudly as what was said. Reverend Winwood was to replace his brother-in-law as Archdeacon—the Winwoods would be quitting Highbury before the paint was dry on the refurbished walls. Naturally this development annoyed and offended him. The living was within his gift and he ought to have been consulted before the incumbent made any alterations to the arrangements. He had spent considerable sums in improving the vicarage to the Winwoods' requirements. It was entirely commensurate with Mrs Winwood's high-handed behaviour to have manipulated this promotion for her husband on the back of her brother-in-law's elevation. That the reverend himself was embarrassed by it explained his shrinking reticence for the duration of the afternoon. On the other hand, the Winwoods' incumbency had been an unmitigated failure. A change might well be the best thing.

It did not take the squire long to ascertain Mr Paling's

role. Once the ladies had withdrawn, conversation between the bishop and his host turned to matters theological and doctrinal. The bishop was very much the authority—or believed himself to be so—Reverend Winwood purported to agree with every syllable. Mr Knightley moved his seat next to Mr Paling so as to discreetly draw the young man out.

'You will take orders soon, I believe Mr Paling?'

'Oh yes,' the young man stammered, 'in May, I think.'

'You are from the North Country, I surmise?'

'Yes. My father was Reverend Winwood's curate in Derbyshire. He died of influenza. He caught it from a parishioner during the epidemic. Reverend Winwood had taken his family away—naturally, he feared for the health of his daughters—so it fell to my father to minister to the sick. On his return, Reverend Winwood was so good as to undertake the completion of my education. He placed me at St Luke's college. I am very grateful to him.'

'Indeed,' said the squire. 'Was any other occupation offered to you? The military perhaps, or the law?'

Mr Paling shook his head. 'No, sir, but I wanted no

other. The church is my calling.'

The squire nodded. 'I wish all young men were as fixed on their course as you seem to be. And following ordination, have you any prospects in view?'

Mr Paling blushed to the roots of his hair. 'Reverend Winwood has been so good as to … and the bishop seems to endorse … but I fear, sir, I am not at liberty …'

'Do not concern yourself,' said Mr Knightley, finishing his claret. 'The situation is entirely clear to me. Mr Winwood intends to retain the living of Highbury and will install you as his curate, at a tiny fraction of the stipend, no doubt. I pray you will not take this personally, Mr Paling. I am certain you are a worthy young man and would serve the parish admirably. But I am the benefactor of this living and I will decide who occupies it. Excuse me, I will join the ladies.'

Chapter 20

The ladies—or more likely their servants—had been busy while the gentlemen took their wine. The drawing room had been transformed into an auditorium, with every chair pressed into service and placed around the new doors to the old morning room. These were thrown open, revealing the pianoforte and harp splendidly displayed. New French doors opened out to a freshly laid terrace. The carpentry seemed excellent, the decoration of the walls and ceilings most proficient. There was no want to taste or elegance. Thus far the squire was pleased with the improvements to the vicarage—the effect was certainly to enhance a space which was, by nature of the age of the building, rather confined.

Mrs Winwood's scheme was to extend her hospitality into the marquee, but the wind had increased during dinner; torches intended to light up the garden guttered and smoked, candles within the marquee likewise blew out repeatedly. Two footmen circled with tapers trying in vain to keep them alight. Tables covered with linen bore the beginnings of supper. The fire in the parlour had burned down—a screen deterred anyone from interfering with it—and the draught from the French doors meant that there was little warmth to be had.

'Mama, we shall have to abandon the marquee,' Miss Winwood said. 'It is too cold and windy. It was always a risk; the climate in April is unreliable.'

'On no account!' Mrs Winwood cried. 'After all the trouble and expense of it? The lower orders are to sup there—I shall lead them in myself. If I distinguish them by my condescension, they will think it the finest thing in the world. Meanwhile the premier guests—the Claytons, the squire, the Bitterns and the ecclesiastical contingent—will sup in the dining room. It will be up to you girls to make sure than none of the hoi polloi get in there by mistake. I have the Bateses particularly in mind; she must under no circumstance to be permitted to presume. Do you understand? Now, where is Sophia?'

'She is preening. She thinks Bolton has not done her hair properly. I fear she is going to make a terrible exhibition of herself.'

'Go and hurry her along. The evening guests will begin

to arrive directly and I would have you all on hand to assist me. Your father can by no means be relied upon. I am disgusted with him. The bishop has all but trodden him into the dust. Oh! Mr Knightley. I did not see you there in the doorway. I hope the other gentlemen will be as alacritous as you.'

'They follow directly, ma'am.'

The Winwood girls put the finishing touches to the room, adjusting draperies, rearranging displays of trinkets, tweaking flowers. Arabella and Cordelia found themselves very much opposed on the matter of an antimacassar, one declaring it too horrid to be seen, the other defensive of its merits. Their difference of opinion threatened to become ugly, even physical, until their mama separated them with a cuff which sent both scurrying upstairs in tears. Ursula, unmoved by her sisters' distress, shuffled her music and adjusted the music stand. Mr Knightley could make no contribution other than to keep out of the way. He found a glass-fronted display cabinet and pretended to examine its contents with fixed attention until the other gentlemen came through.

A jostle in the hallway and the evening guests began to

arrive. The ladies took off their outerwear and gentlemen handed over their hats before forming what amounted to a procession past the stairs and into the room. The bishop arrested their progress by a prolonged greeting addressed to each in turn. His stature and manner pushed Mrs Winwood absolutely into the shadows; she could not by any means subjugate him or silence him. His protracted preamble caused a back-log in the hall, through the door and down the path.

Mr and Mrs Weston with their married children and spouses were amongst those first to survive the ordeal by bishop and gain the parlour, The Snells and the Bitterns followed closely behind. Several clerical acquaintance from the diocese and some of the masters from St Luke's soon joined them. The numerous chairs and the small side tables prohibited easy movement; a collection of cameos and miniatures was all-but knocked asunder by a lady's gown. Candles guttered in a dozen candelabra, their reaching flames threatening the new curtains which billowed either side of the open doors. The room was soon uncomfortably full and oppressively warm.

Mr Knightley hovered by the door, his ear alert for the arrival of his carriage. At last, discerning the voice of his coachman, he hurried out, pushing with difficulty past the press of people in the hallway and on the vicarage path. But only Mrs Stokes and her son were within, she with her bandaged foot resting on the velvet seat, he lounging opposite, an expression of extreme complacency on his fresh-scrubbed face.

'I did not expect to see you here, Simon,' Mr Knightley said.

'I was invited,' the young man re-joined, bullishly. 'The young ladies expect me in particular and I am the last man to let a lady down.'

'You will behave yourself like a gentleman, sir,' Mr Knightley warned.

'Oh, as to that, you know, I always do,' Simon Stokes replied, with a supercilious grin.

Mr Knightley assisted Mrs Stokes from the carriage. The steps to the vicarage were narrow and awkward, the path filled with people. At last he swept her up into his arms to carry her inside. Just at that moment Mrs Bates and her daughters stepped into view. She and Mr Knightley exchanged a look across the prone figure of Mrs Stokes, which was loaded on both sides, awkward, embarrassed, pained. Then he carried his burden past the waiting queue of guests and into the vicarage.

Mrs Winwood had been generous with her invitations, assuming the marquee would accommodate the overflow from the parlour, but the canvas sides of the tent flapped and shuddered in the wind and nobody seemed inclined to venture into it, least of all the ladies in their thin gowns. Those lesser guests who had been destined to be relegated to the marquee pressed in preference into the vicarage parlour after their greater neighbours. Abel Larkins and his wife, John Abdy, Mr and Mrs Pellins, Mr Wilcox, the apothecary from Kingston. All were agog to see the broadly publicized improvements to the vicarage, the promised style and panache of Mrs Winwood's hospitality, and did not see why they should be marooned in a draughty, dark pavilion when all was light and bright and laughter in the main house. No. Much she had promised and much, they felt, they deserved to see. Accordingly, they made free; peering into cabinets, examining upholstery assessing makers' marks on porcelain and silver.

'Look at the curtains, Abel,' Mrs Larkins was heard to say, 'there must be ten yards of material in each swag.'

Mrs Winwood looked on helplessly as her belongings were fingered and pored over. 'Utter presumption,' she barked. 'Who do they think they are, to manhandle my bibelots with their grubby, work-worn hands?' In vain did she usher her inferior guests through the French doors and into the marquee. As quickly as she decanted them they returned. 'Very nice,' they said, 'but much too cold. We'll stay in here, ma'am, if it's all the same to you.'

Mr Knightley deposited Mrs Stokes onto a chair and went to find a footstool. 'Your son's presence here disturbs me greatly,' he told her on his return, which was not soon, the crowds and superfluous items of occasional furniture inhibiting his search to an almost insuperable degree.

'Me also, but he would not be left behind,' Mrs Stokes murmured.

There was a hush as Lord and Lady Clayton were announced. Mrs Winwood and the Bishop absolutely tussled in the effort to be the one to greet them, but the bishop overcame and commenced an officious oration of welcome. A way was, with difficulty, made for them through the crush of guests and furniture. They were clearly very much disgusted at what they found. 'A shocking bunfight,' Lady Clayton muttered. 'I hope we shall not have to stay long.'

The awed hush attendant on the Claytons' arrival meant that Miss Bates' diatribe as she described their progress through the hall was clearly audible; a long narrative describing the removal of wraps preceded an account of the weather—excessively windy, beginning to rain quite heavily. Details of their journey were recounted—the road quite wet, puddles a consideration, no cuckoo to be heard—and at last they were in the room.

'I declare, what a tall man the bishop is! I could not understand a syllable he uttered. Was it a blessing of some kind? I confess I did not really listen, I was much too eager to see …' Miss Bates looked around her, 'A transformation indeed, as far as one can … such a lot of guests! Quite the concert hall, is it not, Mama? And the old windows quite gone! Doors in their place—what an innovation indeed! They will get the full force of the north wind when it blows! But to be sure,' with a cautionary finger to her own lip, 'must not criticise … Today it is but in the north north-east, and a little fresh air is always beneficial. Mrs Weston! How do you do? Yes, very well indeed I thank you. Mama is just behind me. I have lost sight of Jane. Such a crowd! So many friends and neighbours I did not expect! The Fords I believe … Yes, yes, I heard the same. She is indisposed. I am very sorry to hear it. Such a good friend and neighbour, Mrs Ford. The Coxes arrived just as we did and Jane got quite besieged by the little ones. Oh? You think Mrs Winwood did not intend the children to come? I wonder if Mrs Coxe did not apprehend ..?' Looking around the room, 'I quite see it might be inconvenient. Such a crowd of people—hardly anywhere to sit! And so many little ornaments and knick-knacks as there are about the place! A profusion, upon my word! Quite charming of course—but rather vulnerable to little hands. We will have to watch little William Coxe near that delicate porcelain … Oh, I see Miss Ursula has seen the danger. She is collecting it all up. Well, I think that highly sensible, do not you? Oh, thank you, no coffee for me—never take coffee—a little tea, by and by. Oh! Here it is! Well, I will take this seat at the back, next to you, Mrs Snell, if I may. Everyone is finding somewhere to sit—or to perch! See Mr Pellins there! I hope that console table can take his weight! The music will begin soon, I suspect. Miss Ursula is taking her seat by the pianoforte. I wonder what her repertoire will be. I own to you, Mrs Snell, it is very strange—very strange indeed to be here, our old home—not that I am not very grateful for the new; so snug as we are, and I must not become maudlin. I must count our blessings. And we can see all the commerce of Highbury you know. Mr Snell's chambers are just opposite—almost—if you sit at the extreme end of the window seat and crane just a little you can see them quite clearly. And all the people coming and going, in and out. Such legal business as they must have. I wonder Mr Snell is not worked to exhaustion. Mrs Stokes alone must keep him occupied on a full-time basis. I cannot conceive what she needs with a lawyer—not that it is any of my business, of course—but she certainly must have some for she visits ever so often—almost daily. Oh Mrs Snell, are you quite well? Let me get you a little brandy. You suddenly look so pale. Where is Mr Snell? Shall I fetch him? Oh, there

he is, with Mrs Stokes—he is handing her tea. Mr
Snell! Oh Mr Snell! I fear your wife is not quite well,
sir.'

The musical portion of the entertainment was delayed
by Mrs Snell's being suddenly unwell and having to be
taken home. Those who had found seats were obliged
to vacate them while the lady was assisted from the
room, Hetty helpfully explaining the while that Mrs
Snell had become ill just as they had been discussing
the curious frequency of Mrs Stokes' consultations
with Mr Snell. Those more able to put two and two
together than Hetty busily did so, and while by no
means all of Mrs Winwood's guests were tolerant of
gossip, sufficient of them were susceptible to it that
before five minutes had elapsed Mrs Stokes found that
she was the recipient of sly stares and whispered
innuendo. Chairs were edged away from her, backs
turned. Whether on this account or not, Lord and
Lady Clayton found they must leave urgently.

In the meantime, the Coxe children were hastily taken
to the church school room—they could not by any
means be allowed to disrupt the recital. Miss Ursula
made some difficulty about the draught from the

French doors, the smoke from the candles, the noise of the canvas, which, now, as well as being flapped by stiff gusts of wind was also being drummed by rain. The doors must be closed. Those few gentlemen who had submitted to being pushed outside were now urged to come back in again. They brought the news that the marquee was leaking. Instructions were given to take the supper from there into the dining room. This could only be achieved using an outdoor route—the passageway being thronged with people who could not be seated in the parlour. The effect of the rain on the exotic hors d'oeuvres and delicately wrought canapés was deleterious in the extreme, but could not be helped.

Everyone knew that Mrs Bates detested tittle-tattle and while the rest of the room buzzed with speculation about Mrs Stokes she was left alone. Mr Knightley took advantage of a vacant seat at her side.

'How was dinner?' she enquired, a bright, determinedly brave look in her eye. 'I hope you were edified by the august company. The bishop is very intimidating. I hardly dare look in his direction in case I catch his eye.'

Mr Knightley snorted. 'I was disgusted by the Blands. Our Bishop is worth ten of him. The dinner was passable. I could have had better at home.'

'Oh dear. I am sorry to hear it. Mrs Winwood will be sorrier still. She has set great store by this evening, I think.'

'She invited the wrong guests then,' Mr Knightley said. 'If she had wished me to enjoy myself she should have invited …' he hesitated for a moment before concluding his sentence with the word 'others.'

Mrs Bates looked across the room to where Mrs Stokes sat in isolation with her foot elevated on a stool. 'For my part, I was glad to be excluded. It would have been too difficult, I think. The Winwoods are quite different from Frederick and me—but being different does not mean they are wrong. They must be allowed to establish themselves and I must disappear into the background while they do so. Mrs Winwood does not want to be reminded of what went before.'

'You are right,' Mr Knightley agreed. 'She only has eyes for what is to come. But it looks like the music is going to begin at last. I ought to stand. Mrs Wilcox has no seat.'

'There are seats near Mrs Stokes,' Marie observed, 'I wonder why nobody takes them.'

Mr Knightley followed her gaze. 'Indeed,' he frowned. They both knew Highbury too well. Something was afoot. They exchanged a quizzical look before Mr Knightley moved away.

The room had just settled again when it was discovered that Miss Sophia was absent. Two of her sisters went in search of her and she presently appeared in the morning room looking very flushed, her dress and hair disarranged. Her mama was wedged between the bishop and another clerical gentleman and quite powerless either to obfuscate her daughter's shame or to box her ears for it, both of which things she looked like she very much wished to do. A moment or two later Simon Stokes slouched into the room and took up a nonchalant position against a glass-fronted cabinet. The connection between himself and Miss Sophia's dishevelment was apparent to everyone but rather than being embarrassed he looked very pleased with himself indeed. He helped himself to two glasses of wine from a passing footman and drank them both in quick succession.

Mrs Bates looked across to where Mr Knightley stood. His face was like thunder, his eyes relaying messages of the most imperative and irate nature to Simon Stokes, who smoothly ignored them. That the squire wished to cross the room to confront the miscreant was all too clear, but the jumble of chairs, the tightly packed-in crowd and the imminent commencement of the recital made it impossible. Mrs Stokes gave evidence of being so extremely uncomfortable that Marie almost felt sorry for her. She, too, no doubt, wished to quit the room, or hoped that she would be swallowed whole by the new Turkey rug, but she sat on in misery, throwing the occasional reproachful look at her son but meeting no other eye.

Miss Ursula played a startling chord, setting teeth on edge and causing one lady to spill her tea. She corrected her fingering and played it again. The room fell silent, and she began.

Let others describe the musical delights of Mrs Winwood's party. We need not dwell on the fumbled notes of Miss Ursula's murderous rendition of Mr Bach's most beautiful compositions. The shrillness of Miss Sophia's off-key warblings can be passed over as well as the percussive contribution of Mrs Winwood's jangling ire. Let the terrible twangings of the epic battle between Miss Ursula and her harp be a subject for another time, when our nerves have recovered and our headaches gone.

As soon as the final chord had reverberated to its agonised end there was a corporate sigh of relief, a polite smattering of applause and the audience rose almost as one from the cramped confinement of their seats. Under cover of this mass movement Mr Knightley mobilised himself across the room and all-but manhandled young Stokes from the premises. Champagne was hurriedly served—an unprecedented display of luxury as well as a handy diversion as Miss Sophia was forcibly bundled from the room by her irate mama. Some of the gentlemen spoke of making up fours of bridge but found that no card tables had been provided. Someone had the excellent notion of opening up the church school room—the venue of the regular Wednesday whist club—but found it to be swarming with little Coxes who had run amok during the musical recital. Supper was announced but those who ventured into the dining chamber were cornered by the Venerable Bishop Bland who delivered an interminable sermon on abstinence while loading his plate with the choicest *amuse-bouches*. The crush was overwhelming, the delicacies on offer hardly compensated for by the extreme inconvenience of gathering them. The chief beneficiaries of the lavish supper were the Coxe children who, ousted from the school room, had taken shelter beneath the dining room table from whence they were able to gorge themselves on smoked salmon vol-au-vents, lobster toasts and savoury *palmiers* and to spit mouthfuls of caviar onto the new carpet.

Mr Knightley reappeared to collect Mrs Stokes—his carriage had been brought round and was ready to bear her homeward. Mrs Bates watched his receding back as he carried her from the room. That he had rescued her from the ignominy of her son's behaviour was evident, but she suspected some other disgrace to be attendant on the lady herself.

She expected to see no more of him that evening, so was surprised to find him once more by her side.

'The carriage shall come back for you, if you wish it,' he said in a low voice, 'at your convenience. There is no need to hurry. For myself, I shall walk back to Donwell. The rain has stopped. It is wet underfoot but it does not signify. The fresh air, the opportunity to work off my angst. Such a display! Insupportable!'

Indeed, he looked so heated, so very wrathful that Marie was almost afraid, but she said, 'My dear friend, do not exercise yourself. Whatever that callow young man has done it does not reflect on you. I feel very sorry for his mother. She must be mortified.'

'Feel sorry for the mother?' Mr Knightley burst out, his voice however still muted. 'Only you, saint that you are, could summon an ounce of charity for her. I am not so good.'

'It is natural that she will wish to excuse her boy, I suppose,' Marie ventured.

'Excuse him? Oh no. At least in that she is as angry as I am. She realises he has thrown away any chance of redemption. Nothing will induce me now … But on her own account she will admit to no shame whatsoever. I am sorely disappointed, Marie. I must walk off my chagrin. I am no fit company. Good night.'

Mrs Bates looked around the room. It seemed that all

the respectable families had taken their leave or were in the process of doing so. Neither host not hostess was to be found. The door to Reverend Winwood's study was fast shut as though wedged from behind with a chair. Noises from the upper floor suggested the Winwood girls were being soundly whipped by their mama. Marie gathered Hetty and Jane to her. They located their wraps in the hall and slipped quietly away.

The Venerable Bishop Bland and his wife sat on, occupying two substantial chairs near the fireplace. The less respectable contingent of Highbury society remained also, guzzling champagne and scoffing such remnants of the supper as the Coxe children had spared. From time-to-time Mrs Bland cast a mischievous eye at the fire, where a few coals glowed dully. Presently she announced, 'The rain has stopped and I shall inspect the damage to the marquee. Will you join me, Bishop? In the meantime, let us put some of this wood on the fire. I would not have our sister's guests be cold.

Chapter 21

The following day was Saturday—market day in Kingston and the day of the assizes. Hetty had engaged to go to town with Hermia Winwood and accordingly set off immediately after breakfast. Jane was promised to Miss Weston and quit the Bates' little door soon after her sister.

Whether from the aftermath of the Winwoods' party, or due to the draw of the market and the court proceedings, Highbury was quiet, the High Street almost deserted. It was tempting to Mrs Bates to remain indoors, to wallow in misery—the image of Mrs Stokes in Mr Knightley's arms quite haunted her—or to allow her mind to speculate on the meaning of Mr Knightley's parting words. But she would allow herself to do neither. She determined to show the captain's letter to Mrs Bittern, fetched her wrap and bonnet and took her walk towards that lady's residence. But when she arrived at Grange Spinney she found her friend to be from home.

'Gone to Kingston this morning early, ma'am,' the

housekeeper said. 'The master is to sit on the bench, you know, and the mistress decided to accompany him.'

Marie walked back to Highbury via the woods and fields which flanked the river. The way took her into Donwell land, through woods thick with bluebells and alive with birdsong. She did not walk fast—the day was exceptionally fine and Marie enjoyed the solitude—a commodity in short supply in the cramped quarters above Mrs Pellins' shop.

It was just past the dinner hour when she finally returned home, to find Hetty there before her and agitated to some considerable degree.

'Mama!' she cried, 'there you are! I have been quite worried about you. I imagined … but I told myself very sternly that no possible harm could have come to you. Martha says the pie crust will be charcoal by the time we eat it. See, the table is all ready and when you have removed your bonnet we will sit down. Jane is late as well—perhaps she dines at the Westons'. If so, she ought to have sent word. Martha will be very cross.'

Marie and Hetty sat down together and Martha served

the pie in an extremely curmudgeonly manner.

'Do not frown, so, Martha,' Marie told her. 'I was but a few moments late.'

'A pie is a thing what can only be cooked the once, ma'am,' Martha retorted, flouncing from the room.

'So, Mama, I have news. I am quite bursting with it although Hermia told me in strict confidence.'

'Then you ought to keep it to yourself, Hetty. A secret is a sacred trust, unless it reflects dishonour on the keeper.' Marie said. 'Pass me the potatoes, please.'

'Certainly Mama. Here you are. Boiled again, I see— but a roast potato would be too great a luxury for an ordinary day and I must not complain. As to Hermia's secret, I know I can confide in you without there being the least danger of it being passed on elsewhere. You are the soul of discretion, so sharing it with you is like keeping it to myself. But if you do not wish me to tell you I shall confide in this bowl of vegetables and you may eavesdrop if you wish. She and Mr Paling are engaged! I assure you nothing could have astonished me more. We had met him a handful of times in Kingston. It seemed to me that it was quite by chance but now I suspect they had arranged it. He was at the dinner last night, and the entertainment afterwards. I did not see him, did you? To be sure he is a retiring and self-effacing young man. I expect he was squashed to the back. But after the performance—and what an execrable performance it was, too—he took Hermia out for some air and proposed to her. And she accepted! But it is to be kept secret for the time being. The vicarage is in uproar. Let me pass you the kale, Mama. I am weary of it myself—it seems to have been our staple fayre all through winter. Of course, we must be grateful—such good neighbours that we have, to provision us with such generosity. And I must say Martha has been most inventive. She has a hundred and one ways with kale, has she not? What a treasure she is! And I shall tell Jane when she returns that it was most inconsiderate of her not to let us know she would be dining from home. Where did you walk today, Mama? Whom did you meet?'

In spite of herself, Marie's interest was piqued. 'I think you have lost your thread a little, and the vegetables are eager to know what distresses the people at the vicarage.'

'Oh! So you are listening! I thought as much,' Hetty

said with a smile. 'Miss Sophia's shocking behaviour has caused extreme consternation. It seems she has been slipping away to meet with Mr Stokes for the fortnight past. Her sisters—excepting Hermia, of course—have been complicit, telling their mama she was running errands or calling on Miss Snell when in fact she was trysting with Mr Stokes. Mrs Winwood is in high dudgeon, as you can imagine—and who can blame her—such reprehensible behaviour! I am appalled at Miss Sophia. But the upshot is that they are all—that is, almost all—to depart the vicarage tomorrow to stay with the Blands. Sophia was to go anyway, you know, but now Mrs Winwood says she will not trust Sophia out of her sight. So Hermia is to stay behind to look after Reverend Winwood and the two little girls, and the others are to go to the Archdeaconry, and thence to London. Hermia is quite delighted. To be spared the continual quarrels of her sisters will be a blessing, she says, and she suspects her father feels the same way.'

'Well, I do feel sorry for Mrs Winwood,' Marie said. 'A daughter so disgraced is a dreadful thing—and with such a person as Mr Stokes, who has nothing to recommend him whatsoever. I do not mean to impugn the Stokeses. I am sure she is a respectable woman, although, after last night ...'

'Simon Stokes will be halfway to Newgate gaol by now. That is the other news I have. He was convicted of theft and fraud today at the assizes. It seems he stole a horse and sold it to someone else. He is like to be transported but that is yet to be determined. Perhaps Mr Knightley will intervene.' Hetty laid down her knife and fork. 'That pie was delicious. The crust only a little burned at the edge. Jane has missed a treat. I hope there is to be a baked apple for dessert. My stocking has a hole in the toe. Will you darn it for me, Mama? For you know if I try it will not last five minutes before my toe is out again. Where can Jane be? Shall I walk to the Westons after dinner, Mama?'

'What has Simon Stokes to do with Mr Knightley, Hetty?'

'Oh! He has behaved most correctly, in my opinion although some thought him wrong. Mrs Cropley was at market, you know, her stall is just outside the court building and she hears everything fresh from those who go in and out. It seems Mr Knightley has stood surety for Simon Stokes since the arraignment last year. But for the squire Simon would have been held on remand all this time, but he has had his liberty. Much good he has done with it, you may say—to ruin Sophia as he has—but that does not reflect on Mr Knightley's good intentions, in my opinion.'

'No indeed, it rather enhances their altruism,' Marie agreed, 'to have been so staunch in an all-but hopeless case.'

'It may be that Mr Knightley did not consider it hopeless,' Hetty observed. 'I suspect him of trying to rehabilitate Simon Stokes. It would explain his attentiveness at the Crown, of late.'

'Indeed, it would,' said Marie, a cloud lifting on her understanding, her heart swelling at this new and oh so preferable interpretation of past events. 'Yes, it certainly would. And it is just like Mr Knightley to try to save a young man like Simon, a man whose father was so lacking.'

'I would not go so far as to say he wished to 'save' him, Mama,' Hetty said. 'If he had wanted to be certain of that he would not have recused himself from the bench. Mr Coxe, who, you know, acts as one of the clerks to the court, informed us during a recess that Mr Knightley refused to sit, stating that he could not trust himself to be wholly impartial. So it was left to Mr Bittern and Lord Clayton alone to hear the case and pass judgement.'

'Well, that was proper, too,' Marie murmured.

'That was my opinion, but there were others who thought differently. Mrs Jackson, who kindly brought us back to Highbury in her cart, thought the squire would have done better to stay on the bench where he could influence the other men to acquit Simon. But then she is a close friend of Mrs Stokes, you know. I think the squire did right; the law, you know, must transcend friendship, it must be above everything. If he was guilty he should not have been acquitted because a magistrate was biased in his favour. Oh, thank you, Martha, baked apples! How delicious. I think you should eat Jane's, for she does not deserve such a delicacy. Custard too! You are spoiling us! So, Mama, to continue, Mr Snell acted for Simon Stokes but made a poor show of defending him, apparently and would on no account have any intercourse with Mrs Stokes, much as she implored him to do so—she was anxious to impress upon him the very great necessity that he should exert himself, I surmise. I do not blame her, with so much at stake. In the end Mr Knightley was called to give character witness and he declared that he could not, in all honesty, vouch for the good character of a young man who had resisted all inducements to be steered into a better way of life, had refused the offer of a commission in either the militia or the Navy and also an apprenticeship with a local businessman. Mrs Stokes quite fainted away at that. Mrs Jackson was warm in her indignation against the squire although she did admit that seeing the poor lady insensible did distress him to a strong degree.'

'It must have done, indeed. What a difficult position the squire found himself in.'

'Very difficult—to do all that he honourably could, without doing more than was legally or morally incumbent on him. I do not envy the squire, I assure you.'

'Mrs Stokes will not forgive him.'

'Perhaps she will, in time. She cannot be so blind to her son's character. Even Mrs Jackson was mollified when I suggested that, with Simon Stokes no longer at the Crown, her son —who is currently pot-man, you know—may rise to a higher position. It is an ill wind which blows nobody any good, they say.'

'Indeed, they do,' Marie mused. 'Hetty. I wonder if you will be so good as to ask Martha to clear, and then to walk towards Mrs Weston's house. I find I am increasingly anxious about Jane. I will lie down. I have walked a long way today, and I have much on my mind.'

Jane had been detained at Mrs Weston's by a crisis incurred by the arrival, in a woeful state, of Mrs Snell and Miss Lavinia. Both were in hysterics, or as near to them as made no difference. It had taken all Mrs Weston's powers to calm both ladies to a state where they could explain their distress.

Lavinia's angst was easier to clarify—she was heavily implicated in the flirtation between Miss Sophia Winwood and Mr Stokes. Mrs Winwood had been at the Snells' house early to interrogate the girl—so early that the family had not breakfasted or even dressed. Lavinia had been hauled downstairs in her nightgown to be harangued by Mrs Winwood, closely questioned, disbelieved, lectured, vilified and finally cast off into the very deepest, darkest pit of utter and irrevocable ignominy.

'I am not completely blameless,' the girl stutteringly admitted after a good half hour of inarticulate sobbing and wailing. 'I knew Sophia was receiving notes from Simon Stokes. I believed she was returning them—she told me that by feigning disinterest she was sure to inflame his passion—I had no notion she was writing back to him, or that she had met him, unchaperoned. If I had known that she had used me as an alibi I would never have sanctioned it. But Mrs Winwood says I am complicit. Indeed, she says that before Sophia befriended me, she would never have dreamed of such reprehensible behaviour, would never have noticed such a puppy as Simon Stokes. Befriended me! I like that! It was I who took pity on Sophia. She would have had no friend in the world if I had not admitted her into my circle. Nobody liked her from the start. You did not, did you Jane?'

'No, I did not, but then I was prejudiced against all the Winwoods,' Jane agreed.

'Sophia has a vicious nature,' Miss Weston said. 'Jane, I am very happy that you are not tarnished by association with her.'

'Oh!' Miss Lavinia started up again, a crescendo of blubbering dismay, 'but you think I am tainted?'

'Time will diminish it,' Miss Weston said, wisely. 'In future you shall associate with Jane and me. You say the Winwoods are going away? All the better. They will soon be lost to memory and your part in the scandal will be seen as incidental and then forgotten altogether.'

Mrs Snell's distress was harder to fathom, especially for the younger girls who were excluded from the parlour while she poured out her woes to Mrs Weston. Lavinia was able only partly to explain it. 'It is something to do with Papa,' she said. 'He has been preparing the case to defend Simon Stokes—he is to be tried today, you know. Mrs Stokes has felt it necessary to consult with him extensively. Mama takes exception to it. I do not know why.'

Jane and Miss Weston exchanged meaningful glances but kept silent.

The dinner hour came and went, and still the Snell women were unable to leave the sanctuary of Mrs Weston's house; the idea of going home, of meeting people, of further perfidious revelations all undoing the good the Weston ladies had painstakingly done. Copious quantities of patient soothing and the liberal dispensation of tea were lost in a moment when it was suggested that the time had come to go home. At last, Hetty arrived to enquire after Jane, the Snells reluctantly departed and Mrs and Miss Weston were left utterly exhausted.

When they returned home, Martha was serving tea. 'I suppose you have dined, young lady?' she asked, her tone acerbic.

'No, I have not. I have had tea and some bread and butter, but nothing else since breakfast,' Jane said. She looked pale and wan. Martha bustled off to fetch sustenance. Marie poured a glass of Madeira.

'I fear there has been some impropriety between Mrs Stokes and Mr Snell, Mama,' Jane whispered, when she had taken both and felt somewhat restored. 'Mrs Snell is distraught. Thankfully I do not think Lavinia comprehends. Do not tell Hetty. It is too private and delicate a thing. She would not mean to let any hint of it slip, but …'

'I understand,' Marie put her hand on her daughter's.

'Although I think she is somewhat improved of late. Something has at last occurred to restrain her wayward tongue. I do not say she has ceased talking—that will never be, I apprehend—but she is more disciplined. Nevertheless, we will not speak of Mr and Mrs Snell's affairs, or of Mrs Stokes' either. They are none of our business. But I shall pray for them all.'

'So shall I, Mama.'

Much had Marie Bates to pray—and think—about. That she had utterly misconstrued Mr Knightley's interest in the Stokeses was manifestly clear. The squire had been visiting Simon Stokes, not his mother. His proper, paternal interest in all of Highbury's residents would have permitted him to do no other than exert himself on the lad's account: to do what he honourably and honestly could. Of course, he had entertained no romantic notions about Mrs Stokes. He—who was as good a judge of character as it was possible to find—would have allowed no room in his heart for such a one. Marie's own flaw—of seeing too much good in people—had caused her to be blinded; she had tried to persuade herself that Mrs Stokes' want of elegance, a certain coarseness of manner, could be overcome, might be a result of her situation in life rather than inherent to the lady's character. But Mr Knightley's pragmatic and clear eye would never have suffered him to make such a mistake. How could she have so misjudged him? How could she have supposed for one moment that a man of such natural good taste and superlative breeding could have lowered himself by such an alliance?

Whatever had gone on in Mr Snell's chambers would never be certainly known, but Mrs Stokes' visiting him there so frequently was in itself an error of judgement difficult to pardon. It provided all the evidence required to illuminate that lady's want of propriety. It would seriously bruise the reputation of both. Mr Snell, on his own account as well as on hers, should have deterred her. Mr Knightley's reputation, however, was unblemished; indeed, his endeavours to sponsor Simon Stokes were admirable; philanthropic, disinterested, kind. They were everything she would have expected of him. She was ashamed, now, to think of her cutting, almost spiteful remarks concerning Mrs Stokes, the slurs she had cast on his visits to the Crown. She had much to upbraid herself with on that account. But he had been stoic in his reserve. How easy it would have been for him to explain himself. But he had not done so—and why should he? What business was it of hers? Naturally he had not broadcast his benevolence—he was the last man to allow his left hand know what his right was doing. In the same way as he had quietly, discreetly aided her—providing a home and an income—so he had been unobtrusively active for Simon Stokes' good. It was not a secret, as such, but it was private.

But Mr Knightley did have a secret, of that Marie was quite sure. She had seen it in his eyes, in his demeanour. He had even broached the topic on their journey home from the Bitterns'. It was something delicate, something very near his heart She saw now that she had been selfish and cruel; whatever troubled him she should, as his friend, have been ready to listen. But she had been caught up with her own misery—her own jealousy. That she knew, was the crux of the matter.

Well, she would listen, she resolved, if he were ever to try to confide in her again, she would listen, as his friend.

Chapter 22

Marie Bates did not have her opportunity to listen to Mr Knightley for some time; he was absent from the parish for two weeks. By the time he returned Mrs Winwood and two of her daughters had quit Highbury. Intelligence concerning the dramatic termination of their elegant entertainment was soon abroad. Mrs Winwood had quickly descended from disciplining her girls when the first cries of alarm had resounded from below. She had entered the parlour to discover a thick pall of black acrid smoke hanging in the room, everything coated with greasy soot, her guests in choking discomfort, their eyes streaming. Only the Blands, who had been in the marquee, had been spared. When the smoke and fumes had cleared Mrs Winwood had been found lying lifeless on the new Turkish carpet. An apoplectic seizure had been feared—thank heavens Mr Wilcox had been present. He had diagnosed a swoon and soon roused Mrs Winwood back to life by the application of some smartish smacks to the face. The following day it was put about that an invitation to Mrs Winwood, Sophia and Ursula to accompany the Venerable Bishop Bland and Mrs Bland to the Archdeaconry and afterwards to London had been too pressing to refuse. Ursula's music, it was posited, would benefit from the superior tutelage that London could offer; nobody, certainly, could argue with that. Miss Ursula and Miss Sophia were both apparently in need of new dresses which could by no means be procured more locally. They would stay for the remainder of the season, after which time—well, Mrs Winwood had hinted, heavily, there was no knowing what might occur.

By the time the squire returned to Donwell the vicarage was an oasis of calm. Reverend Winwood was happily cloistered in his study, Hermia had calmly and efficiently supervised the clearing up. The surplus staff had been dismissed, the marquee taken down and hauled away. The governess had taken Arabella and Cordelia firmly in hand. The two youngest Misses Winwood were responding well to the new tranquillity of the vicarage, less confectionery, earlier nights and the composed, reasonable supervision of their eldest sister.

May arrived, and with it a spell of mild, agreeable

weather. Jane and Miss Weston were often outdoors adding to their compendium of wildflowers. Donwell woods was a carpet of flora, the fields sprouting new growth, the trees laden with blossom. Miss Snell generally accompanied the other girls. She had no hand at drawing and knew few of the flowers' names but she was so grateful for their company that they could not exclude her from their outings. Jane did not neglect little John Knightley, whose nurse frequently brought him to wherever the girls were.

Marie Bates spent a great deal of time outdoors also. When she was not visiting the poor she walked with Mrs Bittern, whose doctors advised a little exercise to be taken daily. Plans for their removal to France were already in an advanced stage; almost every day a cartload of crates went off. 'Soon we shall be reduced to only two chairs and a spoon apiece,' Mrs Bittern joked, 'then I suppose it will be time to follow the furniture. But it will be hard to leave Highbury in the springtime. I doubt anywhere is more beautiful.'

'Vichy will have equal charms, if different,' Marie said with a sigh.

'I hope you will come to visit us,' Mrs Bittern said.

'You could come for a stay of a long duration.'

'I doubt I could travel so far,' Marie said. 'And to be away from the girls …'

'I understand,' her friend soothed. 'But it is not impossible that one day the girls will be away from you. Jane has her opportunity in Brighton, if you decide to accept it, and Hetty …'

'Oh, I think Hetty will be always with me.'

Marie found the period of the squire's absence one of extraordinary calm and pleasure. Being in the daily company of her friend was a benefit to her in every way; the weather was dulcet and benign; her girls content. The leak in the bedroom had dried up, putting off the need for the interference of builders and thatchers. She felt strangely buoyed, optimistic for the future without having any specific idea of what that future may hold. She only knew it was an unutterable relief that the nuptials of Mr Knightley and Mrs Stokes would form no part of it.

Returning from Grange Spinney one evening, having dined there, the early dusk being exceptionally fine, Marie decided to take the track along the river and through Donwell woods. The canopy was full of leaf, now, the forest floor thick with bracken, the pathway meandering through the trees like a magical trail. She was but halfway along the path when she met Mr Knightley coming toward her. It happened at a spot which was particularly beautiful, a verdant dell bright with spikes of foxglove. The descending sun glinted off the river making it shine like a mirror as it slid between mossy banks.

Marie's sense of pleasure at seeing him was quite overwhelming; it deluged her. It was all she could do to keep her voice calm and even. 'So, you are returned to us,' she said with a broad smile as he approached.

'Yes indeed. I got home this afternoon and have been playing with John. What a fellow he is! And so happy to see me again.'

'You have been missed,' Marie said, sincerely, significantly. 'Do you walk to the Bitterns'?'

'Not particularly. I simply wanted to stretch my legs. Do you come from there?'

Marie nodded. 'I have walked this way several times in the past weeks. It is a delightful path. I felt sure of my way even if the light was to fade. I suppose I am trespassing! But I feel the landowner will not prosecute me!'

'He is lenient, where you are concerned,' Mr Knightley smiled. 'May I walk with you? I would not intrude, however.'

'It would be a pleasure. I would very much like the company.'

Mr Knightley turned and they sauntered on together. 'I have been to see George,' Mr Knightley said at last. 'He does very well as school. I wanted to see him, to discuss something with him. It will affect him very nearly. John also, but he is too young to be consulted.'

'George has all the good sense of his papa,' Marie replied. 'I am sure he gave you good counsel.'

'He gave me excellent counsel.'

The way narrowed and they were obliged to walk separately for a while. Mr Knightley did not speak. Perhaps he intended Mrs Bates to enquire as to the nature of his conference with young George, but she was the last person to pry.

When they were able to be side-by-side Marie said, 'The Winwoods have departed, or at least some of them have.'

'I believe so. She is no sad loss to our society, I think. An overweening show-off who set out to make us look provincial and ridiculous, but it miscarried; she is the one to look ridiculous. She exhibited daughters who had better have been kept hidden and exposed her husband to scorn. But we need not worry about her. Reverend Winwood is to be the new Archdeacon. They will all quit Highbury before midsummer.'

'But who will minister to the parish?' Mrs Bates asked, aghast. 'The flock needs a shepherd.'

'It is just like you to be concerned about them,' Mr Knightley said, in a voice strangely hoarse, 'and I admire you the more for it. Winwood thinks to put his protégé in as curate—young Paling. He is not yet ordained but I think he has a genuine vocation. However, the living is mine to dispose of and I am by no means sure that I shall agree to it.'

By this time they had gained Donwell Park proper. The sun, at its lowest, lit all the windows of the Abbey like amber lamps; it was an exceptionally beautiful old building. A long avenue of lime trees led from the river to the Abbey, its shadows stretched over the adjacent parkland. Two figures could be seen in the gloom beneath the trees—two figures but pressed very closely together so as to appear almost as one—until the approach of Mrs Bates and Mr Knightley caused them to spring apart. There was nowhere to hide and to do them credit the two lovers made no attempt to do so. A moment brought them into speaking range.

Mr Paling said, 'Good evening sir. Ma'am.'

Mr Knightley bowed. 'Good evening Miss Winwood, Mr Paling. The air is pleasant, is it not?'

'Most refreshing, sir. Miss Winwood felt the need of some air … She takes care of her father and sisters now, you know.'

'And very excellently she does it,' Mrs Bates smiled. 'But the night closes in. I think you should escort her home.'

'Yes, ma'am.'

The couples went their separate ways and presently Marie said, 'I do not think you should be too hasty in refusing that young man the living of Highbury. A single curate is one thing, but one with a wife is quite another. Miss Hermia Winwood is not like her mother, I think. She will not baulk at visiting the poor.'

'I will consider your advice,' Mr Knightley said. He drew Marie's arm through his and pressed her hand.

'I thank you,' Marie said, 'and in return I would ask your advice, if you could spare half an hour tomorrow. I have had a letter from Frederick's brother.'

'I am delighted to wait on you at any time, for any reason, you know that,' the squire said.

They had arrived at the sweep in front of Donwell. 'Will you come in? It must be past the hour for tea. I shall have the gig drive you home.'

Marie shook her head. 'I will continue to walk. The evening is so fine. If I go on I shall be home before it is quite dark. But I hope to see you tomorrow.'

'I will accompany you,' Mr Knightley said. 'I would speak with you more.'

They continued up the drive. Behind them the sun dipped so low that their shadows were twenty feet long, the two side by side on the grey dust of the road. In spite of having declared a desire to talk, the squire remained silent.

At last Marie said, 'Would you tell me about Simon

Stokes? Your efforts with that young man have only lately come to my attention.'

Mr Knightley sighed. 'He was a lost cause from the beginning. His mother begged me to take him under my wing and I did so to oblige her. But he has always been a profligate—too much like his father. He was indulged as a child by both parents, and now Mrs Stokes reaps the dubious reward. I stood his bail in order to give myself an opportunity of earning his trust and putting him on a better road. But after his behaviour with the Winwood girl I knew it was all in vain. If I am honest, even before that, I knew. He is on a determined path to whatever is wicked, debased or dishonest.'

'You behaved very honourably at the trial. What an impossible situation to find yourself in.'

'I fear Mrs Stokes will never forgive me. But she is a lady with an unreliable moral compass.'

'That, I think, I always knew. I have had an instinctive reluctance to be more than very distantly associated with her, but on the other hand, almost in opposition to myself, I have been trying to convince myself that she has admirable qualities: fortitude, tenacity, resilience, that I ought not to judge her too harshly.'

'She has those—one cannot help but admire the way she runs the Crown—no one is wholly bad and neither is she. But you have innate good sense, Marie; your instinct—that she was not quite respectable—was true.'

Mrs Bates hesitated. 'My instinct has led me seriously astray these past months. I am sorry to say that I misjudged you.'

'Oh really?' Mr Knightley stopped and looked at her directly. It was by now that time when day slips into night. The air around them was purple, a gloaming which was neither one nor the other. The birds in the copse had settled to rest.

'It is all tied up with my trying to see good in Mrs Stokes,' Marie went on. She was glad that, in the dusk, he could not see her face. 'I misconstrued entirely your interest in the Crown,' she admitted at last, her voice low.

'Ah.' Mr Knightley considered a moment. 'And that gave you … pain?'

Marie nodded.

They walked on. Presently Mr Knightley said, 'It explains a good deal. For my part, I have felt, these past few months, that you and I were separated by a gulf—a gulf I have crossed but which I believed still enveloped you. It is a difficult journey, and one which each must make at his—or her—own pace. I hesitated to speak to you as plainly as I wished. That no doubt has exacerbated the misapprehension between us. I would have spoken to you of Simon Stokes … And other things. I badly wanted your advice. But I felt you were too bemired in your loss to spare me any attention.'

'I am sorry I gave you that impression. I was bemired, but not in grief.'

They gained the gates to Donwell and began to walk along the road to the village. It was quiet, very dark— the moon had not yet risen—but the two of them knew the road as they knew their own faces; as they knew each other's faces.

'So,' Mr Knightley said at last, 'we are not separated at all?'

'At last, after months of confusion, I know where I stand,' Marie replied.

They passed the few small houses which led to Highbury proper. To their right, Vicarage Lane was lost in gloom. Somewhere within it the church stood sentinel, Frederick and the late Mrs Knightley lay in the churchyard in dreamless sleep. They passed Mrs Grace's cottage. The lantern over the Crown's doorway shone through the darkness.

'I wish we did not need to say goodnight,' Mr Knightley burst out. 'I would take you home with me and have you there with me always. You will say that I am a stupid old man to think of it, but I do.'

Marie turned to face him. A slight breeze loosed her hair and blew it across her face. He wanted more than anything to push it back with his finger.

'I do not think you are old or stupid,' Marie said. She reached up and touched his dear, dear face. More she did not say. More she did not need to say.

It was sufficient for Mr Knightley, who smiled and allowed himself to lift the lock of hair gently and tuck it away. 'So it will be, then,' he said in a low voice.

She nodded. 'So it will be.'

Chapter 23

Mr Knightley was not behindhand with his visit to Mrs Bates the following day. She showed him the letter from Captain Bates and asked him to provide the references requested. His response, considering his otherwise energised spirits and extreme good humour, was as sober and careful as she could wish.

'If your brother-in-law recommends the situation—that is reassuring,' he said. 'But you have had no contact with Captain Jeremy Bates for many years and you do not know his situation in life, his habits or his circle. If I were you I would wish to know more of this Mrs Sealy before I committed my daughter to her care. I have connections in Sussex. Fairfax—an old school fellow of mine with whom I have kept in touch these many years—has a son who resides there. If you will allow me, I will write and ask him to make discreet enquiries.'

They were alone in the parlour, Jane and Hetty having gone for a walk. Mr Knightley put the letter down on the table and advanced a few steps towards Mrs Bates where she stood before the unlit fire. He took her hands in his. 'It might be—that is to say—I hope it *will* be—that Jane may not need to leave Highbury at all; that is, there will be no pecuniary reasons for her to do so. She might find it convenient to make her home here as long as she may wish.' His direct look recalled to both their minds the evening before, and their words, in the moonless night. Mrs Bates found herself suddenly very warm and rather desirous that he should place his arm around her waist. She stared fixedly at a button on his waistcoat until this feeling should pass.

At last she recollected herself and said, 'I am extremely grateful to you, sir. Please do write your letter. I think the truth is that regardless of other matters, Jane will rather wish for this opportunity than not. Lieutenant Weston is in Brighton, you know. There are some who will say I allow her to run after him but the Westons are, after all, old family friends. I trust him to watch over her. I conjecture she will wish it not just in relation to Lieutenant Weston (although, of course I would be deceiving myself if I did not admit that he is a powerful draw on her thoughts) but for the adventure of it. If your research does not uncover anything against it, I think I will encourage her to go. If she is unhappy, she will come back.'

Mr Knightley retained his hold on her hands—such small hands they were, he noted, the fingers slim. She still wore her wedding ring. 'It goes without saying,' he said, 'that, whatever changes may occur to your circumstances, your daughters will …'

'Oh,' Marie interrupted, 'I would make no change to my personal situation that did not allow for both my girls to be with me for as long as they should wish.'

Mr Knightley nodded. It was understood.

Mr Knightley's letter was written and despatched that afternoon. Mrs Bates wrote by the same post to her brother-in-law thanking him most warmly for his thoughtfulness. 'It was always a matter of regret to my dear Frederick,' she concluded, 'that relations with his brothers were not kept up. His mama cautioned against it but he did always hope to be called back to Hazelwoods to minister in the church there. Your kindness in recommending us to your estimable friend Mrs Sealy is all the more signal in that there has been, between your establishment and ours, some regrettable distance. I am considering your offer very carefully and will write again when my mind is settled on the question.'

She received a brief reply almost by return, informing her that Mrs Sealy had quit Brighton for the continent, where the mountain air of Switzerland had been recommended for her health, and enclosing her address there. The post of companion, if taken up, would commence in the autumn. Concerning the estranged relations between the Bates brothers, Captain Jeremy made no comment at all.

Towards the end of May Mr Paling took holy orders. Reverend Winwood's sermons improved considerably in that he rarely preached any. Increasingly, Mr Paling mounted the pulpit. His homilies were more suited to the agricultural mind, the homely, domestic concerns of farmers and milkmaids. Wheat and chaff, loaves and fishes, lost lambs—these were things they understood. They nodded, sagely, as he spoke.

'Tis quite like having the Reverend Bates back amongst us,' Mrs Hopley declared, and it was universally recognised that she meant it as high praise.

There was no question of Mrs Winwood's return to Highbury and on the whole the remnant of the

Winwood family did not seem unduly unhappy without its absent members. Miss Winwood smiled a great deal more than formerly. Without her mother's overbearing presence she came quite out of her shell. The ladies of Highbury declared her a pleasant, well-mannered girl without airs, compassionate and kind.

June came. The fruit trees at Donwell had blossomed luxuriantly and now the nascent fruit could be seen in good abundance. The brown, ploughed earth had disappeared beneath green as wheat and barley flourished. Marie Bates was often abroad in Donwell parish, calling on the tenants and cottars there, familiarising herself with the arrangement of its meadows and pastures, the topography of its orchards, woodlands and streams. Nothing pleased Mr Knightley more than to find her drinking tea at a scrubbed farmhouse kitchen table, exchanging receipts with the farmer's wife, or roaming the paths and byways of his estate collecting elderflowers for her excellent cordial. He delighted in her company, and made himself late for estate meetings with Abel Larkins so often that Abel was moved to remark to his wife, 'Summat's odd about the squire. Reckon 'es got 'iself a ladylove.'

Mrs Larkins, who knew everything about everybody, replied, 'Abel, you're slow on the uptake, aren't you? I could've told you at Christmas it was on the cards.'

The reply from Mr Fairfax—the son of Mr Knightley's friend—was satisfactory in every way. Mrs Sealy was a respectable widow lady held in high regard by Brighton society. Any gentleman's daughter could do no better than place herself under Mrs Sealy's ample and comfortable wing. Jane was informed of the opportunity which had presented itself to her, and embraced it with open arms. She would spend the summer at Highbury, visiting all the old familiar places, and in September she would take coach to Brighton.

Highbury saw the sudden and unexpected departure of the Snell family; the lawyer closed his practice and moved away. Whatever affairs Mrs Stokes had had, legal or otherwise, were left in abeyance. Their house was bought by a Mr Cole, a mercantile man, who brought his new wife to Highbury to put some distance between themselves and the commercial source of their income, a feat which they were never fully able to accomplish. But Mrs Bates was very far from holding herself aloof on that, or any, account, and she frequently drank tea there, finding Mr and Mrs Cole a well-mannered couple, eager to be liked, disposed to be delighted by everything Highbury had to offer. Mr Perry, a newly qualified apothecary, set up a practice in Mr Snell's old chambers, adding considerably to the amenities of Highbury. Squire Knightley held a dance in his threshing barn to celebrate the return from school of his son, and killed two pigs to roast over the fire. Trestle tables were set out along the length of the building, there was food and laughter and cider. Mr Paling and Miss Hermia Winwood announced their engagement. Mr Knightley took Marie Bates away from the noise and the dancing into the quiet of the shrubbery and kissed her there very thoroughly, by the light of the new moon. The following morning Marie Bates exchanged her bereaved black for a gently sad sable.

In July Mr and Mrs Bittern moved permanently to the continent and Mrs Goddard, a gentlewoman tragically widowed at only twenty-nine years of age, opened a school for young ladies at Grange Spinney. Mrs Bates happily encompassed Mrs Goddard into the growing society of the busy little town. Randalls was bought and refurbished by a retired military man for accommodation of his wife and extended family. What Lieutenant Weston felt when he received this news in a letter from his mama was not known, only that his regiment was to leave Brighton for manoeuvres in Yorkshire.

'He says it's temporary but you can never be sure,' Mrs Weston said, a cautionary look in her eye which encompassed Jane as much as it did Marie. 'We will not see him in Highbury again this year, of that I am certain.'

Jane looked back at her very directly. 'I wish him a safe journey to Yorkshire,' she said, boldly. 'I shall be sorry not to see him in Brighton, but I expect my time will be fully occupied with Mrs Sealy.'

The Lieutenant's removal to Yorkshire was a blow to Marie Bates, however. She had trusted to him to meet Jane from the coach, to call on her at Mrs Sealy's, in short to be her friend, the only familiar face in a town full of strangers.

'I am afraid Jane will be lonely,' she confessed to Mr

Knightley. 'Brighton is such a vast distance from us here. She will not know a soul.'

'Jane is such a young woman as will recommend herself wherever she goes,' the squire said. 'Mrs Sealy will ensure she is made to feel at home, I am sure. And I imagine that her first few weeks will be taken up with getting to know her new employer, in learning her ways. She may not have much liberty to feel lonely.'

'I hope you are right,' Marie said, but doubtfully. 'I wish I could go with her, and see her new situation for myself. It would put my mind at ease, I do not mind owning to you. But,' with a sigh, 'it cannot be so. Jane must make her own way.'

Reverend Winwood announced that he was to be inducted as the new archdeacon and would leave Highbury to take up his position. Mr Paling would succeed him as incumbent at Highbury. This news was broadly welcomed although, without Mrs Winwood, Highbury had found Reverend Winwood less taciturn, more approachable. Before two weeks had passed, he had gone, taking Hermia with him for the time being, until she should return as Mrs Paling.

'But I am to be bridesmaid,' Hetty announced.

'Hermia will get married from the archdeaconry in the first week of September, and I am to go a few days beforehand, and stay there with her. She says my chatter will distract her and calm her nerves! Whoever would have thought that I could calm anyone's nerves? I—who have been more used to exacerbating everyone's fears and exaggerating everything out of all proportion! Well, I do declare! And to be bridesmaid is a very great thing—when she has so many sisters to choose from! I am quite overwhelmed! I do not think I was ever so singled out before, was I Mama? Oh! But whatever shall I wear? My sprigged muslin is torn—the hem is quite ruined—and the moth got into my silk last year, so that is no good either. Hermia is to wear satin. But I shall not worry about it. No one will be looking at me, this grey costume will be quite suitable. Except grey is not very pretty, is it? A little too funereal for a wedding. Well, I shall have to decline, that is all. Hermia will not mind. She has four sisters, all of whom I am sure will be delighted to stand with her. Ah, well. I am content to have been asked.'

'Hetty, dear,' said her mama, thinking what histrionics

would at one time have been attendant on such a circumstance as this, and how her daughter had mellowed. 'We will go and see Mrs Ford. Time is short, but I am sure she will have something suitable. Mrs Ford is so very good, and, as an old friend, she will not charge us more than she can help. And I daresay Mrs Grace will undertake to make your gown up, too.'

'Oh Mama, you are too good. I shall go straight away and see what is in Ford's. Do you go to Donwell?'

'Indeed I do, and Jane accompanies me. They begin to cut the wheat today. But we will be back in time for dinner.'

When they returned it was to find Hetty wild with news.

'And what do you suppose?' she enquired, hardly giving Marie time to remove her shawl or bonnet, 'I do not think you will have heard it for Donwell lies in quite the opposite direction, unless you heard it from Mrs Hopley. She was at Mrs Cropley's farm when I passed it. The Hopleys' girl Sarah is to go to Clayton Park as parlour maid now that she is not needed at the vicarage. Well, well. She will find a vast difference at

Clayton, I conjecture, to what she has been used to at the vicarage. Since Mrs Winwood's departure it has been all easiness there. Not that what I am sure Sarah will do very well at Clayton. Mrs Cropley's boy Daniel is under-gardener at Clayton Park. He says the housekeeper at Clayton Park is a scourge with a high-pitched voice likely to shatter the chandeliers and he would rather sew his own ears closed than hear her shrieking at the kitchen maids when they have burnt the bread or curdled the custard. He does not envy Sarah her position in the house, he says, and I must say, the housekeeper does sound … but one mustn't judge. I think it is right to maintain discipline—one cannot have burned bread or curdled custard at a house like Clayton Park—or anywhere. And in fairness Clayton is a vast house and the running of it cannot be easy—it would fray anyone's nerves, I would think. To be sure, Mrs Cropley is such an easy-going woman that I expect Daniel is not used to hearing a raised voice. Probably the housekeeper at Clayton is not so very strident at all! But that is by the by, and I cannot imagine how you got me onto the topic of Clayton Park, for it is nothing to the purpose of what I want to tell you. After I had been to Ford's I walked out this afternoon towards the Hartfield pastures and they were full of men and horses! The ground is being broken! Young Mr Weston was there overseeing a delivery of stone and he told me the foundations would be dug before Christmas. What do you think? So Mr Woodhouse is to come back to Highbury after all. A very nice man, I thought, and who is not to say that he does have all the ill health he claims? And one should feel rather sorry for him, indeed. I did, at one time, I do not mind owning to you Mama. Such an eligible man in so many ways and, if things had been different, perhaps one could have … but that is all behind us now, and he must live somewhere I suppose and where better than here?'

Mr Knightley heard from Mr Woodhouse shortly afterwards. He was due to be married, he said, to Miss Charlotte O'Brien, middle daughter of his late father's estimable and long-time friend Mr Oswald O'Brien. The ceremony would take place in September and thereafter the wedding couple would proceed to Germany, where the air was especially healthful, to bathe in the thermal waters at Baden Baden. In the meantime he requested the squire to take a friendly interest in the construction of his new property.

'Which I shall be happy to do,' Mr Knightley said. 'Young Pole, the architect, seems to me to be a very sensible young man with a thoroughgoing knowledge of his craft. If I were to have alterations done at the Abbey, I would certainly engage his services.'

'The Abbey has stood in its current state for three hundred years, more or less,' Marie teased, 'I cannot imagine you changing a single stone of it.'

Mr Knightley gave a rueful smile. 'The truth is,' he said, 'word is abroad of the modern kitchen arrangements being installed by General Bramhall at Randalls. My cook begins to think her old range and draughty larders decidedly inferior. Hartfield, I understand, will have the most up-to-date of necessaries. Anyone might look at the Abbey's primitive arrangements and feel disinclined to consider removing themselves there.'

'Anyone?' Marie gave him a mischievous smile.

'Indeed,' was all his reply, but his look said a great deal more.

August came and the harvest was brought in; a period

of fine, dry weather meant a very bountiful crop.

'I am very pleased,' the squire said as he walked with Marie across the last field to be mown. 'The mill will work night and day for the next fortnight, to lay up sufficient flour, and then work will commence on the new workings.'

The squire oversaw the work personally, often stripped to his breeches and waist-deep in the race, handling timbers and hauling on ropes. For the duration of the works he had arranged for a supper to be served to the workers, brought down from the Abbey and laid out on trestles on the meadow beside the mill pond. The weather continued extraordinarily benign. Marie often helped the cook and the housekeeper to serve the food. It was a pleasure to her, to walk to Donwell, to discuss arrangements with the household staff, to walk with them, or to ride on the gig. And then to watch the squire as he worked amongst his tenants, to see him clap them on the back, shake their hands, exchange jokes, give directions. She liked to see the estate children run to him, the women and girls deferential but easy in his company. He was extremely well-liked, respected, almost loved, she thought. And then he would look up and see her, and his eye would brighten, his lips curl into a smile, his hand rise in greeting.

'The son of my acquaintance Fairfax invites you to stay with him,' the squire announced on one such evening. He and Marie sat side by side on a rug spread on the grass. Most of the workers had gone home for the day, the sunset was fast approaching. George and William Larkins were swimming in the mill pond while the household staff busied themselves clearing the dishes and packing up the remains of the food. 'I had his letter this morning. He has taken a house in Brighton, in the same area as Mrs Sealy's. She is due back the first week of September, I believe. He suggests you travel with Jane and stay as his guest for as long as you feel you need to ensure the girl is settled in her new position.'

'Mr Fairfax is all kindness,' Marie exclaimed. 'It is of all things that which I most desire. To see Jane settled, to meet Mrs Sealy. Perhaps even to call on Captain Bates and see for myself what kind of man he is, to see whether he can be relied on to help Jane, should she need it.' She turned her smile on Mr Knightley. 'I see your hand in this, Mr Knightley. You wrote to him, did you not? Confess it! Ah, I see by the quiver in your lip that you did, and you are heartily pleased with the outcome of your endeavour.'

'I am pleased by anything that pleases you, ma'am,' Mr Knightley said, 'and any concern of yours, be it ever so small and insignificant, I delight in taking upon myself. I would spare you any unhappiness, any anxiety, any inconvenience.'

Mrs Bates thought she might weep. 'You are too good,' she said, her voice trembling. 'Much, much too good.' She reached out and pressed his hand. He lifted hers to his lips, and kissed it.

Presently she said, 'Would next week be convenient for Mr and Mrs Fairfax, do you suppose? I will secure seats for Jane and me on the London coach.'

'You will do no such thing,' Mr Knightley said, a look of mock sternness on his brow. 'The Donwell coach shall take you. When you get back the new wheel will be working and another year will have turned at Donwell.'

'A whole year,' Marie murmured, thinking back to last September.

Mr Knightley leaned towards her. The field was empty now, the rumble of the trap's wheels on the track and George's squeals in the pond were the only sounds. 'In September, we will announce our engagement,' he said, his mouth very close to her ear, 'and by Christmas, we shall be married.'

Marie was overtaken by a thrill so exquisite she could not reply.

He got to his feet. 'The moon is almost up. It is time George got out of the water and home to bed.' He held out his hand to Marie Bates. 'Come, my dear. Let us go together.'

YOUR REVIEW MATTERS

Thank you for reading this book. As a self-published author I don't have the support of a marketing department behind me to promote my books. I rely on you, the reader, to spread the word.

A short review provides great feedback and encouragement to the writer, and is a helpful way for others to know if they might enjoy the book. Please write a few words along with your star rating.

Jane Bates has left Highbury to become the companion of the invalid widow Mrs Sealy in Brighton. Life in the new, fashionable seaside resort is exciting indeed. A wide circle of interesting acquaintance and a rich tapestry of new experiences—balls at the Assembly rooms, carriage rides and promenades on the Steyne—make her new life all Jane had hoped for.

While Jane's sister Hetty can be a tiresome conversationalist she proves to be a surprisingly good correspondent and Jane is kept minutely up-to-date with developments in Highbury, particularly the tragic news from Donwell Abbey.

When the handsome Lieutenant Weston returns to Brighton Jane expects their attachment to pick up where it left off in Highbury the previous Christmas, but the determined Miss Louisa Churchill, newly arrived with her brother and sister-in-law from Enscombe in Yorkshire, seems to have a different plan in mind.

Jane Fairfax, orphaned at the age of three, spends her early years as the darling of her grandmamma and aunt Hetty in Highbury. She seems likely to remain there permanently, with only her own pleasing person and good understanding to augment what their limited means and middling connections can provide. But the return from oversees of Colonel Campbell, with every reason of duty and gratitude to take up the daughter of his fallen friend, changes Jane's circumstances—and her destiny. At eight years of age she is adopted into the family of Colonel Campbell. Though brought up as a second daughter and given every advantage of education, culture and accomplishment that wealth and affection can supply, the colonel's provision cannot extend further. Jane is destined at last to earn her own independence as a governess until a holiday in Weymouth throws her plans into disarray and tests her character and loyalty to breaking point.

Jane Fairfax's early years get only a few paragraphs in Jane Austen's Emma and what really occurred in Weymouth is left largely for Emma Woodhouse to speculate upon. What was the real nature of the relationship between Mr Dixon and Miss Fairfax? How and why did he transfer his affections to Miss Campbell?

This novel answers those questions and more. What was it like for Jane to live in the household of the Campbells, the eternal guest who must never allow herself to outshine their mousey and dull-witted daughter? How would knowing that she must quit the luxury and affection of the Campbells to earn her own competency taint her enjoyment of them while they lasted? What on earth would make a sensible girl like Jane engage herself, in secret, to a feckless and unreliable man like Frank Churchill?

ABOUT THE AUTHOR

Allie Cresswell was born in Stockport, UK and began writing fiction as soon as she could hold a pencil.

She did a BA in English Literature at Birmingham University and an MA at Queen Mary College, London.

She has been a print-buyer, a pub landlady, a book-keeper, run a B & B and a group of boutique holiday cottages. Nowadays Allie writes full time having retired from teaching literature to lifelong learners.

She has two grown-up children, two granddaughters, two grandsons and two cockapoos but just one husband – Tim. They live in Cumbria, NW England.

Mrs Bates of Highbury is her seventh novel.

ALSO IN LARGE PRINT BY ALLIE CRESSWELL

The Talbot Saga (so far) comprising
The House in the Hollow
The Lady in the Veil
Tall Chimneys
The Highbury Trilogy inspired by Jane Austen's *Emma*, comprising:
Mrs Bates of Highbury
The Other Miss Bates
Dear Jane